KEY WEST
LOST AND FOUND

KEY WEST
LOST AND FOUND

Robert Haines

ABSOLUTELY AMAZING eBOOKS

ABSOLUTELY AMAZING eBOOKS

For Mom.
Thanks for believing.

KEY WEST

LOST AND FOUND

CHAPTER 1

April 1966
Saturday

Sam Torres lay on the beach where the tide had deposited him. Seaweed, tangled in his hair, partially obscured the gash in his scalp. There was no blood; the sea had washed that away and, since his heart wasn't beating, none circulated to ooze from the wound. Except for the blue tinge to his otherwise tanned skin, he could have been asleep.

Sam was a conch, the Key West term for a local, born and raised on the island. Other than a hitch in the Navy during the last war, the furthest away he'd been was Miami. Havana is closer.

As a cop I've seen the victims of death before, whether by accident or design. I know the procedures necessary to determine the cause as well as the steps to take to find out why and, if warranted, who. This was the first time I'd had such a close, personal connection to a victim.

Sam was not just a local fishing guide to me. He was a long time friend of the family since before I was born. The kind of non-relative who becomes an honorary 'uncle.' Now I had to investigate his death. The Chief was off-island and, as Detective Lieutenant, it had fallen to me to oversee the department in his absence. Even if I hadn't been in charge, I would have wanted this case because it was Sam.

The call had come in before I'd even had time for morning coffee and my empty gut churned. Grief, sorrow and anger mingled together. Grief at Sam's death, sorrow at the loss of a dear friend who had been there since my childhood, and anger that something or someone had done this to a man who, throughout his life, had gone out of his way to help those who needed it.

1

But those emotions had to be controlled, repressed, while my professional side found out what, or who, had killed Sam.

The last time I'd seen Sam was Thursday evening. He'd been getting his boat, *Greta*, ready to take a fishing party out Friday morning; loading supplies, checking fuel, charts, all the things a good skipper does to keep his boat and passengers safe. Sam was one of our best guides here at the end of the road. Now it was early Saturday. The sun was rising out of the ocean. A slight breeze that probably wouldn't last rustled the palm trees along Atlantic Avenue and his body lay washed up on the beach. What had happened between then and now? Had *Greta* been hijacked? Was Sam the victim of piracy? Was this a horrible accident? All I was getting were questions. I needed facts.

Doctor Stearns Elliott, a local GP and part-time medical examiner, finished his preliminary examination and slowly stood, stretching to ease his back after being bent over the corpse.

"Any guesses, Doc?" I asked, knowing full well that was all he could give at this time.

He looked at me over the tops of his glasses as he ran his fingers through his sparse, gray hair. "Looks like he took a pretty good hit to the head, but I can't tell yet if that did it or if he drowned. I don't see any other marks."

Sam was dark, partly from heritage, partly from his constant exposure to the sun on the water. Like many old conch families, he was mostly Cuban with some Caribe Indian in him. But, somewhere in his lineage, there had been someone, male or female, who'd had an African connection. That and a lifetime in the sun had given him a darker complexion such that, to some people, Sam was colored.

Segregation had officially ended. President Johnson had signed the Civil Rights Act two years previously and, although racial prejudice still existed in Key West, most of us who lived and worked here could care less about the color of a man's skin or what he did in life. The important thing was how he did it. Even if he wasn't successful, as long as a man gave it his best and was honest, he could expect a fair deal from most of the rest of us on the island. Sam was no different. It didn't matter if they were black, white, islander, mainlander, Cuban or American, Sam would help if he could and usually received help in return.

Sam was also the best man I knew on a boat. He didn't make mistakes on board which was why the evidence of a significant blow to the head bothered me. *Greta* was a powerboat so there was no boom to swing around and catch someone unaware. Even the outriggers she had to hold trolling lines out to the sides couldn't swing so that they'd knock someone overboard. If Sam had slipped and hit his head on something, odds were that he'd still be on the boat with some fishing client frantically trying to radio for help, not lying dead on the beach.

"Let me know as soon as you can, Doc. I guess I better go see Elyse."

"Will do, Tom. Tell her I'll drop by later. Break it to her gently; you know how her heart is."

"Yeah, Doc."

A small knot of people had begun to gather, early risers, probably locals, and on the way back to my car, I noticed Amy Petersen, reporter for the *Key West Current*, one of our local papers, and a sometime date of mine. She was a transplant from up north and had arrived on our island about four years ago. The first time we'd met, I'd had to arrest her to keep her out of the Navy brig.

Amy was an intelligent, attractive blonde. Slim, about 5'8" but with curves in all the right places and legs that wouldn't quit. Indeed, it was her legs that I'd first noticed when we met, helped by the fact that, at the time and in deference to our tropical weather, she'd been wearing shorts. Her most arresting feature, though, was her eyes. Green eyes, but like no other green I had ever seen. In a moment they could change from translucent like light jade to the impenetrable dark green of the Gulf when a storm comes flying across. Since she covered the police beat for the paper, we saw each other when our respective professions crossed and, whenever possible, socially. Recently, we'd been tiptoeing around the idea of our relationship becoming more serious.

It seemed like we spent most of our time trying to get around the stereotypical situation of a cop and a reporter where the reporter wants to know everything and the cop doesn't want to say anything. We'd reached an impasse where we kind of knew just how far we could push each other before it got ugly. I realized that she needed facts on which to base her stories and she seemed to have grudgingly accepted that I couldn't always provide them without jeopardizing whatever the case was.

Although early, the day was already warm and giving every indication of getting warmer. Amy was wearing khaki shorts and a semi-transparent, white, long sleeved shirt open over a soft yellow T-shirt. Sandals on her feet and a wide brimmed hat completed the ensemble. Since arriving in the Keys she had acquired a smooth, even tan. However, she was smart enough to know that too much sun would turn her skin into something resembling an old leather wallet so she always had a bottle of a popular sun and skin lotion in the large bag she called her portable desk. That bag was her constant companion. I don't think I had ever detected any other scent but the coconut of that lotion on her. Fortunately, I liked it. I just hoped she didn't have a camera in her bag. The last thing I wanted to see were pictures of Sam on the front page.

I knew she would be pestering me for details: who,

what, when, where, why, and would carefully fill in her own speculations. But I also knew that, when given the facts, she stuck to them. She also knew Elyse, Sam's wife, so I called her over.

"What's all the excitement, Tom?"

"We've got a body on the beach. Doc doesn't know yet if it's an accidental drowning or what."

"I hope it's not a visitor 'cause that sure won't help the tourist business."

"No, not a tourist, unfortunately," I sighed, thinking of the loss we had suffered. "I don't want this on the record yet, but it's Sam Torres."

"Oh, my God!" Her eyes flashed wide and bright at the news, then darkened. "Are you going to tell Elyse?"

"I have to before she gets the news from someone else. That's why I called you over. I want you to go with me if you can. I don't have anyone else I can take and she knows you."

"Sure, but –"

I knew that "but." The reporter in her always looked for the story.

"Yes, Amy, you get the story, but stick to the facts," I cautioned. "And right now the facts are we don't know anything except that Sam's dead. I'll make sure you get an official copy of the autopsy report as soon as Doc's finished."

Back down the beach, Doc had the body on a stretcher and covered before anyone else could see it.

Amy had walked to the beach, easy on our two by four island, so we headed for my car. I would take her home later, but she would probably want to come by the station after we saw Elyse.

I have always liked police work. The only part I find difficult is delivering the kind of news I had to now. I was glad Amy was with me. Although, procedurally, it was odd taking a reporter on a call like this, I trusted Amy and she and Elyse knew each other. It also helps to have another woman present when you have to deliver bad news to a new widow.

Elyse Torres knew something was wrong when she opened the door of the small, but neat, cottage on Grinnell Street that she and Sam had shared for thirty-five years. She saw it in my face. Amy and I got her to sit down before telling her then Amy held her while I went to the kitchen for a glass and some brandy. The brandy was used for cooking and medicinal purposes. This was definitely the latter.

I had to ask Elyse some questions. So after things had calmed down I began.

"Elyse, I saw Sam Thursday in the harbor getting the boat ready. He told me he had a charter Friday morning. Did he come home that night?"

She took a dainty sip of the brandy and looked at me, a profound sadness in her eyes. "Thursday? Si, Thursday he came home and then left early Friday."

"When did he get back on Friday?"

"I do not think he did. He did not tell me they would be back yesterday so I assumed it was an 'overnight.' Sometimes he would get a group that wanted to go out beyond the Tortugas and they would spend the night at Fort Jefferson. Sam had a permit for that."

I made a note to check that. "Do you know who booked the charter or where they were from?"

"No, Senor Tom, I do not, but perhaps it is in his book over there." She pointed to a small desk in the corner.

There was nothing on the top except a small bank calendar and a cup with some pencils in it. I opened the drawers, but all I found were a few old letters and some blank paper

"Is this where Sam always kept his charter book?" I asked.

She nodded. "Si, except when he was out stocking the

boat. He took the book to list the gear and supplies he put on board. He must have left it there when he came home Thursday evening."

Gently, and hoping I wouldn't have to start looking for a second body, I said, "I didn't see Julio in the kitchen. Did he go out on the charter with Sam?"

Julio was Sam and Elyse's "adopted" son. Sam had found him floating with some wreckage off Big Pine Key about seven years ago when the boy was 11. Julio said he had escaped from Havana and the "Revolutionistas" and had no family back in Cuba.

Not having children of her own, Elyse would not think of turning him in to the authorities. With the help of Father Stephen, the local priest, she convinced Social Services to place Julio in her and Sam's care. They both taught him English and soon he was helping Elyse at neighborhood functions and Sam on the boat when he wasn't in school. Although to my knowledge Sam never took him on his overnight charters, I wanted to make sure that Julio was here after Sam had left Friday morning.

"No, no," Elyse insisted. "Julio did not go. Not since I started having my heart problem has Sam taken Julio with him. Sam always wants to be sure someone is close by."

"Where is he then?" I asked.

"Julio went early to Padre Stephen to help with today's fiesta. He should be back soon. Oh, Senor Tom," Elyse said, the tears flowing again, "how could this happen? How could my Sam fall off his boat?"

"I don't know, but I will find out. And if someone did this to Sam I will find them. Now, tell me, are you going to be all right? Doctor Elliott said he would come by later to see you and I have to get back to the station, but I don't want to leave you by yourself."

Amy, sitting on the small couch next to Elyse, put her arm around the older woman's shoulder. "Don't worry Tom,

I'll stay with her. I'll call Eddie to let him know where I am and I can walk back later. It's a small island."

Eddie Harris was a copy boy at the paper. He was a couple of years younger than Julio but they often palled around.

"You go ahead," she said. "I'll call you later."

As I left casa Torres, Rita Gomez from next door came running over. Rita and Elyse had come to Key West from Cuba when they were children and both married into Cuban conch families. I had never known if she and Elyse were related, but they could have been, they looked so much alike; both barely five feet tall and what my Grandmother had always described as "pleasantly plump," with dark hair always wound up on their heads. "Senor Tom, is it true, about Sam?"

Rita Gomez and Elyse Torres were both in their upper fifties, old enough to be my mother, but both insisted on calling me 'Mr. Tom.' When I was a kid they had called me 'Tomasito' or 'little Thomas,' even when I was a good foot taller than both of them. It was only when I came back to Key West after time on the force in Miami that I became 'Mr. Tom.' With Sam, however, it had always just been 'Thomas.'

"Yes, Mrs. Gomez, I'm afraid it is."

"Oh, poor Elyse, poor Elyse," she said, shaking her head and muttering what I presumed was a Spanish prayer.

"Mrs. Gomez, would you please do me a favor?"

"Si, Senor Tom, anything. You catch who did this to Sam?" she said wagging her finger at me. Clearly Rita didn't think Sam's death was accidental.

"Yes, I will catch whoever did this, but right now, would you please stay with Elyse."

"Yes, yes, of course. I have already sent for Padre Stephen in case he has not yet heard, although I am sure that he already knows and is on his way."

"Good, thank you," I said. "Doctor Elliott will be stopping by later to check on her, so keep her calm and please tell Miss Petersen that she doesn't need to stay. I'll wait for her in the car."

"Si, yes, I will."

As she went inside, I got in the car and reached for the radio microphone.

"Headquarters, Car 12. Sally are you there?"

"Go ahead Car 12. What's up Tom?" the voice of Sally Fitzgerald, our shared secretary and daytime dispatcher came through the speaker.

"Sally, is Dennis there?"

"Yes, he just came in."

"Good. I'll be back shortly. Make sure Dennis stays there, I'm going to need him. If anything else comes up have someone else handle it."

"Okay, Tom. Is it true about Sam Torres?"

"Yes, I'm afraid so." Word moves fast on this island.

"Damn. The Chief's not going to be happy. He liked fishing with Sam." It didn't seem like our Chief was ever happy about anything, but I didn't say that to Sally.

"No, I don't think he will be, but there's no need to call him up in Tallahassee. Let's see if we can solve this before he gets home. Car 12 out."

The passenger side door opened and Amy slid in.

"Everything okay?" I asked her.

"Yes, Mrs. Gomez just made tea and Doc called. He said he's on his way here and will be over to see you later."

"He didn't say anything else, did he?"

"No, Tom. He knows better; and no, I didn't ask. I know you'll tell me when you can."

I pulled my door closed. "Okay. You want me to drop you at home?"

"No, but if you would run me over to the paper, I would appreciate it. I promised Elyse I would write a piece about

9

Sam for tomorrow's edition, so I need to get started."

"No speculation, Amy," I warned.

She scowled at me, her eyes darkening. Sam's death had angered her too. "Come on Tom, you know me better than that. Besides, I don't have anything to speculate about. All I know is that Sam's dead and that he washed up on the beach. Right now how he got there is anybody's guess and your job to find out."

"Okay, fine. Just don't do any guessing, at least not yet. Remember, Elyse reads everything you write."

I started the car, and we headed over to the newspaper office. Amy had her notebook out and was already scribbling while I was thinking about the things I wanted Dennis to get busy with.

CHAPTER 2

Back at KWPD Headquarters, Dennis was waiting at my desk. I stopped at the machine for a cup of coffee and joined him. Dennis Early was a lanky 20-year-old and had only been on the force two years. He'd joined soon after finishing High School, but he knew these islands. More importantly, he was observant and had a level of common sense not often seen in someone his age; I'd grabbed him for my investigations team as soon as I could. As I sat down, he pulled out his notebook.

"I've already called the marina where Sam docks and, according to the harbor master, *Greta's* not in her slip. Also, Sam didn't file a projected course."

I raised an eyebrow and before I could say anything Dennis continued. "I know it's not a requirement; but you know Sam, he'd do it just to be safe."

"I know," I said. "The fact that he didn't bothers me. What about the neighboring boats? Anyone see or hear anything Friday morning or evening?"

"Don't know yet. Those questions are easier asked in person and you told Sally to make sure I waited here for you."

"Right, I did. Okay, get on over there and start asking." Dennis started to stand and I held up my hand. "Don't limit it to Friday, though. I saw Sam early Thursday evening when he was getting the boat ready. Find out if anyone saw him after that, but also if they saw anyone around *Greta* before or after. Elyse said he had a charter scheduled, but we couldn't find Sam's book so see if anyone actually saw him leave Friday morning. Maybe we'll get lucky and get a description of who was with him."

Dennis finished scribbling in his notebook and got up

to leave. "You don't think this was an accident."

It was a statement, not a question. The kid was smart, but I hadn't realized that he'd figured out how to read me.

"You're right, Dennis, I don't."

"Neither do I," he said and left.

Dennis would start at Sam's marina, but I knew he wouldn't stop there. He'd check every dock, slip, marina, boat yard, creek and canal in our jurisdiction, even the private ones. But he didn't have the authority to contact the Sheriff's Office or the other towns up the highway. That was my job.

An hour later I was making my last call to the local Coast Guard command.

"U.S. Coast Guard, Key West, Captain Stander," the voice on the other end answered.

"Lee, it's Tom Jackson. What are you doing answering your own phone? I thought a Captain merited a yeoman to do that."

He laughed, "My yeoman's out sick, the cutter crews are out on patrol, it's lunchtime and I drew the short straw for this weekend, just like you, I guess. I heard the Chief's off island. What can I do for you?"

"Lee, I've got a possible missing boat."

"What do you mean 'possible'?"

"I've got an officer out checking and he hasn't called in yet to say he's found it, but I don't think he will."

"Why not?"

"Because it's Sam Torres' boat, *Greta*, Lee. And Sam's not on her."

"And I presume that he's not at home either?"

I could tell from his voice that Lee's personal radar was up.

"No, he's in the morgue. We found him on the beach this morning."

"You suspect foul play?" Lee queried.

"Given the circumstances, yes. I don't believe Sam was involved in anything directly, but I'm not ruling it out yet. I think it's more likely someone stole *Greta* to make a run in a boat that wouldn't be questioned and somehow Sam got in the way."

"Okay, I'll get the word out to the cutters. Have you called everyone else up the line?"

"Yeah, got them all the way up to Jewfish Creek, and the Sheriff'll put the word out to Miami-Dade, Collier and the rest."

Paper rustled in the background then Lee said, "Hang on a minute, Tom." His handset clunked as he put it down. More paper rustled then Lee was back on the line.

"I thought I remembered something as soon as you mentioned Sam's name. One of the cutters stopped him a month ago, about half way between here and Cuba. They put it down as a routine safety check, but given the location they gave him a closer inspection than usual. Didn't find anything, but there's a note here that his passengers didn't look like the usual fishing charter types."

I laughed, "Come on Lee, what is a 'usual fishing charter type'?"

"You know. Pale businessmen from up North, down for a week and already sporting a good sunburn," he said. "The cutter skipper said these guys were tanned, like locals or at least Floridians, and definitely more comfortable around his guys than the usual charters. Like they were used to dealing with us or other authorities. Two of them he described as large with significant muscle who never took their eyes off his crewmen, while the one who was clearly in charge was described as about sixtyish, tall, fit, silver haired, not gray. He stayed relaxed in the chair enjoying a very good smelling cigar. There's also a note that one of the muscle men referred to him as 'Mr. D.' Sounds like they were some of the kind of boys you might have met in

Miami."

"What? Did your boys think Sam was running something illegal?" I asked.

"No, it was a combination of location and heading that triggered the initial stop and then the observation of his passengers as fitting a type," said Lee.

"Personally, I don't think Sam ever knowingly took on anything shady," I said. "But professionally, I have to say that I've seen it happen with someone you wouldn't expect. I can tell you we've never had any reports of anything Sam did that could be considered suspicious. I don't suppose your crew was able to get any ID's for those guys?"

"No, since it was simply represented as a safety stop, there was no legitimate reason to ask. You want a copy of the report?"

"Yes, I would, if it's possible."

"Not a problem, Tom. I'll have one of the secretaries type up a copy when they get back from lunch and have it sent over as soon as possible. In the meantime, I'll post a description of *Greta* as missing, possibly stolen or hijacked."

"Thanks Lee. I'll keep you in the loop on this if we find anything."

As I rang off, Sally buzzed to let me know that Dennis was on line 2. Had he found something already?

CHAPTER 3

I punched the flashing button on the phone. "Hi Dennis, what've you got?"

"Nothing yet, Lieutenant. I've canvassed Sam's dock area, but I haven't been able to speak with everyone 'cause some of them aren't here right now. Those whose boats are here, I'll check their addresses at the dock office and get them at home if necessary. However, some boats are out, so I'll have to come back and check them this evening. But that's not why I called."

"I figured that, Dennis. What's bothering you?"

"When you were with Mrs. Torres this morning did you see Sam's truck there?"

"No, I didn't. I presume it's not at the marina either."

"That's correct, Sir. A couple of people remembered seeing Sam leave Thursday evening and one person thought they saw it here Friday, but I couldn't confirm it. They weren't even sure it was Sam's. There're a lot of blue pickups around town and I was thinking it'd be a good idea if we stop and check all of them."

Some years ago, the local Ford dealer got a shipment of pickups, the majority of which were blue. It seemed to be a popular color and several were still running around here.

"Good point, Dennis. I'll get the word out and call the Sheriff. If the truck has been stolen, hopefully it hasn't made it off the Keys. Where are you going next?"

"I'm going to take a boat out and check with some of the live-aboards outside the harbor. Then I figured I'd nose around some of the areas up by Garrison Bight and drop in at the Navy. Find out if they saw anything, if that's okay? I'll call in when I get back."

"Okay. Watch yourself out there and remember, all we

know for sure is that the boat is missing. We're trying to establish where and when it was last seen and if Sam was on board. Although I'm treating his death as suspicious, that isn't official until we get the autopsy report."

"Right, Sir. I'll be circumspect," said Dennis as he hung up.

Replacing the phone I thought 'circumspect,' that's not a word I'd expect to hear from a typical Key West police officer. But then, I don't consider Dennis 'typical.' He's a local, but he's definitely a few points higher on the scale than your average Key West native. Sally's got him active in amateur dramatics and just last week I saw him reading Shakespeare during lunch. If any of the other officers read anything approaching literature during their lunch hour, it's more likely to be the latest Hammer novel from Mickey Spillane. I had the distinct feeling that Dennis would not stay in Key West.

Before putting out a broadcast on Sam's truck, I called his house to confirm that it wasn't parked around the corner. The phone was picked up before the first ring finished.

"Si, hello."

"Mrs. Gomez? Is that you?"

"Si, Senor Tom. Thank heaven you called."

"What is it? Is Elyse all right?" I was suddenly worried that she'd suffered a heart attack with only Mrs. Gomez there.

"Si, Senor, she is all right, Doctor Elliott is with her. It is Julio."

"Julio, what's wrong with Julio?"

"He is missing. Padre Stephen was just here and was surprised that Julio was not."

"But Elyse said Julio went over to the church this morning to help with the fiesta. You're telling me he didn't come with Father Stephen?"

"Si, Tomas. The Padre said he saw Julio this morning but could not find him when he heard about Samuel. He thought Julio had come home."

"I'll be over as soon as I can, Mrs. Gomez, but first tell me one thing. Is Sam's pickup there?"

"Wait, I will look."

She put the phone down and I heard her walk away. As I waited I started roughing out a description of the truck and Julio then someone picked up the phone and Doc's voice came over the line.

"Tom, is that you?"

"Yeah, Doc. What's going on over there?"

"First of all, Elyse is okay. I'd like her to spend the night over at the hospital. I think it would be calming, but she won't go for it, so I'll get one of the nurses over to stay with her. The other thing is that no one has seen Julio all day. At least not since early this morning, just after he got to the church."

"Damn! I don't like that Doc, not at all."

"I didn't think you would. Here's Mrs. Gomez," and he handed the phone over.

"Senor Tom, the truck is not here."

"Could Julio have taken it?"

"I do not think so, Senor. He rode his bicycle to the church and according to Padre Stephen, it is still there. Also, I do not remember seeing the truck this morning."

"Okay, Mrs. Gomez. I'll be over directly. Thanks."

I hung up and went out to Sally's desk. "Sally, I want an 'all points' out on Sam's pickup. Call everyone out on patrol and make sure they get the word. Nothing half-assed either. They're to stop and check licenses and registration information on all blue pickups." I handed her the paper with my descriptions. "Also, tell them to be on the lookout for Julio Torres. It's not official yet, but he may be missing. Alert the Sheriff's office too, especially about the truck, since I think it's a good bet that it's already outside the city. I'm going back over to the Torres.' Call me if anything comes in."

She was on the radio as I walked out the door. Just as I got to the car I heard someone call me.

"Tom, you got a minute?"

I turned toward the voice. It was Andy Hardy from the *Current* coming toward me. Andy was Amy's editor and a general pain in the ass. He couldn't write worth a damn but apparently kept his job because of who, or maybe what, he knew and what he got out of the other reporters. Sucking up to the boss probably helped too. He was also the last person I wanted to talk to.

We were the same age, both grew up here and went to the same schools. Although we weren't friends, on this island we couldn't help but run into each other. I remember Andy got a lot of ribbing over his name in elementary school, what with the series of Mickey Rooney and Judy Garland movies. In high school he started going by Andrew and considered himself a ladies man, but I never knew anyone who ever went out with him more than once and I don't think that had changed. The name jokes changed though, such as 'Andy Hardly' among others, referring more to his considerable record of strikeouts rather than Rooney's character.

As a kid he'd always been somewhat of a snitch. If you got called to the principal's office the question in the back of your mind was always "what did Andy squeal about this time?" As adults, most of us referred to him as a rat, though some used stronger language, and we all watched our backs when he was around.

In high school he somehow wangled his way onto the school newspaper and had delusions of being the next Edward R. Murrow, or something like that. The problem was that he didn't look for news so much as gossip or dirt and whatever he could find that would bring anyone, except Andy Hardy, into question. His other problem was that he couldn't write his way out of a paper bag. I never did figure out how he got his way onto the school paper in the first place and, second of all, how he stayed. He probably knew something about someone that they didn't want known. That became his MO, digging up and, sometimes, fabricating information on people so as to have control over them. It got to the point where some of us in school just wouldn't talk to him.

He was also a cheap bastard. If he was out with someone, he always managed to get away without paying the lunch or bar tab; forgotten wallet or a trip to the head at the right moment. When the other party readily agreed to pay, odds were that Andy had reminded them about something they didn't want generally known. However, if pushed, he would charge it to the paper so even then it didn't come out of his own pocket. This behavior had continued into his adult life.

When Andy left high school and went off to college the impression was that he was glad to be out of Key West and had no intention of coming back. He would never say what his major was going to be but I suspected it would be journalism because of his behavior in high school. The question then became whether he would pass his courses.

I was surprised when I came back to visit Dad and found out that Andy was back on the island working at the *Current* for Larry Reynolds of all people. Larry had pretty good standards. The fact that he hired Andy told me that there was some reason other than any alleged journalistic abilities. I suspected that Hardy knew something about Reynolds or one of his friends that they would rather keep quiet and the job was his payoff. But he was also good at making people meet their deadlines, getting them to produce, and keeping things running on time. It turned out that management was his forté. Whether through blackmail or he was just good at it, I didn't know. But anyway, here was Andy back in Key West and again creating problems for people; nothing that I, as a member of the Department, could do anything about, but problems nonetheless.

There'd been some instances when individuals he'd been pressing for information on supposed stories had called to complain. A couple of times I'd been present when he came pretty close to stepping over the line and I had to warn him to back off. He'd even filed assault complaints on two people who had punched him out when he wouldn't leave them alone, but our local magistrate knew Andy as well. His complaints didn't go anywhere once it became clear that he'd repeatedly ignored their warnings.

I had always been careful to avoid getting involved with Andy, particularly after coming back to Key West after my time in Miami, and I didn't think he had anything he could use against me. At least he'd never tried. But he'd also been bothering Amy. Not that she'd made a formal complaint, just casually mentioned it when we were having coffee at Rosa's one morning. It was probably more that than the fact that I just plain didn't trust him that, when he stopped me, I was short with him.

"No, Andy, I don't have a minute," I said curtly, opening the car door.

"C'mon Tom, what's so important that you don't have time to talk to the press?"

I looked down at him; Andy was barely about 5'8" and I'm 6'2."

"Andy," I said, my temper quickly rising to its boiling point, "send over a decent reporter and, when I have the time and something to say, I'll talk to him. I will not talk to you about anything. I don't like talking to you on a good day and this certainly isn't one of those."

Andy was nothing if not persistent. "C'mon, Tom. All I

want is some information on the Sam Torres situation. I've got a deadline to meet."

"Bullshit, Andy. You and I both know you make your own deadlines and you've got as much chance of getting anything out of me as you have of getting a date with Amy Petersen."

He looked surprised.

"Yes, she's mentioned your attempts and the fact that she's told you to get lost on more than one occasion. No, she hasn't made a formal complaint against you either to me or to Mr. Reynolds. At least, not yet." I stepped toward him being purposely more intimidating. "So take this as a 'friendly' warning and back off. In any case, this isn't your turf. Amy has the police beat and she was on the scene this morning so she gets first crack at the story, when there is one. Her work relies on facts, not gossip and innuendo."

Andy stepped backward, scribbling on his notepad, probably something about me not being a cooperative public servant. I got in the car and started the engine. I think the possibility of Amy complaining to Larry Reynolds bothered him more than anything I could do to him.

I backed the car out of the space, stopped and looked at him, and added, "Also, I wouldn't recommend any professional retaliation against her. You know how Mr. Reynolds feels about that."

The last time someone at the paper tried to malign one of the female employees, Larry Reynolds had literally kicked the guy out the door and into the street. It was only due to his contacts in the Mayor's office and a quiet payment to the individual involved that Reynolds had avoided an assault charge. He may have other faults, but Larry Reynolds does not put up with anyone showing disrespect to his "girls."

CHAPTER 4

I turned onto Grinnell from Southard Street. A cyclist pedaled furiously up ahead of me. It was Julio. I gave the siren a quick sounding to get his attention, and pulled up in front of the house as he dropped his bike and ran toward the front door.

Through the open car window I called, "Julio, hold up a minute. I need to talk to you."

I picked up the microphone, and called Sally. "Headquarters, car 12. Cancel the alert for Julio Torres. I found him and he's okay. Car 12 out."

I got out of the car and walked over to Julio. "Now, quickly tell me where you've been and then get inside. Elyse needs you right now."

Tears welled in his eyes. I could tell he knew and was trying to be brave, but he was fighting a losing battle. His voice broke with emotion. "Is it true what they are saying about Papa Sam? Is he dead?"

I took hold of his shoulders and looked him in the eyes. "Yes, Julio. I'm sorry, but it is true." His tears flowed freely as he leaned against me and I remembered my feelings when I'd been told of my father's passing. I'd been much older than Julio, but that didn't make it any easier.

"How Senor Tom? What happened?" he sobbed.

"I don't know yet, son. But I will find out. Doc Elliott needs to do a post mortem and later he'll be able to tell us more. Right now I need to know where you've been."

Julio sniffed and wiped his eyes. "I only went to the movies."

"The movies? I thought you were supposed to be helping Father Stephen." I gave him a stern look. "Who is she?" I asked, noting the expression on his face.

Julio looked at the ground and mumbled, "Gloria Reynolds."

Now I was surprised. "Gloria Reynolds? Larry Reynolds' daughter?"

Julio looked at me, somewhat of a hurt expression mingling with the sorrow on his face but with a glint of fire in his eyes. "Yes sir, she's a nice girl. We are friends. We're not doing anything wrong."

"Julio, you know who her father is. You know his position and how he feels about his daughter."

Larry Reynolds was 'Old South,' and, like all Southern gentlemen, devoted to his daughter, especially since her mother had died five years ago. However, he could also be bigoted, chauvinistic, and very opinionated. He'd been against desegregation and had often made his feelings known on the editorial page of his paper. Recently, though, he'd been rather silent on that issue, probably because of his rumored political aspirations. He would not be pleased to find out that Gloria, his only child, his precious little girl, was seeing someone who, in his eyes, was nothing more than a Cuban refugee.

"Senor Tom, I know the things her father says and writes; I know that he doesn't like people like me and Papa Sam and Mama Elyse. But Gloria, she is not like that. Gloria is a nice girl who does not say bad things about anyone. She helps Padre Stephen and the sisters even though she is not Catholic. She is helping me to study for my test."

"What test?"

Julio stood up straight and looked directly at me. "My citizenship test. I am eighteen now and I have lived here in the United States more than five years. I have no one back in Cuba. It is time I did this and Gloria is helping me."

"And how does going to the movies, instead of helping Father Steve, relate to studying for your test?" I asked, more to cover my own embarrassment at his revelation than

24

anything else.

Julio's shoulders drooped. "To be honest, it does not. We just wanted some time alone and the movie house is cool. We did not hear about Papa Sam until we came out and I came straight home."

I couldn't deny that fact. The State Theater on Duval was air conditioned, unlike most of the homes in Key West. But then again, so was the church. However, it's difficult to be alone there.

Julio looked up at me. "I still don't know what has happened, only that Papa Sam is dead. What can you tell me?"

I put my arm around his shoulder and walked him up onto the porch while I gave him the short facts that Sam had been found on the beach with a head wound and that we didn't yet know if it was an accident or something else. I also told him that until we had the official medical report we weren't ruling anything out.

"Julio, *Greta* isn't at her mooring and Elyse told me that Sam had a charter booked for Friday. Do you know who that was for?"

"No. I would have to look in the book."

"I was afraid of that. Unfortunately Sam's book is missing. I'm guessing it's on the boat or he left it in his truck. Do you know where the truck is?"

He shook his head. "No, Sir. But Papa Sam never took the book on a cruise. He only took it to the boat when he would load supplies and then he always brought it home and put it on the desk."

"And Sam came home Thursday evening?"

"Yes, Sir, and he left early Friday morning. I helped him put the tackle in the truck. He never leaves it on the boat."

"Did you see the charter book on the desk that morning?"

"Yes sir. It was there when I left later for school." Julio

25

stared at the ground, his brow furrowed, then looked up at me. "But I don't remember seeing it this morning. Mama Elyse must have put it in the drawer."

Well, that narrowed our time line on Sam and confirmed that his charter book wasn't on the boat or in the truck. Also, that the truck had to have been at the harbor Friday morning. But where were they now?

"Julio, I want you to search your house for that book. I looked on and in the desk earlier and it wasn't there, but you look again. I know that's where Sam always put it, but it wasn't there this morning. If you find it, call me at the station. If I'm not there, leave a message and they'll get me on the radio."

"Si, Lieutenant. I will look everywhere," he said with confidence. I looked at Julio Torres and saw a different person than the young kid I had been expecting. I put my hand on his shoulder and looked him in the eye.

"Julio, I'm proud of the way you're handling this situation and for what you're planning. I know Elyse is too. She and Sam have taught you well. I'm a little concerned about your relationship with Gloria Reynolds but, as a friend, I will do everything I can to help if that is what you both want. As a police officer, though, I caution you to obey the laws. You may get into situations which could jeopardize your plans, especially if Mr. Reynolds finds out about you and Gloria. He'll view you as an undesirable element in her life. I want you to promise me that you'll both be careful and if anything does happen you come to me, Doctor Elliott or Father Stephen before you do anything else."

"Thank you, Senor Tom. I promise and I will tell Gloria."

At that point the door opened and Doc came out.

"I thought I heard voices out here. So, you found him. Where was he?"

I smiled, "Relax Doc. It was nothing serious. Julio and a friend just went to the movies and didn't know anything until they got out then he came straight home. We both got here together."

Doc turned to Julio.

"Well young man, you'd better get in there. You have a man's work to do and I need to talk to the Lieutenant."

Julio gave one last sniff, wiped his eyes and went inside.

Doc and I sat down on the porch steps.

"All right Tom, who is she?"

"How'd you know?"

"I was young once. And I've had teenagers. I know the signs."

"Would you believe Gloria Reynolds?"

Doc whistled. "I have to admit the kid's got taste and guts. Do you think her old man knows?"

I laughed. "If he did, we'd have heard it across the whole island by now. I don't think it's serious, yet. According to Julio, it's simply friendship and she's helping him study for his citizenship test."

Doc nodded. "Ah, that explains it."

"Explains what?"

"I finally got Elyse to take something to help her sleep. As she was drifting off she mumbled something about Julio and a test but I couldn't make out what it was. That must be it."

"How's she doing?"

"Resting comfortably right now. I think she'll be all right now that Julio's home. She got rather agitated when Father Steve came by and voiced surprise at his absence. I've still got a nurse coming to stay the night though, just in case. Anything come up yet on the investigation?"

"No, nothing yet. Dennis is out with his nose to the ground. There's an 'all points' out for Sam's truck. And the Sheriff and the Coast Guard have been alerted to watch for his boat. I've got some theories trying to form in my mind, but nothing's making sense."

Doc got up and stepped off the porch.

"Well," he said, stretching, "I'm on call tonight so if anything happens here I'll know about it. I'm going to go grab a bite and then get started on the autopsy. You know where to find me if you need me."

"Okay, Doc. Thanks."

I leaned back and tried to think but Doc's mention of food made me realize I'd been running on caffeine all day. I got up and walked back to the car. Julio and Gloria's relationship made me think about my own relationship with Amy, where it was now, where it might go, and whether her father would object to his little girl dating a cop. Then my stomach rumbled and I wondered if she was still at work and hungry too.

CHAPTER 5

Since he wasn't here, I parked my car in the Chief's spot next to the door into KWPD headquarters. We shared space with the fire department on the ground floor of City Hall, a red brick building with a distinctive clock tower, at the corner of Ann and Greene Street. The Mayor's office and City Council were upstairs.

I intended to call the paper and ask Amy to dinner, but Sally was at the door waving an envelope at me. "Tom, this just came for you from the Coast Guard. The Chief called to say he got up to Tallahassee and I'm off to the theatre to work on costumes. Gene is working dispatch tonight so I'll see you tomorrow."

I knew the envelope had to be the report that Lee had promised and my curiosity got the better of me. "Thanks, Sally." I started opening the envelope as I walked into the building.

I pulled out the contents and laid the report on my desk. A note was clipped to the first page. "Tom," Lee had written, "here's a copy of the report on Sam's last safety stop. Hope it helps. There was also a photo in the file that you might find interesting. I had no time to find the negative and make a copy so I'm sending the original. Don't lose it."

The report didn't add much to what Lee had told me over the phone.

The photograph was more interesting.

There were six people in the photo; Sam, a couple of Coasties and three other men grouped around the fighting chair on the stern of *Greta*. I now understood Lee's comment from our conversation about them looking like the kind I might have met in Miami. The size of the photograph, and the distance from which it was taken, made it difficult to make out their features with the naked eye, but the two on either side of the chair were clearly what we would refer to as 'the muscle' for the one sitting in the chair. Remembering that the report noted that this third person had been addressed by the others as 'Mr. D,' it was him I was interested in as I rummaged in the desk for a magnifying glass.

I looked through the magnifier at 'Mr. D' and some of the pieces of the puzzle started to fall into place. I didn't like the picture they were forming.

When I went to college, my father was hoping I would go on to law school and follow him into his practice. Dad's firm, Jackson and Cole, was small but, when I was in school, it was well known in the Keys for anyone who needed a will drafted, a contract written, or representation before the local court on a DUI, speeding ticket, simple assault from a bar fight, etc. In short, it was a general practice firm that pretty much took care of the legal needs of the regular working citizens of Key West and the lower Keys. The wealthy had their fancy lawyers in Miami. The locals had Dad.

I know Dad was disappointed when I told him I planned to study police science, but he never showed it nor did he try to change my mind.

The only time he showed some concern was one afternoon back in 1954. I'd come back home for a visit after getting out of the Army and before taking a position with the Miami PD as a young detective. We were out fishing the flats off Sugarloaf Key, or as Dad always called it, 'feeding the fish,' since he hardly ever caught anything and viewed it more as an opportunity to relax and reflect. Except for this one time, I can't remember ever discussing anything important with him when we were fishing. Serious subjects were always reserved for his office.

This time, however, Dad was not relaxed. Instead of

reclining, he sat hunched over staring at the water as I described the job I would be reporting to the next week. When I finished, he looked at me.

"Tommy, when you were a boy I think I knew that you wouldn't follow me into the legal profession. Had your mother survived then you would probably have siblings and one of them would continue the practice. I've made arrangements with Efrem Cole that when my time comes, he'll settle with you regarding my percentage of the practice."

I looked at him, startled that he would be talking like this.

"Dad," I said, "are you all right? Is there something I should know?"

"No, Tommy, I'm okay according to Doctor Elliott, but I do feel tired more often and I am," he paused, "concerned about this position of yours in Miami."

"Dad, it's a great opportunity. I'll learn more about investigations in two years with the Miami PD than I could hope to learn anywhere else in Florida. Then I can bring that knowledge and my contacts back here to Key West."

"I know that, Tommy; it's just that I get the legal journals and reports from Miami. I see what's going on up there and it bothers me. There are elements working their way into all facets of the city and county which are not going to make your job easy or, indeed, safe. And I'm not referring to the cronyism going on or the land barons. The criminal element is becoming more adventuresome, even brazen, in some of its activities."

"But Dad, that'll be part of my job. I can't avoid that. In fact, that's part of the reason I accepted the position. I want to know what to look for and how to deal with them before they get down here and, if I can, stop them from getting to our island. I'd much rather deal with our own home grown crooks."

My father sighed, his fishing rod, loosely held, dropped mirroring his mood. "I don't think you can stop them, Tommy. But if you can at least slow them down, that would help. However, there is one gentleman that you should watch out for."

The way he said "gentleman" told me he didn't mean it.

"Who's that Dad?"

"There is one Salvatore Donatello in Miami. He's not one of the top men in the organization, at least not yet, but he is one to watch out for."

"What's his position and how do you know him? You've never done any serious criminal prosecution." I'd heard of Donatello, but I was surprised that my father knew about him.

Dad looked at me and gave me a weak smile. I wouldn't call it 'sheepish,' but he definitely looked like a kid who'd been caught with his hand in a cookie jar.

"I've never told you this, but it was just after you went into the Army."

I'd spent two years after college as an MP and I think it was that experience along with my college degree that had gotten me the first level detective job in Miami without having to first spend time in a uniform.

Dad continued. "I had one situation that took me to Miami as part of a larger case involving gambling and murder charges against Mr. Donatello. The allegations were that he ran the illegal gambling organization in Dade and the surrounding counties and had someone murdered for 'non-performance' as the contract lawyers put it.

"My client was a small fish swimming in a large ocean and got caught. A small timer from the lower Keys who ran the bag from here to Miami, he got scared when he heard about the murder and started naming names. As a local attorney, I was requested by the bar to provide his defense so they could be sure there was no collusion between a

32

public defender from Miami and the Miami Police.

"What my client told the police led them to Donatello and his associates. Unfortunately, the prosecutor's office wasn't able to prove anything against Donatello." Dad reeled in his line and stared at the empty hook. "Personally, I believe that he pulled some strings in the Mayor's Office, maybe even the police department, and was able to walk away without so much as a smudge against his name. It didn't even make the newspapers."

I rebaited his hook and he tossed it back into the water. "What happened to your client?"

"He got a reduced sentence of three years because of his cooperation with the police and lost his life in prison, probably for the same thing. Allegedly, it happened during a fight, but most likely it was sanctioned as a warning to others."

"I remember that incident. It involved gambling in connection with a college football team. The quarterback was supposed to keep the points down but got carried away with the way the game was going and forgot. They found him later in the Everglades, or rather what was left of him, but the 'gators hadn't obscured the cause of death, two bullets to the head." I felt something tug my line and started reeling in.

"Yes, that's the case," Dad said. "Somebody wanted to put Mr. Donatello away for murder, but somebody with more pull wanted him free. They couldn't even get him for running an illegal book. His lawyers completely discredited my client and his testimony, even his confession about his own activities. Unfortunately, that was after he had been found guilty based on that confession. Shortly after that the prison fight took place."

"So what happened to Donatello?" My line went slack.

"After the trial he left Miami. Word was that he got sent to Havana to run the casinos and, as far as I know, he's still there; although I would presume that he returns to Miami periodically. Just be careful up there, whether it's with Donatello or anyone else in that organization. Remember also that they have friends somewhere with the ability to keep them out of jail and out of the news."

"Don't worry, Dad, I will. I think I'll also check up on Mr. Donatello just to see where he is."

"Just do it quietly and not on the record, okay?"

We didn't catch anything that day and I was never able to confirm Sal Donatello's whereabouts. No one would talk, although there were rumors. I think I saw him once at City Hall. I was getting out of the car as someone who appeared to resemble him was getting into a limo with darkened windows. I had no reason to follow him and was on my way to a meeting at the prosecutor's office on an unrelated matter. I did note down the license plate number of the limo for future reference. That was in 1957.

As for the murder of the young quarterback, that remained an open case.

As I said, there were rumors about Sal Donatello, but nothing confirmed until Spring of 1959 when he was seen and positively identified in a Miami Beach restaurant that was well above my pay grade. What was even more interesting was the identity of his dinner companion, none other than the former lead prosecutor from the quarterback case who had recently retired. According to the person who saw them, they were chatting like old friends. The former prosecutor was later listed as a partner of the high dollar firm that provided Donatello's defense team in that old case.

I left Miami that fall and came back to Key West as planned. Dad was gone by then; a heart attack that neither he nor Doc Elliott had foreseen. But Key West was still home, the old house was paid for and land prices hadn't yet started to take off like the rockets at Cape Canaveral.

The name Salvatore Donatello had fallen off my personal radar.

Now, seven years later, it was back on. 'Mr. D' was Sal Donatello. But what would he and his boys be doing on Sam's boat half way between here and Cuba? Had Sam been running contraband for Donatello? Was that why Sam was now in the morgue? Did Elyse know anything? Might she and Julio be in danger? Too many questions and not enough answers.

The ringing of the telephone jerked me back to the present. I picked up the handset and punched the flashing button. "Jackson." It sounded more like a bark than anything else.

"Tom, are you okay? It's Amy."

I'd forgotten I was going to call and ask her to dinner.

"Amy, I'm sorry, my mind was somewhere else."

"That's all right. I was wondering if you were hungry? Knowing how you work, I'm guessing you haven't had anything all day."

"You know me too well. How about The Harbour? We can see what came in on the boats today. Are you still at the paper?"

Ordinarily I would have suggested a pizza or something simple, but Amy's cooperation this morning merited something nicer. The Harbour was one of the better restaurants in Key West. Its location along Caroline Street next to the docks guaranteed that what they served was fresh caught that day.

"Yes, I just put my piece on Sam to bed. I think Elyse will like it. As for your selection, I'd be happy with carryout and the sunset at Mallory Square, but I'm not going to turn down a proper meal."

"Okay. I'll pick you up in about 20 minutes. I've got a call I have to make."

"Give me an hour. I have to go home and change if I'm

35

going to be seen with you at The Harbour. Pick me up there."

We both hung up. I pulled out my private telephone list and dialed a number at my old precinct in Miami.

"Miami PD, Sergeant Zachiarelli, how may I help you?"

"You can put down the cannoli, Lou, and get to work."

"Stonewall Jackson! Well I'll be damned. What's wrong? Things so quiet down there in paradise that you got to call up and bother a hard working cop?"

Lou Zachiarelli was the only one who habitually used the nickname I'd been saddled with as a kid. He'd been a desk sergeant when I was in Miami and was always on my case about how to do my paperwork. I was actually a little surprised he was still there this late in the day. Then I remembered that he'd switched from days to swing shift when his wife, Iris, got sick. I guess he'd never gone back.

"Hi, Lou. Since when did you start answering the phone so nicely?"

"We're under orders from up top, 'be pleasant when you answer the phone since you don't know who's on the other end' bullshit. Apparently some society dame called and didn't like the way the conversation went so she complained to her husband who then complained to his councilman and so on up the line. Then the shit started to flow down hill. You know how that works."

"Yeah Lou, I do. That's one reason I got out of Miami."

"And so am I, just as soon as I retire in two years. Then I'm going to come down there and bug you."

I laughed. It could well happen with Iris gone and the kids grown.

"You know I have a room for you Lou, anytime you're ready. In the meantime, I need some information on Salvatore Donatello. What's he up to these days?"

Lou whistled in surprise at my question. "Donatello? Jeeze, Tom, don't tell me he's messing around down there?"

"Not yet, as far as I know. But he was spotted by the Coast Guard about a month ago on a charter boat that operates out of here and it got me wondering."

"Well I haven't heard anything up here, but then I'm not on that detail any more Tom. They've got me working West Miami, what they call 'Little Havana' now, where things are starting to warm up. Donatello, as far as I know, still has his operations downtown, although I hear he's got legitimate interests in some fancy places in Miami Beach, probably trying to clean up some of his ill gotten gains."

"I take it you all still think he's in charge of the gambling and prostitution up there, but any noise about him branching out into other areas?"

"You know none of that's ever been proven, Tom, and if you mention it in public, you'll have his lawyers all over you."

"I know, I know, he's got an in with the Prosecutor's Office, the City Council, maybe even the Department itself. For all I know even the mayor jumps when Donatello speaks. I just want to know what the word on the street is Lou."

"Okay, Tom, okay. Like I said, I'm not on that detail anymore and I haven't heard anything so maybe he's not making any moves, just running his end of things. To be honest, I don't think you have anything to worry about down there from the likes of Donatello. Most likely what you're going to start seeing are the gangs from West Miami moving down and causing trouble.

"We're getting some chatter around here that they're moving, or have moved, into the drug business and some of them have contacts in Cuba and elsewhere for the stuff. When you consider their cost and the rate of return, it's a hell of a better investment than gambling or prostitution. Plus there's the possibility that Castro may be helping by not putting up many roadblocks to bringing the stuff through Cuba. It would be a good way for him to score some hard currency since Kennedy slapped the embargo on him in '62. I'll try to get you put on the 'memo list' for anything we get. Meanwhile, as far as Donatello goes, I'll see what I can find out and let you know. Remember who you're dealing with though and be careful."

"I will Lou, don't worry, and thanks."

I hung up the phone, shoved Lee's report into my desk and walked out of the squad room.

"Gene, any word from Dennis?" I asked as I passed the dispatch desk.

"Yes, sir. He called in about half an hour ago to say he had nothing to report and was going home but he'd see you tomorrow."

"Anything on *Greta* or Sam Torres' truck?"

Gene checked the lists.

"No, sir, nothing yet."

"Okay. I'll be at The Harbour and then I'm going home. Call me if anything comes in."

"Yes, sir. I hear they got some good grouper and red snapper in today so enjoy your meal."

"Thanks Gene."

As I walked out to the car I was still trying to think of what possible connection there could be between Sam Torres and Sal Donatello. I'd known Sam all my life. He taught me to fish, even showed me a couple of his special spots. As far as I knew he'd never even had a parking ticket. He was too disciplined. His boat was the best cared for in the harbor and his truck still looked like it'd just come out of the showroom, which down here surrounded by sea air was something.

As for smuggling, I couldn't see Sam doing that either. Not even the occasional "square grouper" or bale of marijuana found floating in the ocean. Some boat captains will haul those in with the idea of selling the stuff to make a few bucks. They usually find out otherwise when we get them. The other thing is that, once you bring anything in, there's only one road out for 110 miles to the mainland and that can easily be blocked. No, Sam wouldn't mess with anything like that. He'd have had too much to lose if he got caught. He wouldn't risk *Greta* that way. Also, Elyse would have strangled him.

No matter which way I looked at it, it just didn't square for Sam to be mixed up with the likes of Donatello.

Of course there was also nothing to indicate that Donatello was trying to move in down here. I would have definitely known about that. There was no way that a big time gambling or prostitution operation could move into Key West without the police hearing something. Sure we had a few floating crap games, some illicit poker games, even some betting on sports events which I was sure went through the boys in Miami. At times we even got some girls coming down here from Miami and elsewhere to, shall we say, 'ply their trade.' But none of it was of a scale to warrant a large investment down here. It was strictly small potatoes.

No, if you were looking for a large-scale operation to interest someone like Salvatore Donatello, it wasn't here. We just didn't present a large enough market for him. Besides, in all of the information I had on Donatello, there'd never been any indication that he had an interest in anything but gambling and prostitution. Also, the only suspicious death or murder that he'd ever been linked to was the case of the quarterback, and even that was questionable.

Face it Jackson, I told myself as I pulled up at home and went in for a quick shower and change before going to pick up Amy, the only thing that can put Sal Donatello on Sam's boat was that they were out fishing. Donatello was simply a charter. But how did he and Sam meet?

CHAPTER 6

Sunday

I woke up the next morning to the smell of fresh coffee and the sounds of pots and pans knocking together like someone was looking for the correct one. Rolling over, I wondered for an instant who the hell was in my kitchen. Then I remembered the previous evening.

Amy had been waiting for me when I got to her place. I couldn't help but notice her casual elegance. Instead of her usual attire of shorts or Capri pants, she wore a pair of cream-colored linen slacks and an open shirt of the same hue over a soft green T-shirt. Her only jewelry was a pair of jade earrings. The combination with her eyes was stunning. A light shade of lipstick that matched her nail polish completed the outfit. She neither wore nor needed any additional makeup. I liked what I saw and told her so.

"Why, thank you, sir," she said, giving me a little curtsey. "You look particularly dashing yourself."

I looked down at my gray slacks, navy sport coat and light blue shirt. "Same me," I said. "Just a different wrapper."

"Well I like this wrapper. It sure beats that uniform you're always in. This outfit makes you look human and I don't have to worry that someone might think I'm being arrested for something." She took my arm. "Come on, I'm hungry," she said and grabbed her bag as we walked out the door.

At The Harbour, we were shown to a table overlooking the waterfront. I asked the waiter about the snapper and grouper and he confirmed that they were both fresh off the boats. We ordered one of each so we could share and I left it to the waiter to select the wine knowing he wouldn't pick anything outrageous.

As we waited for our appetizers, Amy pulled out a copy of the piece she'd written on Sam and asked me to read it saying that she wanted to be sure there was nothing in it that would upset Elyse.

She watched me intently as I read her piece. Finishing it, I looked up. She raised one eyebrow and said questioningly, "Well?"

I smiled at her. "Don't change a word. It's perfect. You know, Sam had many repeat clients from all up the East coast, even some from out West. You should put this on the wire."

"I was hoping you'd say that. I almost did it before I left, but I wanted you to see it first so I've got Eddie waiting for me to call and tell him to go ahead."

"So go call him. Here's a dime," I said fishing in my pocket. "Can he do that without Andy's say so?"

"Screw Andy," Amy replied.

"Please don't," I responded. "That thought is just too horrible to entertain. But seriously, can Eddie put something out on just your say-so?"

Amy stood up, taking the proffered coin, "In this case, yes. I went over Andy's head and cleared it with Mr. Reynolds, he likes what I write. Besides, the little weasel wasn't there, thank God." Somehow, the fact that Andy wasn't at the paper when Amy was writing bothered me. Where was he instead of ogling her? Had he taken my warning to heart? I doubted it. He was probably out making trouble for someone. I just hoped it wasn't for me or Amy.

The appetizers and wine came while Amy was on the phone. I poured a couple of glasses and was just taking a sip when she came back to the table. I could tell from her expression that storm warnings were up. "What's wrong?" I asked.

"Andy." She almost spat the name. "He came into the

office while I was on the phone with Eddie and wanted to know what was going on since it was obvious that something was going out and he hadn't approved it."

"Did Eddie tell him?"

"He didn't have any choice. But he was able to stall until it was too late to pull it back. Needless to say Andy was pissed and he lit into Eddie something awful. I may have to go see Mr. Reynolds tomorrow to make sure Eddie doesn't get fired. By the way, Andy knows we're here," she said over her wine glass.

"Damn. How did that happen?" I asked annoyed that, once again, Andy Hardy had infringed on what little privacy I had.

"Apparently he called the station wanting to talk to you about the case. Whoever was on duty told him you weren't available. Then he demanded to know where you were and what was going on in the investigation claiming freedom of the press and the public's right to know. He threatened to go to the City Council and have this guy fired."

I sighed, "That would be Gene. He's a good kid, but he hasn't yet developed the skin to stand up to the likes of Andy Hardy."

"Anyway, according to Eddie, the only thing Gene would tell Andy was where you were, but nothing about the case. Apparently, that's about when I called and Andy heard Eddie talking to me."

"How did you get all this?"

"I'm a reporter, Tom. It's my job to get information." Her eyes darkened. "Do you have a problem with that?"

"Okay, okay. Down, Tiger," I said, holding my hands up. "I'm not angry with you; I just can't figure how Eddie could tell you all this with Andy right there."

Her face softened as her brief anger subsided. "A little trick I taught him. Eddie didn't hang up when Andy came in, he just laid the phone down and I stayed on the line and listened. After Andy left, Eddie got back on and filled me in. By the way, I heard about your run in with him earlier today; thanks for your support. I think this could be a good story if you would give me some facts to work with."

"As soon as I've got something solid, I'll let you know. Like I told Andy, you were first on the scene so it's your story. Besides, he'd only screw it up."

Amy raised her glass and toasted. "Amen to that. I just hope he doesn't do something tonight."

"Well you don't have to worry about him coming here. He knows I'd throw his ass in jail if he created a disturbance in public and Reynolds wouldn't like that. Besides, I understand Mel has barred him from the place." Mel Kauffman was the owner of The Harbour and a former boxer who would just as soon knock Andy into next week as let him through the door of the place. "Now quit worrying about Andrew Hardy and enjoy your dinner. With you on his side I think Eddie's safe too."

The rest of the evening passed quietly. Although we'd often shared lunches, quickly grabbed carryout, as well as the occasional pizza and beer after hours, a real sit-down dinner like this one was a rarity for us. We'd known each other for four years, been to friends' parties together, caught the occasional movie, even attended some fancy events at Casa Marina or the Key West Country Club, but those had been because I was representing the Department or Amy was there for the *Current*. Surprisingly, in all that time, this evening was our first what you could call "fancy dinner date," just the two of us. It was sad that it coincided with the loss of a good friend.

I was fairly certain we wouldn't be interrupted tonight. Even though I was technically "on call" for anything, Gene wouldn't call unless it was a real emergency. Even then, knowing where I was and who I was with, I think he'd probably call Sally first to ask if he should disturb me. I knew Dennis wouldn't call until tomorrow since he'd already reported in. And with the sun down, if anyone found *Greta* we wouldn't be able to do anything until daylight anyway.

Looking at Amy in the candlelight, I thought back to the time, almost four years ago, when she and I first met, shortly after she'd arrived in the Keys, just in time for the missile crisis in 1962 when everyone thought the Cubans and the Russians were going to invade. She'd been covering the story as a freelance journalist, working on her Masters degree and reporting back to her professor in Chicago. I'd had to arrest her for trespassing and creating a public disturbance in order to keep the Navy from trying to charge her with espionage. Then Larry Reynolds got involved, the charges were dropped and he hired her full time.

Since then she'd finished her degree and covered every subject she could from the police beat on down to local interest stuff, and I had followed her stories. Her writing was first class and her facts were always correct, especially on any story dealing with the KWPD or Sheriff's Office. Amy could have been a top reporter on a big city paper but she never showed any interest in moving in that direction.

We talked about the little nonsensical things that most people do when they want to avoid talking shop. When those were exhausted we talked about each other. She asked me about growing up in Key West and I asked her about Wisconsin where she'd spent her childhood. Amy told me about the winters and how, after a spring break trip to Florida, she vowed to avoid them again if at all possible.

After getting her BA in English she'd interned at a newspaper in Pittsburgh; then went to papers in St Louis, Chattanooga and Atlanta, slowly working her way back to Florida at the same time working up her resume and doing her Master's by correspondence. She probably could've gotten a good job at the Miami *Herald* but for some reason that she said she hadn't yet figured out, she bypassed Miami and as soon as she hit the overseas highway decided to go all the way to the end. So far, she hadn't considered going back, though I was sure she'd had offers.

I'd asked about her family on other occasions and she'd always been defensive. I knew she had a sister who'd been married but was now divorced and the way she talked about her parents made me suspect they weren't together either. Amy had gone back north only a couple of times since we met and both of those trips had been for her sister's sake. My job and a fear of failure or loss held me back from commitment in relationships. I often wondered if Amy's hesitancy had something to do with the same fears due to her sister's experience.

I wanted to know more about her family but this evening wasn't the time to ask. I'd been getting a feeling recently that something between us was changing, a good change, and I didn't want to spoil it by asking or saying the wrong thing. Instead, I told her about my conversation with Julio and his plans to become a U.S. citizen. I even mentioned that Gloria Reynolds was helping him. Amy had the same concerns I did about Gloria's father and said she'd help Julio if he needed it. I was glad that she offered since I was afraid that if I'd asked her she would have hesitated because of her boss.

After dinner we walked by the water under a clear night sky heavy with stars, holding hands like a couple of high school kids. A light breeze stirred the palm fronds which clicked and clacked like horse's hooves on cobblestones. Mixed fragrances, the tang of salt, the faint ammonia odor of rotting seaweed, the sweet perfume of hibiscus and bougainvillea and other tropical blossoms wafted across the island and moderated the warmth of the day that seeped from the buildings and streets. I pointed out some of the constellations and explained the basics of celestial navigation. When she asked me how I'd learned all of that, I told her that my Dad had been an amateur astronomer, I still had his telescope, but that it was Sam who'd taught me navigation.

She asked me about Dad and I gave her the short answers about how he'd come down to the Keys as a new lawyer, struggled to get a practice going and get accepted by the people as one of them, how he'd helped those who needed it even when they'd had nothing with which to pay for his services. That was during the depression. She kept prodding, using her reporter's knack to get more out of her subject than they were sometimes willing to give. I was surprised at some of the things I remembered because of it.

Then she started asking me about Sam.

Amy had once done a series of stories about the charter skippers of Key West, but when she got to Sam, he wouldn't talk. "It'd be too much like advertising," he told her, "to talk about myself." Sam was the only person I've known that Amy couldn't get anything out of. She got it out of me.

We strolled along, now arm in arm, and I told her about how his great, great grandfather came over from Cuba with the cigar business; then the story about his great grandfather being a 'wrecker' saving passengers and crew from ships that hit the reef and profiting from the salvage of their cargoes. I told her about his grandfather who went to sea as a simple hand and rose to become first mate of his last ship before it was lost in a hurricane with all hands. Finally, I told her how his father had started as a hired hand on a commercial fishing boat and worked his way up to owning his own boat. When he passed away, Sam took it over and turned it into what, I considered, the best charter boat in the Keys.

Then she looked at me with the reflection of the stars in her clear, green eyes and said, "Yes, but what about Sam?"

I looked into those eyes, saw honesty and the depth of

kindness that had been in the piece she'd written today and I opened my mind and told her everything I knew. How, when my mother died when I was three and Dad was still struggling to make the practice work, Sam would bring us fresh fish and some of whatever Elyse had baked that day so he was sure we had something to eat. How he'd told my father that a boy needs to know how to fish and how to find his way around, so he taught me like I was his own son.

I also told her how neither Sam nor Elyse would ever take anything in payment for their kindness until one day when he came to Dad with a problem concerning a charter client who refused to pay because he hadn't caught anything and blamed Sam for it. Because Sam was part black and from a Cuban family, this person thought he could get away with it. Dad proved otherwise and the word got out among the locals. From then on, Dad's practice among the Cubans, Blacks and other minorities in the Keys grew and no one with a problem was ever turned away because they couldn't pay, were of a different color, or didn't speak English that well.

Sam and Dad both, in their own way, taught me about family and community. I think that's why I went into police work and why I came back to Key West, because it's a community where you can know the people and their needs and can work to keep it safe for everyone. To me, this island is family.

When we finally stopped and looked around, I realized we were half way up Duval Street. At some point along the way, Amy had wrapped her arm around my waist and I'd put mine around hers. I felt her warmth against me; her scent mingled with the island's.

"You should have stopped me," I said. "We've got a long walk back to the car."

She turned and put both arms around me, hugging close. "I don't care," she said almost into my chest. "I feel as if I finally know you after all this time and I like it. I feel safe. Let's go home."

I looked at her and, holding my breath, asked, "Yours or mine?"

Amy replied, "Does it matter?"

I breathed in the combined aromas of Key West and Amy Petersen and something inside me snapped into place. I knew that this was what I wanted, to be here, now, with her, and it seemed that was what she wanted too. We kissed long and hard under the street lamp. When Amy pointed out that people could see what we were doing I said "so what" and hailed a passing cab to take us back to the restaurant and my car.

Now it was morning, I was in my bed and the woman I had just spent the night with was making breakfast for me in my kitchen. It felt good. Would it continue? Could we make it work? I didn't know, but I found myself deciding I was ready to try. I hoped she felt the same.

The smell of fresh brewed coffee was tantalizing and I figured that breakfast in bed the first morning was probably too much to expect so I got up and slipped into my robe. I walked down the hall and quietly entered the kitchen. Amy was in front of the stove, her back to me, wearing one of my shirts. Her own clothes were still in a pile on the bedroom floor where they had fallen last night.

My gaze started at her feet and travelled up her legs noting the shape of her calves, the hollow at the back of her knees and the swelling of her thighs as they disappeared under the tail of my shirt. I remembered the feel of those thighs wrapped around me last night. The shirt itself draped over her hips, gently caressing her buttocks and hinted at the inward curve to her waist as I continued my tour up her back to her shoulders, the shoulders of a good swimmer.

"When you've finished undressing me again you can take the juice and coffee out to the patio. I hope you like

49

your eggs scrambled," she said.

"How did you know I was here?"

Amy turned around. Only the bottom couple of buttons on the shirt were fastened. Damn, my shirts never looked that good on me.

Smiling, she said, "A woman always knows when her man is around."

I felt things stirring and started toward her. Amy waved a spatula at me. "Uh, uh, not before breakfast."

Picking up the juice and coffee, I went through the open French doors to the back patio, my mind focused on the words she'd used, "her man." I took that as a good omen. Amy followed shortly after with the eggs and bacon.

We sat there enjoying a quiet Sunday breakfast like any respectable couple, except that we were anything but. I had never thought that the simple act of drinking coffee could be so infused with desire until that morning. The way Amy looked at me across the table as she sipped from her cup was enough to weaken stronger men than I. That together with the knowledge of what was barely hidden by my shirt resulted in my untouched eggs going cold while I got progressively warmer.

It was a good thing I hadn't bothered to thin the vegetation around the back yard; otherwise my neighbors would have had a shock.

I was about to get up and lead her back to the bedroom when Amy came around to my side of the table, unbuttoning those bottom buttons as she came. I pivoted my chair around to meet her. Reaching down, she spread my robe open, smiling at what she saw. Straddling my lap, she eased herself slowly on to me, moaning slightly. I put my arms around her; slipped my hands under the shirt and up her back pulling her against me, feeling her breasts flatten against my chest as my lips met hers.

We sat there for a few moments, neither of us

breathing, then she began to rock her hips gently back and forth, massaging me with a slow steady motion that reminded me of the easy rocking of a ship at sea and part of me wondered if this could be why sailors considered ships female. However, the other, and major part of me just wanted this to continue, albeit in a more comfortable location. Moving my hands down to Amy's derriere, I stood up holding her as she wrapped her legs around me and I walked us back into the house to the bedroom where we spent the rest of the morning.

CHAPTER 7

The ringing of the telephone woke us both up. Amy's head was on my chest and my arms were around her. The light breeze from the ceiling fan helped to evaporate our combined perspiration in the heat of the tropical afternoon.

I picked the receiver off the cradle, "Yeah, this is Tom Jackson," I said lazily.

"Good afternoon Mr. Jackson, this is your wake-up call."

I recognized Sally's voice and looked at the clock on the nightstand, 2:00 p.m. "What's up Sally?"

"Sorry Tom, I know it's technically your day off, but Dennis called looking for you and I thought you'd want to know."

I remembered that Dennis had said he was going to follow-up on those boats and owners who weren't in the marina yesterday. Sunday morning in Key West is usually the best time to find anyone. The religious ones are at church, the partiers from the night before are sleeping it off at home or in the holding cells, and everyone else is generally just taking it easy.

"Thanks Sally. Did he say where he was?"

"Yes, he's at the marina. Are you going to meet him there?"

I was still waking up and yawned, "Yeah, call him back and tell him I'll be there in about thirty minutes. I'll meet him at the Coffee Shack."

"Will do, Tom. Oh, by the way, Eddie called. Tell Amy that Larry Reynolds is looking for her and wants to see her at the *Current* as soon as possible."

Without thinking I said, "I will Sally," and hung up. Only then did what she'd said register and I thought how did she know?

As I sat up on the edge of the bed, Amy snuggled up against my back. "What was that about?"

"Dennis wants to see me over at the marina. Maybe he found someone who saw Sam on Friday. Also, Sally said to tell you that Reynolds is looking for you."

Amy looked at me quizzically, "How did she know I was here?"

"Damned if I know, but we'd both better get going. I'll drop you at your place."

"I could use a bath before I see Larry."

"Would you settle for a quick shared shower? You scrub my back and I'll scrub yours."

Twenty minutes later, showered and dressed, I'd taken Amy home and was on my way to the marina. I found Dennis at the Coffee Shack by the dock master's office.

"Sorry to drag you out Lieutenant, but I thought you might want to talk to Gus yourself," he said as he handed me a much needed large coffee.

Taking a sip, I felt that first refreshing surge of fresh brewed coffee as it slips down the throat. The Coffee Shack was just that, a shack, but for my money they had the best coffee on the island.

"Why? What's Gus been up to?"

Augustus Habermann was 75 if he was a day. I'm not really sure even he knew what his true age was, but I hoped I was half as sharp as he when I hit that milestone. Gus had come to the island shortly after World War I, arriving on a tramp steamer. He'd always maintained that he was a simple fisherman who'd been shanghaied into the Kaiser's Kriegsmarine and was lucky enough to survive. Deciding he liked Key West he'd stayed, taking jobs on commercial fishing boats before eventually getting his own boat and going into the charter business. He and Sam were good friends and his slip was four over from where *Greta* normally tied up.

"Nothing unusual," Dennis said. "But the dock master told me that Gus left Friday morning around the same time Sam did and I figured he might know something. I thought you'd want to be here when I talk to him."

"You haven't been over to his boat yet?"

"No sir. He just came in about an hour ago and had clients with him so I didn't want to bother him while they were around."

I looked toward Gus's slip. He was hosing down the deck. "Looks like they're gone now. Let's go talk to him."

As we approached his boat, Gus saw us and waved, "Guten tag, Tommy. Wie gehts?" Gus still had a strong accent and frequently lapsed into his native German.

"Hi Gus, I'm good, yourself?"

"Ach, I cannot complain."

"Gus, have you been out all weekend?"

"Ja, Tommy. We left Friday morning right behind Sammy in *Greta*. Warum? Why?"

"Did you actually see Sam on Friday Gus?"

"Nein, it was not quite light enough to see clearly. Was ist los Tommy? What is wrong?"

I decided to give it to him straight. "I'm afraid I have bad news Gus. Sam is dead."

"Todt, Sammy ist todt?" Gus gasped with surprise then looked, beseechingly, upward. "Ach du lieber Himmel. What happened?"

"We don't know yet Gus. He was found on Smather's Beach yesterday morning and, so far, it looks like you might have been the last person to have seen him. Was Sam at the wheel when you followed *Greta* out Friday?"

Gus started coiling his hose and Dennis took out his notebook and pencil. "Nein, it was not Sammy, about the same height but not so big. Maybe it was Julio piloting?"

"No it wasn't Julio. He didn't go out with Sam that trip. Did you see who went aboard *Greta* before she left the slip, or hear anything?"

"Nein," said Gus, shaking his head. "I could not see across the other boats in the way and I was busy getting my party aboard and settled. If it was not Julio piloting, then who? Sammy not let anyone else handle *Greta*."

"I don't know, Gus," I sighed. "I was hoping you might've been able to identify whoever it was."

"I am sorry Tommy. I do not know anything else." He picked up a long handled squeegee and began pushing the excess water to the scuppers. "Now, you excuse me, Ja? I must finish here; then I go see Elyse."

"Sure Gus. Thanks for your time. If you remember anything else call me."

"Ja, Tommy, I will."

Dennis and I headed back up the dock to our cars. I asked him if he had found anyone else who might have seen or heard anything.

"No, Sir, Gus was the last one on my list."

"Well, we now know what time *Greta* left and we have to presume that Sam was on board regardless of what Gus said about him not being at the wheel." I stopped as something passed through my mind. "Dennis, *Greta* has dual controls, one set in the wheel house and another up on the flying bridge. If the person Gus saw was on the bridge, it might've been because he wanted a better view of where he was going. Sam never used the bridge going out or coming back. He didn't need to be up high to see the way. Hell, Sam could go in and out of here with his eyes closed. Go back and find out where Gus saw this person and also which way they turned when they left the basin."

I sipped my coffee, thinking, while Dennis trotted back to Gus. One of the first things I learned in my police science courses was never assume. Get the facts and always check and double check. From the facts you then performed deductive reasoning and if your conclusions didn't make sense then you went back and checked your facts again. I was getting more facts but, so far, it didn't make sense that Sam was dead.

Dennis came back and, checking his notebook, said, "According to Gus, the person he saw was on the flying bridge. He also said it was possible that someone was in the wheel house, but he couldn't be sure, it was still too dark. As for the direction *Greta* took, Gus said they turned West then Southward to pass Mallory Square. Gus himself went North along Fleming Key. He also volunteered that *Greta* was not travelling fast and that it looked to him that she was moving a little slower than Sam usually had her go."

I looked up at this bit of information. *Greta* was a modified hull vessel with features of a displacement and a planing hull and running twin marine diesels. She had the ability to get up on plane and run fast, if needed. She wouldn't win any races, but she'd run all day without complaining and could handle most seas including some that a lot of boats similar in size couldn't.

Sam knew his boat intimately. I remember one time he took me out and let me pilot while he took the opportunity to act like one of his customers and fish from the stern chair. He'd told me what speed to run and I thought I had the throttles set correctly. I was watching my heading when he came up behind me, reached around, and just barely nudged the throttle levers forward what couldn't have been more than the thickness of a human hair. He paused a moment and then said, "There, Thomas, now you are at the correct speed," and went back to his chair. I couldn't tell any difference. I asked him later how he could. "*Greta* talks to me, Thomas. She tells me what she wants and, like most women, she knows best; so I listen."

57

If someone else had been at the wheel and was running her slower than Sam usually did he would have come up and made the change. The fact that Gus noted *Greta* was going slower than normal as she moved into open water told me that Sam was not at the wheel and, more importantly, that he couldn't come to the wheel. The question was, why? And who was keeping him from doing so?

Leaving the marina in the direction Gus said he was, Sam could have continued Westerly out to the Dry Tortugas. He could also have come around the tip of Key West and run South toward Cuba or continued around and run East to the Gulf Stream then North up the Keys toward Miami. The first fact in this case was that Sam was found on Smather's Beach which is on the South side of the island. That alone told me which way *Greta* went Friday morning.

If, as seemed likely, Sam was dead when he went into the water, then whoever had been at the helm had to be far enough out that he wouldn't have been seen from shore because, given the apparent speed they were going, it would have been full daylight by the time they got around to that side of the island. Also, since Sam washed up on shore, they weren't far enough out to be over deep water which told me that whoever was piloting wasn't that familiar with the local waters.

We weren't looking for a Keys native. Nor were we looking for someone with knowledge of currents, wind direction or tides. Hell, he probably wasn't even that good with boats in general which, if that was the case, could be very good for us. The waters around the Keys can be tricky if you don't know what you're doing.

It occurred to me then that Dennis was saying something and I turned my attention to him.

"Lieutenant, hey Lieutenant, are you okay?"

"Huh? What's that, Dennis? Yeah, yeah, I'm fine, just a lot of things going through my mind."

"Do you need me for anything else today?"

"No, that's all." I looked at my watch. "It's after 4 o'clock and you were supposed to be off today. Go home and get some rest. I have a feeling this week is going to be busy. I'll see you tomorrow morning."

"Right. Call me, though, if you need me."

I walked over to my car and got in. We were collecting facts which were starting to build a picture, but something was missing and I couldn't quite put my finger on what it was. Also, I was working the assumption that Sam had been murdered. Although the facts were beginning to support that assumption, it was still just an assumption, which I didn't like. I needed confirmation. I needed Doc Elliott's autopsy report.

Arriving back at the office, I was greeted with an urgent message from Amy to call her at the paper just as soon as I could. When she gave me the message, Sally had sounded concerned and volunteered that Amy had been out of breath when she called and sounded like she might have been crying. That was certainly not characteristic of the Amy Petersen I knew. Forgetting about the autopsy report, I went back to my desk, picked up the phone and dialed.

CHAPTER 8

Amy answered the phone on the first ring.

"Tom? Oh God, I hope that's you." The agitation and anger in her voice were unmistakable.

"Amy, relax, it's me. What's wrong, I thought you were meeting with Reynolds?"

"I did. Oh, that bastard, that rotten, despicable little bastard."

"Who? Larry Reynolds?"

"No Tom. Andy Hardy." The way she said it, I had a horrible thought that I was soon to have another dead body on my hands and that I'd have to arrest the girl that I'd just spent last night and the first half of today making love with.

"Amy, calm down. Tell me exactly what happened and where Andy is."

"He's not here, thank God, otherwise I swear Tom I don't think I could keep myself from wringing his scrawny little neck. That slimy little piece of shit tried to get me fired on a trumped up drug charge on top of embezzlement. Damn him!" she started cursing again and slammed the phone down on her desk. I heard a shuffle like the sound of someone else trying to pick up the phone and then another voice came over the line.

"Lieutenant Jackson, is that you?"

"Yes, Eddie? Is Amy all right? What the hell's going on over there?"

"Hey, Lieutenant," Eddie answered. "Miss Petersen's really upset. I think you oughta get over here."

"Okay, Eddie, I'm on my way. Is Mr. Reynolds still there?"

"Yes, sir, I think he is."

"Good. Tell him I'm coming and that I'd appreciate it if

he could wait for me. From the sound of things, I'm going to need him to make sense of this."

"Right, Lieutenant, I'll go tell him. Here's Miss Petersen."

I stood up. "Amy, I'm on my way over. I want you to stay there. Do not go out of the building and if Andy comes back before I get there, I want you to scream at the top of your lungs before you hit him, that way you've at least got a good chance at a plea of temporary insanity."

She caught her breath and I could tell she was turning over what I'd said in her mind; probably with disgust that I was suggesting that she would be charged with anything. Then, seeing the humor in it, she started to chuckle, which was exactly the effect I hoped for.

"Oh, Tom, you're joking. Don't worry I've got Eddie here to protect me, but don't take too long." And she hung up.

Ten minutes later I was at the *Current* situated in a two story wood frame building a few blocks over on Fleming St. The presses were on the ground floor and the reporters' 'bull pen' and offices upstairs. We were in Reynolds' office where he was filling me in. Reynolds was at his desk while Amy and I were in the "interview chairs" opposite.

"Mr. Hardy came to see me at home about noon today, Lieutenant, claiming to have proof that Miss Petersen was engaged in activities which could bring serious damage to myself and the paper. When I asked him what he meant, he claimed that this would be better dealt with here and with Miss Petersen in attendance."

"What did you do then, Sir?" I had my notebook out and was conducting this interview in an official manner, just in case it turned into something serious.

Reynolds leaned back in his desk chair, an old, well-worn wooden swivel chair like the one in the Chief's office, but without the squeak. Reynolds had his fingers steepled in front of him. "You know, Lieutenant, that I do not take lightly to anyone proffering unfounded charges against any of my employees, least of all the ladies. I questioned Mr. Hardy further telling him I would need to know just what it was that he was prepared to allege was going on. I knew that Miss Petersen was working on the death of Mr. Torres and I had given her permission to put her piece on him out over the wire last night."

Reynolds might have been an Old South bigot at times, but he was always proper with regard to his address of an individual even when he didn't like them. Truth be told, I suspected that he had a grudging respect for Sam, not that Larry would've willingly sat down to dinner at the same table with him.

"I knew of nothing that she was working on which could be considered to bring the paper's reputation into question," he continued.

Larry Reynolds had a natural formality when speaking with other than family or close friends. As a police officer, I was neither and adopted the same formality.

"I presume then that Mr. Hardy gave forth with something that led you to call Miss Petersen and ask her to meet you here?"

"Yes, he alleged that it involved falsification of financial reports and," he physically shuddered as he almost whispered the word, "marijuana, and that he had the evidence locked in his desk here."

I looked at Amy but didn't say anything. She was starting to fidget, wanting to ask her own questions like a good reporter, but she read my face and stayed calm. Her turn would come. For myself, I was starting to get a little steamed at Andy for ignoring my pointed advice of yesterday.

"At that point," Reynolds continued, "I called the office here and asked if Miss Petersen was in. Upon being advised that she was not, I looked up her home number and called there but received no answer. I then redialed the office and asked Edward to find her and request her to meet me here."

"Was Miss Petersen here when you arrived?" I asked, knowing full well that she wasn't, and made a note of the approximate time of Reynold's call compared to when Sally had called me.

"No, she was not. She arrived some twenty minutes after we did. I have since been advised that she was having Sunday breakfast with a close friend."

He said this with no hint of emotion so I gathered that either Amy or Eddie had been discrete about any mention of who that "close friend" was or, as a gentleman, he chose not to mention our liaison. I appreciated that reserve as I, for one, was not sure how Larry would view our activities of the last few hours.

"And what happened then, sir."

Reynolds leaned forward, his well-oiled chair silent. "Mr. Hardy stated that he had been going over the reporters' monthly expense reports and had found evidence to show that Miss Petersen had submitted false vouchers and padded her summaries on more than one occasion and that it appeared that this activity had been ongoing for longer than six months," said Reynolds.

I looked at them both and could see the anger rising again in Amy's eyes.

"Apart from the fact that, frankly sir, I don't believe a word of it, this sounds like it would be a matter for your accountants and yourself, not the editor. Besides that, it hardly seems to be a matter which could seriously affect the paper's reputation." Matching Larry's formality helped me remain focused on the interview instead of thinking of what I wanted to do to Andy Hardy.

"Yes, Lieutenant, you are correct. It is properly a matter for the accountants and, in fact, we just had our monthly meeting last week at which nothing of this nature concerning Miss Petersen was raised. Accordingly, I was suspicious of Mr. Hardy's allegations and asked if he could identify any specific instance of such irregularity."

"Did he?" My pencil was poised, ready to note specifics.

"Yes, he mentioned entries on two dates for items which, in his view, were impossible to justify in Key West. Unfortunately for him they were items coinciding with two dates last fall during a week when Mr. Hardy was absent and Miss Petersen accompanied me to Tallahassee on official newspaper business."

I remembered that week. Amy had been excited about being chosen to accompany Larry on the trip during which she would have the opportunity to meet the Governor and some members of Congress who were coming down to Tallahassee from Washington.

"I presume that you pointed this out to Mr. Hardy?"

"Yes, Lieutenant, I did and I suggested at that point that he apologize to Miss Petersen."

"I am going to guess that he failed to follow your advice."

"That is correct." Reynolds said. Why was I not surprised? Andy Hardy rarely followed anyone's advice, preferring to find ways to get around whatever he was advised to not do and ways to avoid what he was advised to do. Reynolds continued, "Rather, he proceeded to advise me that there was another matter he wished to raise that he was sure I would consider serious enough to warrant Miss Petersen's dismissal. Mr. Hardy then proceeded to describe how he had been looking for a small piece of office equipment and, upon opening a drawer of Miss Petersen's desk, came upon that."

With an absolute look of disgust, Reynolds pointed to a clear plastic bag at the extreme front edge of his desk, as far away from himself as he could possibly get it and still have it visible.

I Picked up the bag and inspected the contents, which appeared to be primarily a quantity of something that looked like tobacco, but probably wasn't, and a packet of rolling papers. I opened the bag and took a brief sniff. The contents were definitely not tobacco.

"Did Mr. Hardy identify the 'small piece of office equipment' he was looking for when he found this 'evidence'?" I asked, the last word being uttered in a tone that clearly indicated my suspicion as to its accuracy.

"Yes, Detective, he said he was looking for a pair of scissors."

I turned to Amy.

"Miss Petersen, do you keep a pair of scissors in your desk drawer?"

I deliberately kept my address formal to avoid any possible complaints of bias on the part of the investigating officer, but inside I was thinking more like a defense lawyer working for Amy and wanting to make Hardy pay. I had learned some things from Dad in that regard.

"No, Lieutenant," she answered, in a manner equally as formal as mine. Her eyes were still dark, but the beginning of a grin was playing at the corners of her mouth.

Smart girl, I thought, she knew that this was on the record and that it was looking like I finally had something to pin on Andy. "I keep them in a cup on the top of my desk where they are readily available and visible."

"Do you keep anything in your desk drawers?" I asked her.

"Yes," she ticked items off on her fingers. "I have spare blank pads in the bottom right hand drawer, blank typing paper is in the bottom left hand drawer, blank envelopes are in the top left hand drawer and my address book is in the center drawer."

"Do you keep anything else in your desk?"

"No."

"What about the top right hand drawer?" I asked.

"As far as I know, it's empty. However, I couldn't swear to that as I've never opened it."

I was a little surprised at that. "You've never opened that drawer in your desk in all the time you've been here? Why not?"

Amy shrugged. "Because it's locked and has been since I started working here. No one has ever found a key that fits it."

"That is true, Lieutenant," volunteered Reynolds.

"But why didn't you drill the lock or get a locksmith in to open it and make a new key?" I asked Larry.

"Simple, Miss Petersen never requested that we do so and did not require the drawer for anything."

"That's correct, Lieutenant, I didn't need the drawer so I forgot about it and I guess everyone else did too," said Amy.

Yeah, I thought, everyone except Andy Hardy. Then I asked the kicker question.

"Which drawer did Mr. Hardy say he found the evidence in?"

Amy and Reynolds looked at each other then at me and in perfect unison said, "The top right."

I got up and went out to Amy's desk and tugged on the handle of the top right hand drawer. It didn't move. Reentering Reynolds's office I stood next to Amy and asked, "Where is Mr. Hardy at this moment?"

Reynolds answered first, his expression stern, "I have no idea, Lieutenant, but when you find him you can tell him that he no longer has a job here. I will not countenance employees attempting to unjustly implicate their coworkers. Also, should Mr. Hardy attempt to press charges against Miss Petersen, I will provide appropriate legal counsel for her. Also, if he attempts any form of coercion he will be prosecuted to the fullest extent of the law." Apparently, regardless of any information Andy might have, Reynolds was fed up with him. But charges against Amy?

"Charges? What charges?" I said looking alternately at Reynolds and Amy and unable to disguise the surprise in my voice.

"Probably assault and battery, Tom," Amy said, looking up at me, a little sheepish now, her hands clasped demurely in her lap. "When he said he found the stuff in the top right hand drawer, I lost my temper and hit him. The next thing I remember, Mr. Reynolds was pulling me off him and Andy was heading for the door yelling that he would get even. I believe I gave him a bloody nose. I know I scratched his face." She turned to Reynolds and added, "Mr. Reynolds, I am sorry for my lack of control, but I'd had all I could take from Andy Hardy at that point, what with his constant harassment, snide comments, innuendos and blatantly false allegations."

"That is quite all right Miss Petersen," replied Reynolds, one hand raised as if he were giving a blessing. "Your actions are perfectly understandable, although I wish you had come to me; together we might have been able to avoid all of this unpleasantness." In a more serious tone to me he said, "Quite frankly, Lieutenant, I had noticed some instability in Mr. Hardy of late and had been looking for a way to terminate his employment. At the time, however, I could not find a replacement editor. Now, I suppose I will have to take on the job for the foreseeable future."

Just thinking of Amy trying to beat Andy to a pulp made me want burst out laughing, take her in my arms and give her a great big kiss with Larry Reynolds watching. With difficulty I controlled that urge and maintained the level of formality the interview had started with.

"Mr. Reynolds," I said, "which is Mr. Hardy's desk? I

would like to search it and inventory the contents if you don't mind."

"Not at all. Miss Petersen will show you and if you do not require my presence further I do have a dinner to get ready for."

"No sir, I don't see any need to detain you further, although it may be necessary to speak with you again on this matter. I thank you for your time and for your consideration of Miss Petersen. Also, sir, for the record, I was the close friend with whom she was having breakfast this morning."

Reynolds smiled as he stood and retrieved his jacket from the tree by the door. "I thought as much Lieutenant," he said as he left. "Good evening to you both."

Together Amy and I said "Good evening," and I thought, what? Does everyone on the island know about us?

Amy took me into Andy's office which was really nothing more than one corner of the large bullpen that had been partitioned off. Whereas Larry's office had proper walls, Andy's were mostly glass, presumably so he could see what everyone else was doing, but with blinds on the inside so they couldn't see him if he didn't want them to. Where Amy's desk could be described as spare as to its contents, Andy's looked like a hurricane had been through it. This was going to take time to do properly.

The first thing I did was check the drawers. All of them opened except the large file drawer and they looked just as bad as the desktop.

"Amy, are there any spare keys for this desk?"

"They'd be in Larry's safe if there are."

"Great. I want to see what's in that file drawer, but I don't want to bother Reynolds any more than I have to."

I picked up the phone, called headquarters and gave instructions to send a couple of the technical guys around to the *Current* offices and to make sure they brought plenty of film for the camera. I wanted pictures of everything on and in Andy's desk.

While waiting for the techs to arrive, Amy and I went back out to her desk. I looked around and found the coffee pot, which was still warm, and poured two cups.

"Careful, Tom," she said. "That stuff has been on for hours. It's likely to reach out of the cup and grab you."

I took a sniff and put it down.

"That's worse than anything we have at the station. How can you drink it?"

"I don't, Eddie and I go across the street to Rosa's."

As I looked at my watch to check the time, Eddie came into the room with two tall cups of fresh Cuban coffee.

"Son," I said, "you must be psychic."

Eddie handed a cup to Amy. "No, sir, I just figured you and Miss Petersen might want some and Rosa was getting ready to close."

Taking the other cup from him, I noticed a fresh abrasion on his hand that was oozing blood.

"Eddie, how did you do that," I asked pointing at his hand. He looked surprised.

"Gee, Lieutenant, I hadn't noticed it what with all the yelling up here and Mr. Hardy running down the stairs. I was just starting up when he came down and pushed me aside. I guess I must have done it then."

"You were here when Mr. Reynolds and Mr. Hardy arrived?"

"Yes, sir. I was here when Mr. Hardy came in earlier too, but he didn't notice me I guess."

I looked at Amy and gave my head a little shake as I saw her start to say something.

"Eddie, what time did Mr. Hardy come in earlier today?"

He looked at a large wall clock, thinking. "I think it was about 10:30 this morning."

"And what time did Mr. Reynolds call looking for Miss

Petersen?"

"That was about 1:45, sir."

That fit in the time line for the day. Sally's call had been about 2 o'clock.

"Eddie, when Mr. Hardy was here earlier did he go anywhere near Miss Petersen's desk?"

"No, sir," he shook his head. "He went straight into his office stayed there for about an hour and then left."

Amy was scribbling notes on her pad. "Could you see what he was doing in there?" she asked.

"No Ma'am, he closed his door and blinds, but I heard sounds like he was opening and closing drawers and tearing paper." Eddie turned to me, a worried look on his face, "Lieutenant, is Miss Petersen in trouble?"

"No, Eddie," I smiled at him. "But when we catch Mr. Hardy, he will be. Meanwhile, you might want to put something on your hand."

When the tech boys arrived I took them into Andy's office and told them that I wanted a complete inventory of everything on and in the desk and a similar inventory of everything else in the room. Any papers in the wastebasket were to be retrieved and included as desk contents. Everything was to be photographed. They both looked at me and said, "Everything?"

"Everything. But first," and I pointed to the locked drawer, "can you get that open without damaging the lock or the surrounding wood?"

One of the techs looked at the lock and said "Sure, piece of cake." He rummaged in his bag and pulled out a small pouch which, when opened, revealed a complete set of lock picks. Within 30 seconds he had the drawer unlocked and opened and I just stared. It was full of small bags just like the one Reynolds had shown me.

"Photographs, now!" I barked. "One of the open drawer as it is then each bag individually numbered and logged before anything else."

"Lieutenant," the other tech said pointing at the wastebasket, "you might want to see this."

I looked and clumsily hidden under a crumpled piece of paper was an empty box of .38 cartridges.

"Eddie, Amy," I called, "Does Hardy own a gun?"

"Don't know sir," said Eddie.

"Yes, I think he does Tom," said Amy, "a revolver of some kind. Why?"

I grabbed the phone and called headquarters. Sally answered.

"Key West Police Department."

"Sally," I said, "Is O'Neil there?"

"Mikey? Yes, Tom, he's here. I'll put you through."

Michael O'Neil, is the size of a good full back and looks like he would as soon pull your arm off as listen to anything you had to say. If you said the wrong thing to him, he probably would too. Normally, though, he's one of the gentlest individuals I've ever met, especially with children. He's another Key West local and just about everyone who knows him still calls him 'Mikey' just as they did when he was a kid. I preferred 'Mike.'

"O'Neil here, what's up, Boss?"

"I want you to put an 'all points' out for Andrew Hardy; make it armed and dangerous. Get it to the Sheriff too 'cause he's had time to get out of the city. I want him found and arrested. Make sure they know I want him alive."

"Damn! What's the little bastard done now?" Mike knew Hardy. "What's the charge?"

"Narcotics trafficking to start and possibly embezzlement."

"Trafficking? Andy Hardy? He doesn't have the balls for it," said Mike with surprise.

"Maybe, maybe not, Mike, but I'm looking at the evidence right now. When you've got that bulletin out get on over here to the *Current* and I'll fill you in. Also, put a couple of the boys on his house, just in case, and call Dennis. Tell him I'm sorry, but I want him to go over to Amy Petersen's place and wait for me there."

"Right, Boss. I'll see you in ten minutes." He hung up.

When I turned around Amy was standing in the doorway of Andy's office watching open mouthed as the techs photographed each bag of dope individually.

"My God! Is that what I think it is?"

"Yes, all packaged and ready to sell. I don't know where he got it or who he's working with, but I'm going to find out. I've wanted to get something on that little shit for a long time and now I've got it. I'll be damned if I'm going to let him mess up my town with this crap." Needless to say I was pissed.

"But Tom, you told Mikey to make the bulletin 'armed and dangerous.' Hardy didn't have a weapon with him."

"Maybe not here, Amy," and I pointed to the empty box of ammunition, "but what was in that box fits into something and I'm betting Andy has it. Besides, it gets the Sheriff's boys to sit up and take notice."

"You don't think he'd be stupid enough to actually do something violent do you?"

"I don't know. I wouldn't exactly call it smart to leave all that stuff in a desk drawer. What I do know is that he's angry, at you definitely, most likely at Reynolds, but particularly at you because you got the better of him. Frankly, I hope you did give him a bloody nose. I hope you broke it and maybe something else as well. I do know that I don't trust him. Right now he's like a wounded animal and I have no idea what he may do. I'm not taking any chances."

When Mike showed up I filled him in on what had happened and told him that when the techs were finished with Andy's office, I wanted the entire building searched and anything else related to narcotics photographed, bagged and tagged. When that was done, he was to escort the techs and all the evidence back to headquarters and personally log it in. Given the number of packages of marijuana already found and the empty ammunition box, I thought there was more behind this than just getting back at Amy because she snubbed him and I didn't want anything going astray. Mike was a good cop and a good investigator. He was in line to get his sergeant's stripes so I could be sure nothing would go wrong.

CHAPTER 9

I left Mike and the techs to their work and took Amy and Eddie downstairs to the reception lobby.

"Do either of you know where Larry Reynolds was going this evening?" I asked.

They both shook their heads, dazed expressions on their faces. This whole business with Andy, drugs and possibly embezzlement had thrown them for a loop.

"Gloria probably knows," said Eddie. "He's always calling her when he can't find his calendar."

"What's her number?" I picked up the phone on the receptionist's desk and dialed as Eddie spoke.

"Reynolds residence, how may I help you?" a young voice said on the other end.

"Gloria, this is Lieutenant Jackson. Is your father available?"

"No, Sir, he left about ten minutes ago."

"Can you tell me where he went? It is quite important that I speak with him again this evening."

"Yes, of course, he's having dinner with some businessmen from Tallahassee over at the Club. It's a rather important meeting that he would prefer not to have disturbed, Lieutenant."

"I understand that Gloria and if I didn't have to I wouldn't." Thinking of Andy's parting comment I then asked, "Gloria, are you alone tonight?"

"No, sir, Davis and Elena are here. Why? What's wrong?" Her voice had started to show some concern. "Is everything all right with Daddy?"

Davis and Elena had been with Reynolds for years as butler and cook/housekeeper.

"Yes, your father is fine, but I need to speak with him

again this evening. Thank you, Gloria."

"You are certainly welcome, Lieutenant. Also I think I should thank you for what you said to Julio and, I presume, did not say to my father."

"My advice to Julio applies to you as well, Gloria. I don't want either of you to do anything you could regret in the future."

"Don't worry, Lieutenant. We'll be careful," she said as she rang off.

I turned back to Eddie and Amy. "I have to go talk to Reynolds again. Amy, Dennis should be at your house by now and will be there until I send someone to relieve him later." She started to object but I stopped her. "Listen, right now Andy's an unknown quantity and possibly violent. You are likely to be his primary target, for several reasons. As I said before, I'm not taking any chances. I want you to go home and stay there. Don't give Dennis a hard time."

She leaned over and gave me a quick kiss on the cheek.

"Okay, Tom, I'll behave tonight, but I do have to work and you can't have someone watching me all the time."

"I'll figure something out for tomorrow. Hopefully it won't be for long. Eddie, do you have to be here tonight?"

"No sir, I've just stayed around 'cause I didn't know if you needed me."

"Thanks, but I don't see any reason for you to stay any later tonight. I suggest you go straight home and keep your eyes open. However, I'd appreciate it if you'd come down to the station in the morning and give a formal statement of what you observed today."

"Sure Lieutenant, no problem. G'night, Miss Petersen," he said as he left.

Amy and I headed around back to the parking lot and as we passed through a particularly dark spot, her grip on my arm tightened. "Don't worry," I said, "I doubt that he'll try anything and I'm probably being an alarmist by having someone watch your place tonight. But after the last twenty four hours, I don't want anything to happen to you."

She looked at me and cooed in a fake Southern accent, "Why, Thomas Stonewall Jackson, I do believe that y'all care 'bout li'l ol' me."

I came to a dead stop and Amy continued speaking in her normal voice, "Well, I didn't think it was that much of an earth shattering revelation," thinking that her observation was the cause for my sudden stop. Then she realized where I was looking.

"Oh, shit! That little bastard; that weasel; that ..." Amy was so angry that she couldn't get the rest of her words out, but I had an idea they would have made a sailor cringe.

All four tires on her car were flat. I pulled my flashlight out and switched it on. Every tire had been slashed. Not just a single puncture; the side walls were ribbons of rubber.

"Damn it, Tom, I just got those tires."

"That does it. You are not staying at home by yourself. I don't care how many officers I put outside." I guided her over to my car, "We'll stop there so you can pack a bag and then you're coming home with me after I talk to Reynolds again."

"But Tom, they're only tires. They can be replaced. Yes, I'm angry at him that he did it, but I'm not going into hiding because of it."

I turned her to face me. I was angry, at Hardy, not her, and I was now more than worried. "Listen Amy, tires may be replaceable but you aren't. And that back there isn't simply angry. Angry is one stab through one tire. Two or three tires would be vindictiveness." I pointed back to her car. "All four tires slashed to ribbons like those are is a message. And that message is 'this is what you will look like if you cross me.' I've known Andy Hardy all my life, yes he's sneaky, backhanded and can't be trusted, but I never before considered him to have the guts for violence; something in him has changed. Right now, I wouldn't put anything past him. I'm glad now that I had O'Neil make that bulletin 'armed and dangerous.' I don't want to take a chance on losing you so you are staying with me tonight, end of discussion."

Amy just looked at me and then got in the car. I'm not sure if she was angry at me or just stunned, but at least she didn't argue the point.

When we pulled up in front of her house I didn't see Dennis or his car and was afraid that Mike hadn't been able to get through to him. It was only when I got out of my car that he seemed to materialize out of the darkness. When I commented on this, he simply said that he figured I wouldn't want his presence to be obvious so he covered his uniform and borrowed a neighbor's car that wouldn't stand out. Like I said, he's a smart kid.

I filled Dennis in on what had happened while Amy went inside and packed what she figured she'd need for a few days. In the car she'd come to the realization that I was probably right and suggested that it might be advisable if she brought more of her stuff than just for one night. I didn't ask if it was because neither of us knew how long it would be before Andy was caught or if she wanted to have more than one change of clothes at my house. I was just glad it was her suggestion since it showed an acceptance of the seriousness of the situation both with respect to the potential danger that Andy Hardy presented and to our personal relationship.

Since Amy would be spending the night with me, I didn't see any need for her place to be watched. Instead I sent Dennis over to keep an eye on Larry Reynolds's house until he got home, after which he could go home himself and get what sleep he could. I told him that Gloria was home with the butler and the housekeeper and, unless he saw something unusual, I just wanted him to observe. Of course if Andy showed up Dennis was to arrest him on the spot.

Amy came out with her bags and we headed for the Club.

Located on Stock Island, the Key West Country Club is primarily a social hangout for the upper crust of our little island. It provides a place for the upper classes to meet and greet, to wine and dine without having to rub shoulders with the working class. I wasn't surprised that Larry Reynolds was a member. With his pretensions and contacts, he was probably on the Board of Directors.

My car is unmarked so I pulled up to the gatehouse and showed my badge before proceeding on to the Club House. Leaving the car at the front door, I took my keys so the valet couldn't move it, although the look I gave him when I got out probably told him it would be worth his life if he tried. I wasn't a member and if I blocked one I didn't care. I was on official police business and, as far as I was concerned, that took precedence over some rich snob wanting to get in or out.

Entering the lobby Amy and I went straight to the desk and I asked where Larry Reynolds was. The secretary tried to object, telling me that he had been left with strict instructions not to disturb Mr. Reynolds. I let him know in very clear language that either he disturb Mr. Reynolds right now or I would first arrest him for impeding a police investigation, then I would personally go through the club with badge and gun looking for Mr. Reynolds. With that the secretary scurried off and very soon after returned with Larry Reynolds.

"Lieutenant, what is the reason for this disturbance? I was under the impression that we were finished for the night." Reynolds was clearly not pleased but he managed to maintain his composure.

"Is there somewhere more private where we could speak?" I said.

"Yes, of course. Follow me."

Reynolds led us down a hall and into a private office which I suspected was his own. Sitting behind the desk in that room he fixed his eyes on me. "Now, Lieutenant, I was in a very important meeting for which I had left strict instructions not to be disturbed. However, you were apparently able to persuade Stebbings to disobey those instructions. I trust that you have a very good reason."

Sitting down I motioned to Amy to do the same. "I have issued an 'all points' bulletin for the arrest and confinement of Andrew Hardy on charges of narcotics trafficking and probably embezzlement. I have also advised that he should be considered armed and dangerous."

Reynolds sat up, hands on the arms of his chair, his mouth agape. "Good God, Sir. Why? There was only one small bag of that material, and he displayed no weapon."

I then told Reynolds what we'd found in Hardy's desk and trashcan and what had been done to the tires of Amy's car.

"The actual volume of marijuana found in Mr. Hardy's desk has not yet been determined," I said. "But given the number of bags and the manner of packaging it is clear that it had been prepared for sale or distribution which implicates the paper and yourself as the owner of the property on which the contraband was found."

Reynolds started to protest and I held up my hand.

"Mr. Reynolds, before you say anything I have an obligation to inform you that anything you do say may be used in evidence. However, you should also know that, had this incident involved any one else, I would not now be sitting in front of him telling him what had been found without first serving a warrant for his arrest. I also do not believe that you either knew what Andy Hardy had in his desk or that you are in any way involved with what it would appear he has been doing. Nor do I believe that, had you known, you would have tolerated his presence for one second longer than necessary. But, because of the amount of material involved I have probable cause to search the entire building and everything in it and I currently have a team doing just that. I sincerely hope that they find nothing more. I am also required to make a report to the Monroe County Prosecutor and I wanted you to know what was going on before hand."

Although we didn't run in the same social circles, I knew Larry Reynolds well enough to know what I said was true and that he wouldn't have had anything to do with whatever it was that Andy was involved in. The fact that he was also Amy's boss maybe influenced my decision to tell him a little bit, but not much.

Reynolds sat back, his jaw slack but his anger subsiding.

"Lieutenant, do you believe that Mr. Hardy actually has it in himself to commit violence? I mean, distributing packages of marijuana is one thing, but actual physical violence?"

"At this point, sir, I'm not ruling anything out. I grant you that Hardy's actions today are out of character based on his history. I would have expected him to continue to play the role of a nosey reporter trying to poke and pry to see which way the wind blew, whether we were on to him or not. Frankly, until this afternoon we had no idea he was even considering selling pot, let alone actually in possession of multiple packages ready for distribution. What I would like to know right now is where he is and where he got the stuff."

Amy then asked the question that had been nagging at me, but that I hadn't wanted to acknowledge.

"Tom, do you think Hardy could have been involved in some way with Sam's death and the disappearance of his boat?"

"I don't know. I hope not, but I'm not ruling anything

out which is why you're with me and why," turning back to Reynolds, "I have put an officer on duty outside your house until you get home. He's discrete and won't do anything but observe unless conditions require action. Your daughter and servants won't know he's there unless Hardy tries something."

Andy Hardy, the snitch, had changed his life long pattern and no one could predict what he would do next. The best that I could do right now was to prepare for anything.

"Lieutenant," Reynolds said, leaning forward, "I knew and respected your father. He and I had our differences, but he was always straight in any of his dealings with me and I am happy to see that you take after him so well. I disagreed with his decision to let you proceed with police work, but I respected it. I am now glad he made that decision.

"Steven Barnes, from the prosecutor's office, is one of the gentlemen I am dining with this evening. I would like to call him in here and have you tell him everything you have told me. The sooner the county prosecutor knows about this the better."

With that he pressed a button on the telephone and directed Stebbings to have Barnes join us.

I knew Steve Barnes. In his first year out of law school he had interned at Dad's firm to see if he wanted to be a general practice attorney. Dad had found him to be a quick learner and competent but without the heart necessary to help the people who made up the bulk of Dad's clients. After much discussion, Steve had decided to move into criminal practice and then discovered politics. Moving into the county prosecutor's office made sense to Steve but I suspected that if Larry Reynolds made it to Tallahassee Steve would be there with him.

When Steve entered the back office where we were sitting I gave him a brief summary of what had happened.

He then made it very clear to Amy that everything said there was completely off the record and nothing about this case was to appear in print until she received written authorization from him. Amy's slight squint and sternly set jaw told me she was starting to get a little steamed at Barnes but she was smart and didn't say a word. Larry, on the other hand, betrayed himself as a pure newspaperman and began arguing for freedom of the press and the right of the people to know what was going on in their community. Steve was able to quiet him down by pointing out the effect that early publication of Andy's activities could have on both Larry's attempt to reach the State Capitol and the likelihood of catching and convicting Hardy. After promising Steve that he would get a complete report as soon as possible tomorrow, Amy and I left them discussing how to deal with the situation to Larry's best interest.

Back in the car Amy sat there for a minute and I could see that she was itching to say something, but wasn't sure how I would respond so I started. "Okay, what is it that's bothering you?"

She pounded on the dashboard. "Where does Barnes get off telling me what I can and can't write about? I don't work for him, the county or the State. How can he stop me from writing about this or Larry from publishing it?"

"First of all, I'm not entirely sure that he can stop you from writing about it. However, I don't think that, after he gets through in there tonight, Reynolds will go anywhere near the story until Andrew Hardy is safely in jail and it's been conclusively proven on the record that Larry Reynolds was not in any way involved. I think Larry wants to be in the legislature so bad he can taste it. From my position, as long as Andy is at large, I would prefer that nothing be published that could possibly give him any clue as to what we know."

Amy scowled at me and I didn't need any light to tell me her eyes were darkening to match her mood. Other people were telling her what she could and couldn't do and she wasn't happy about it.

"So what do I do, Tom? I'm a reporter. I have two good crime stories developing here which may or may not be related and you're telling me I can't work them?"

"No, I didn't say that. I said I would prefer that nothing about Andy get published until we have him in custody. As far as Sam's case goes, I'll be honest, right now we don't have much. I haven't even had time to read Doc's autopsy report yet; so officially I don't have anything that conclusively says a crime has been committed there." I hadn't told her about the interview Dennis and I had earlier with Gus. "I'm going to suggest something, but I don't know if you're going to like it."

"What?" she asked, her arms folded, shoulders hunched, mouth a horizontal line, like a little kid refusing to eat her vegetables.

"Did you ever do a ride-along when you worked at any other newspapers?"

"You mean ride with a patrol officer while dispatch gave him all the easy calls just so I'd write something that put the department in a good light? Oh yeah. I've done my share of fluff pieces." She sank deeper into the car seat and her sulk.

"Uh huh, so you know what it's about, only it seems that I don't get the easy calls." At that comment she started to perk up.

"What are you getting at, Tom?"

"I'm suggesting that you stick to me like a shadow. Every call I go on you're there. When I'm in the office you're there. You keep quiet and you take notes. Anything and everything that happens you have first access to. Facts, reports, everything. You write your story or stories as they happen and as soon as I think it won't jeopardize the case you can publish. But there are some conditions."

"Yes?" she asked. "Such as?" Her voice was still defiant

84

but the tone mellowed just a bit.

"If I tell you to stay in the car, you stay in the car. If I tell you to be quiet, you be quiet. And if I yell at you to get down, you crawl under the nearest rock and stay there until I tell you to come out. Can you accept those conditions?"

"If I don't?"

"Then I put you in a cell until Andy Hardy is caught. I'm sorry, but it's the only other way I have to make sure that you stay safe. And if I have to choose between that and catching Andy, your safety wins, hands down."

"You sure know how to sweet talk a girl into spending every hour with you Thomas Jackson," she growled, but smiled. "Okay, we'll do it your way, for now. But having me follow everything you do is going to put you and the department under a microscope. Can you accept that?"

I smiled at her. "If nothing else, it'll keep us all honest," I said, starting the car. "I don't know about you, but I'm hungry. How about Chinese?"

CHAPTER 10

Monday

My alarm went off about a half hour after I fell asleep; at least that's how it seemed. The clock showed 6:00 a.m. Monday morning. I reached over to give Amy a nudge but no one was there. For an instant I panicked, thinking that she'd either changed her mind about staying or that somehow Andy Hardy had been able to sneak in and, without waking me, spirit her away. Then I remembered that when I gave up and went to bed she'd been in Dad's den in front of his old typewriter.

It'd begun after we got back to the house with Chinese carryout, Amy had pulled out a notebook and started asking questions about our cases before I even got plates out: first Sam, then Andy. When I balked, she looked at me and quoted my own words to me.

"'Anything and everything that happens you have first access to. Facts, reports, everything. You write your story or stories as they happen.' That's what you said, Tom. All I'm doing right now is collecting the facts I don't have yet. What happened Saturday and Sunday that I don't know about yet? If I'm going to write these stories the way you expect me to, accurately, I have to know what you know before anything else happens."

So, while we ate, I filled her in on everything to date.

I'd hoped that after dinner we would be able to relax. It'd been a busy afternoon and evening. Amy had other ideas.

"I don't suppose you have a typewriter somewhere? If not, we'll have to go back to my place and get my portable. I don't know why I didn't grab it earlier."

"We're not going anywhere tonight; there's an old Royal

in the den." That had been Dad's original office. "I can't guarantee that the ribbon isn't dried out because I haven't used it in years. But there might be another one in the top drawer."

Amy sauntered down the hall while I wrapped up the leftovers and put them in the refrigerator then started washing the dishes. Pretty soon the banging of Dad's old typewriter echoed through the house. I started a pot of coffee. I'd heard the distinctive clacking of that machine so many times in my life, usually the night before Dad had to argue a case. He always typed his own notes and summaries. His position was that he couldn't leave that part of his job to anyone else since he frequently changed things at the last minute or would think of something the night before. When I was a kid, it wasn't unusual for me to fall asleep to the sound of Dad banging away. It was good to hear it again, especially since it was Amy doing the typing. I found myself wanting this arrangement to continue.

When the coffee was ready I took a cup in to Amy and looked over her shoulder. She was transcribing her notes on the Sam Torres case, most of which she already knew. The only information that she hadn't heard about had been what Dennis and I had got from Gus. I'd told her about that over dinner. What I'd held back were my thoughts about what had happened on *Greta* after she left the marina and her likely position when Sam had wound up in the ocean. At present they were only suspicions and needed to be supported by facts.

As for the Hardy case, Amy knew everything that I knew. All I'd been able to fill in there was background on Andy from before she got to Key West; background that included activities that verged on blackmail but had never been pursued because those involved wouldn't come forward. Recounting Andy's history in light of today's events made me wonder how many others and who may be involved in Andy's activities and when this latest development had begun.

I left her at work and took my coffee out to the patio with the intention of thinking over everything and trying to make sense of what had happened; but as soon as I sat down and started yawning I knew that wasn't going to work.

Going back inside, I closed and locked the patio door, checked the other doors and turned the air conditioner on. Open, the house stayed comfortable with just the ceiling fans as long as there was a breeze. With the doors and windows securely locked, it'd get stuffy without the A/C. When I went back into the den, Amy was still pounding away and barely acknowledged my announcement that the house was secure and I was going to bed. Even when I gave her a kiss on her cheek all I got was a distracted grunt. So this is what it was going to be like when she was on a story.

Now, getting up, I went into the kitchen first. Fortunately I'd turned the burner off under the coffee otherwise it would have boiled dry. I put on a fresh pot and opened the den door expecting to find Amy with her head on the typewriter. Not the most comfortable of pillows. She was asleep, but not at the desk. She had made it to the couch and was lightly snoring covered in her own papers.

Giving her a nudge, I started picking up the scattered pages trying to put them in order as I did but she hadn't numbered them. I gave her another poke and must have hit the right spot because she sat up and blinked with the kind of look you see on someone who has no idea where they are.

"Hey, sleepyhead. There's fresh coffee on and its six fifteen in the morning. Get moving. We have to go to work. You want coffee first or a shower?"

She mumbled something that sounded more like coffee than shower so I went back to the kitchen, poured her a mug and took it back to the den. Holding it under her nose got a reaction and she took the mug out of my hands and held it to her lips. I could almost see the lights turning on as she swallowed. It's amazing what that first sip in the morning can do.

"What time did you move to the couch last night," I asked.

"What time is it now?" was her reply.

I looked at my watch. "About 6:20."

Amy groaned. "Great. An hour's worth of sleep."

"Wonderful," I said. "You're not going to get anything done today. But don't get any ideas. I'm not leaving you here by yourself. There's a cot at the station or you can use the Chief's couch. Now come on, I have to get in and try to make some sense out of the last two days."

While she showered and changed I called in to see if anything had happened during the night. Other than the usual drunks and bar fights, it had been relatively quiet, for which I was thankful. We had enough to deal with right now. Mike had left word that everything from the *Current* was logged in and locked up; also that the search of the rest of the building hadn't turned up anything else. He hadn't left until about 5:30 that morning so I didn't expect to see him before noon, probably not before 2 p.m.

Dennis had called about midnight to say that Larry Reynolds had just gotten home and that everything was quiet so he was going home. I made a note to clock him out at 2 a.m. The city could afford an extra two hours and Dennis had earned it.

Amy and I had a quick breakfast and left for the office, stopping by her place to pick up her portable. I'd offered her one of the machines at the station, but she claimed she was more comfortable on the little one, so I didn't argue.

I spent the morning listening to Eddie give his statement of the events at the *Current* and preparing my report for Steve Barnes. Amy, as I suspected, took one look at the cot in the back room and opted for the couch. I'd just finished my report and put it in an interoffice envelope for delivery to the prosecutor that afternoon when she came out stretching like a cat just waking up from a nap in the sun.

"It's lunchtime. How about a sandwich in Mallory Square? We can watch the tourists, and the walk will do you good." I suggested. "After that we'll go over the autopsy report on Sam and check our time lines to make sure all of the current facts fit. Dennis and Mike should be in by then and we can start tossing some theories back and forth."

"Is that how you investigate, tossing theories back and forth?" she asked, a little surprised at the suggestion.

"Yeah, it's one way to do it. Based on the facts at hand we try out different possibilities to see what fits. If nothing does, then we go back to the facts and try to figure out what's missing. Once we know that, we get back out in the field with our noses to the ground. Bouncing ideas off of each other helps to sort things out and keeps us from being led astray by assumptions."

We walked over to the square, picking up a couple of Cuban sandwiches and coffee on the way, and found a bench where we could observe without ourselves being the subjects. It wasn't quite time for Spring Break, but there was a fair crop of tourists from the northern states wandering around enjoying the tropical warmth and sunshine. You could always tell them from the combination of white skin and incipient sun burns. Apparently it had been a pretty dismal winter up north.

"Tom," Amy started between bites of her sandwich. "I know you think Sam was murdered even though there's no hard evidence for it. I mean, what if he just fell overboard? *Greta* would keep going until she ran out of gas or hit something and that would explain why she hasn't been seen. Why murder? Aren't you just assuming the worst?"

I shook my head while I finished chewing. "No, I don't think so. Apart from the fact that *Greta's* missing, there are facts which would support the possibility of murder. Remember, in addition to *Greta*, his truck is missing. While it's possible it was simply stolen from the marina while he was out, remember that Gus saw at least one person on the boat who he swears was not Sam. Also, Sam did have a charter scheduled for Friday morning. Elyse and Julio both confirmed that. If Sam fell overboard, why didn't his client stop the boat and pick him up or call the Coast Guard? Besides, you've known Sam long enough. Do you think he would slip, hit his head on something and fall overboard? I'll grant you it's a remote possibility that his death was an accident and that *Greta's* out there somewhere with what has to be a complete idiot on board if he can't figure out how to at least stop her or turn her around."

"But why Sam? What would he have that would be worth killing him for?"

I took a sip of coffee and sighed. "Given the circumstances, the only thing that makes sense to me right now is that whoever did it wanted the boat, or something on it, and Sam tried to stop them. The problem with that is I can't think of anything on *Greta* that would be worth killing for. Why not just wait until they get back and Sam's gone home to steal whatever it was? No, Amy, the only thing that makes sense is that, for whatever reason, they wanted *Greta* and they needed Sam. What I need is Sam's charter book to figure out who his client was. I just hope that isn't what they were after."

Amy finished her sandwich and dabbed her mouth with a napkin before daintily folding it and the wrapper into a neat package which she then put in her empty cup. I just scrunched all of mine together.

"But the book wasn't on the boat," she said. "You told me that Julio said he saw it when he left for school Friday after Sam had left for the marina. So it couldn't have been the book they wanted. It has to be at the house somewhere."

"I sure hope so, but I'm beginning to have my doubts. If he'd found it, Julio would have called or brought it over."

I didn't tell Amy, but I was beginning to think that someone had stolen the charter book, not from *Greta* or the truck, but right out of Sam and Elyse's front room.

I looked at my watch. "Dennis and Mike should be in soon," I said, standing up and stretching. We tossed our trash in a convenient can and enjoyed a leisurely stroll back to work. Turning from Duval onto Greene Street, we saw a limo with darkened windows parked in front of headquarters where it was clearly marked 'No Parking.' No one I knew in Key West had a car like that. As we got closer I noticed that the plates were from Miami and I started to get a bad feeling. Mike was on the sidewalk looking at the car with some interest.

As Amy and I walked up, he asked me, "Any idea who it belongs to?"

We walked around the vehicle looking for any indication of official status.

"Never seen it before Mike. Put a ticket on it and let's go inside and find out who our visitor is." Truth was, I had a sinking feeling that I knew who, or at least what organization, the car belonged to so I was glad to see Dennis waiting for us in the lobby.

"Hi, Lieutenant, Miss Petersen. Sally caught me before I went in and suggested I wait for you here. Hi, Mike," as O'Neil came in behind us. "What's with the limo out front?"

"That's what we're about to find out." I turned to Sally, "Where are they and how many?"

"Three, Tom," she said. "An older gentleman, about six foot, well dressed with silver hair and two gorillas. They walked in as free as you please and asked for the officer in charge of the Torres case. I put them in the Chief's office personally, so I know they didn't talk to anyone or start going through anything on the way through the squad

93

room. And, yes, I suspect the gorillas are carrying."

Sally's description tallied with the Coast Guard photo and my recollection from Miami.

"Okay. Amy, you stay here with Sally and if you hear anything amiss, get down behind those file cabinets. Mike, you and Dennis come with me. Be ready, but don't do anything until I tell you." I peered through the squad room to the office. There was enough light in the room to provide silhouettes on the frosted glass walls, one head above where I knew the couch to be and two large indistinct shapes at positions that I guessed to be on either side of the desk, probably watching the door.

"We go quietly."

As we made our way across the squad room, both Mike and Dennis loosened their service revolvers in their holsters but didn't take them out. Motioning them to take up positions on either side of the door, I opened it and walked in.

CHAPTER 11

I'd never seen two individuals so perfectly matched. My first thought was that they had to be twins. Nothing else was possible.

The gorillas, as Sally had described them, stood in opposite corners behind the desk facing the door and were at least six inches taller than my six feet two inches and half again as wide across the shoulders as Mike O'Neil. They were in matching suits, well tailored, even their ties matched. There was nothing I could see to distinguish one from the other. Looking at them I knew I'd hate to have them coming at me. My service issue .38 would be like a pesky mosquito to them. They may have been carrying firearms, but there would be few situations that I could think of where these two would need to use them.

To the left of the door on the couch opposite the desk sat a distinguished looking gentleman. He was about six feet tall, his silver hair complemented by a clearly expensive, gray, tropical weight suit. A perfectly knotted, silvery blue silk tie matched his eyes as well as the silk square that peeked out of his breast pocket. A Panama hat resting on his knee completed the image.

I held out my hand to him.

"Mr. Donatello, what an unexpected pleasure."

I caught movement out of the corner of my eye as Mike and Dennis entered, their guns drawn and covering the two gorillas.

"Would you be kind enough to have Tweedle Dee and Tweedle Dum there slowly remove their weapons, place them carefully on the desk and step back into their respective corners?"

Salvatore Donatello nodded to his associates and I

heard two heavy thuds. I looked and a pair of .45's lay on the desk as his two boys backed away with Dennis and Mike still covering them.

"Now yours, please," I said, still holding out my hand.

"I never carry one," he said, standing up, and I was surprised to hear what, to my ear, sounded like a perfect upper class British accent. Instead he grasped my outstretched hand in his and, smiling, gave me a warm, firm handshake. "You know my name, Officer. Pray tell, what is yours?"

Returning his handshake with equal firmness I replied, "Thomas Jackson, Detective Lieutenant, Key West Police Department."

Now it was Donatello's turn to be surprised, although he didn't show it very much, just the merest flicker of one eyebrow slightly raised.

"Thomas 'Stonewall' Jackson, formerly of the Miami Police?"

"That's correct."

"I thought so," he said. "I had heard you had left the department in Miami, but my source was not forthcoming with your present whereabouts."

So, Donatello had a source in the Miami PD. Not really a surprise as I'd suspected it before I left.

"And who would that source be, Mr. Donatello?"

He chuckled. "Not so fast, Lieutenant. First we must get to know each other." And he sat back down on the couch resuming his previous relaxed air.

"Ah, but before that can happen we have to conduct some business." I said.

Moving over to the desk, I collected the hardware, handed them to Mike and told him to lock them in the gun safe.

"You boys can have those back when you leave town," I said to the pair in their respective corners. "Just stop back here and pick them up. We'll even provide you with an escort. Meanwhile," turning back to Donatello, "who is the registered owner of that car out front? The large black one that is so inconsiderately parked in a very clearly marked 'No Parking' zone."

"That would be me, Detective," admitted Donatello.

"Well, then, you owe the city of Key West some money. And the longer it sits there the higher the fine is going to be so I suggest you have one of these two," indicating Tweedle Dum and Tweedle Dee, "move it 'round the back to the parking lot that we so kindly provide for our visitors. On his way back in, he can stop in at the first room on the right and pay the fine, which, I'm sure, you'll cover. Both of them can then wait outside while you and I become better acquainted."

Donatello looked at me and smiled. Not the shark smile one would expect from someone in his business, but a genuine smile that included his eyes.

"You know something Lieutenant Jackson? I do believe that I like you. Tony," he said to one of the gorillas. "Move the car and take care of the ticket as the Lieutenant said. Frankie wait outside and both of you behave. Don't give any of the officers here any difficulty."

As Tony and Frankie left the room, I asked Donatello, "Are those two twins?"

He laughed. "Most people think so, but no, they're not. They aren't even closely related." Then he turned serious, "Now what about Sam Torres? The article I read in the *Herald* simply said that he was found on the beach but there was no mention of how he died or how he got there."

I sat down behind the desk.

"The investigation into Mr. Torres' death is ongoing and I can't discuss it with the public. However, I do have some questions for you."

I picked up the phone, buzzed out to Dennis and asked

him to bring me the file that held the Coast Guard Report. After he left I opened the file and showed Donatello the photograph.

"Would you tell me what you and the twins were doing on Sam's boat half way to Cuba last month Mr. Donatello?"

"Hmm. Not one of my better photos. I will tell you the truth, Lieutenant. We were fishing, that is all. In fact, Frankie caught his first marlin on that trip. He was quite excited about that." I must have had a disbelieving look on my face because he added, "Check with the taxidermist shop by the marina, he should remember. The fish weighed about 300 pounds and Frankie just carried it into the shop in his arms and placed it on the counter."

I made a note to do just that. Then I asked, "What exactly is your business?"

Without hesitation Donatello answered, "I have several interests, entertainment, restaurants, night clubs, to name just three. All of them legitimate, registered with the City of Miami, and paying their share of taxes."

I wasn't surprised at the last comment. Ever since the Feds got Capone on tax evasion, smart members of the mob, which Donatello obviously was, had gotten themselves excellent accountants and tax lawyers.

"What about gambling?"

"I do go to Hialeah on occasion. I have part interest in a couple of horses that run there."

"Do you wager on anything else, Mr. Donatello?"

"No, Lieutenant, I leave that to others."

"How about international trade?" I ventured. "Do any importing or exporting?"

Sitting forward, Donatello gave me a hard stare. "Lieutenant, you can sit there for as long as you wish asking me oblique questions about what I may or may not do, but you will not get the information that I know you are looking for. Others have tried before under far more persuasive circumstances. Furthermore, none of this will get either one of us closer to the answers to the questions we both have: who killed Sam Torres and why?" He held up his hand as I started to speak. "You know his death was not an accident. Had it been, the reporter from the *Key West Current*, what was her name? Ah, yes, Amy Petersen, would have said so in her article. By the way, that was a very good piece she wrote. I should like to meet her and congratulate her." Again he gave me a genuine smile, then turned serious. "Now, where do you stand on the investigation into the death of Sam Torres?"

Despite the way he praised her, I was concerned that Donatello wanted to meet Amy. She was my responsibility, and not just professionally. With the threat presented by Andy Hardy, I didn't want to expose her to anything else. I also knew what her response to my concerns would be, so I was going to have to play this one very carefully.

Retrieving the photo, I placed it in the file and closed the cover. "As I told you Mr. Donatello, it's an open investigation which I cannot discuss with the public. However, as part of that investigation, I would like to know how you knew Sam Torres?" I picked up my pen and poised over my notebook, ready for answers. "When and under what circumstances did you meet? You must admit that your reputation and that photograph are sufficient to raise questions as to whether or not you are connected with Mr. Torres' death; maybe not directly, but possibly indirectly if he was involved with any of your 'businesses.'"

I knew damn well that Sam would never have agreed to be a willing accomplice to anything even remotely illegal and I was also positive that the only thing he did with Salvatore Donatello was to take him fishing. However, that didn't rule out the possibility that Sam had been killed because someone else thought he might have been involved with Donatello and his organization.

99

Donatello leaned back against the couch, his hands in his lap. "I met Sam about fifteen years ago, in 1951. I had developed an interest in deep-sea fishing and was looking for a good fishing guide. I was told he was the best."

"And you've been coming to Key West on a regular basis to go fishing?"

"Yes, when I need to get away from work. I find it relaxing."

"What about the years you spent in Cuba? Did you come back to Key West then just for the fishing?"

"Sometimes, yes, Lieutenant. At other times Sam would meet me in Havana. You are aware that both he and his wife have relatives in Cuba?" He raised one eyebrow slightly to emphasize the question. I nodded in acknowledgement.

"What about after your return from Cuba just before the revolution?"

"Yes. I happened to be in Miami when Castro's forces took over the country. Since then I have been fishing with Sam about four or five times a year."

"Have you ever been back to Cuba since then, Mr. Donatello? Did you ever prevail upon Mr. Torres to take you back under the guise of a fishing trip?"

Donatello looked at me like I was crazy.

"Lieutenant, do you know that is about the most ridiculous question I think you could possibly ask me. Of course I haven't been back. Nor would I have insulted or endangered Sam by asking that he smuggle me into Cuba. There is nothing in that country for which I would risk the potential penalties which would be imposed by the Castro regime or our own government."

The reaction I got from Donatello was the one I had been hoping for. A simple no would have left me suspicious. Even then, I still had one more question I had to ask, although I knew what the answer would be.

"Mr. Donatello," I began, looking squarely at him, "did

you, at any time, ask Mr. Torres to pick up, transport or otherwise convey any illegal substances from any point outside of the United States to any point within this country?"

Donatello's face remained stern. "Lieutenant Jackson, I know that you have known Sam your entire life. He mentioned you on many occasions. I also know to what you are referring and that you are aware of what Sam's position was in that respect. The simple answer to your question is no. The long answer is that I respected Sam too much and valued his friendship too much to even consider asking him to do anything of that nature." Here his expression softened and a bit of a smile played at the corners of his mouth as he continued. "Had I ever done so, you and I would, most likely, not be having this conversation because, despite the presence of Tony and Frankie, he would have thrown me overboard with an anchor tied to my neck."

I smiled and nodded in agreement. "Yes, quite likely. That's what I would expect and then he'd have returned here and turned himself in."

I thought for a moment and then I said, "Mr. Donatello, I'm going to be blunt. You're perfectly free to get up and walk out after my next question because, as far as I know, you've done nothing for which I could keep you here and there are no outstanding warrants for your arrest." I leaned back in my chair, which squeaked in protest. "For the record, although no one has been able to prove anything, you are suspected of being the person in charge of nearly all of the prostitution and illegal gambling in South Florida, which puts you squarely in the organized crime business. There've been rumors of connections to the disappearances of individuals, but I know of only one instance in which you were suspected of a definite murder, though you were acquitted of that charge." At that moment I thought I saw a shadow of pain pass over his face.

"Because of other circumstances, some directly related to the Torres investigation, I suspect that Sam's death is somehow connected with the movement of marijuana and possibly other substances through the Keys and onto the mainland. I know that Sam wouldn't have willingly participated in such activities and your answers this afternoon lead me to the conclusion that you wouldn't have tried to convince him otherwise. However, my suspicion remains." I sat up, the chair squeaking again, put my pen down and laid both hands on the desk in front of me. "Mr. Donatello, are you in any way connected with the illegal smuggling of narcotics into the United States? And could such involvement have led any of your associates to suspect that Sam knew something which would've made him a liability?"

Donatello sat there on the couch and I could almost see the wheels turning in his head as he mentally weighed the pros and cons of different answers. Then his expression softened.

"Lieutenant, a very good man once told me 'Value your family and value your friends. Do what you can for them because when all is said and done they are all that matters.' Now I have no family. I lost my wife and one son in the war and my other son," Donatello paused and the shadow passed over his face again, "well, he died also. I have very few true friends. In my business you don't encounter many people you can honestly trust. Sam was one of those I could and did. There was another from down here who, like Sam, I could trust. He is also gone, but I believe that, were he and Sam here, they would both tell me to trust you. I hope they would be correct.

"Strictly off the record, yes I am connected with a certain 'organization' in South Florida, but only in an advisory capacity with respect to the finances of their 'entertainment' division. Any suspicions about my involvement in other activities are completely without support. However, even as a mere advisor, I know certain things and must consider my personal security, hence my two associates. The rest of my interests, as I said earlier, are legitimate and I keep them separate. The 'entertainment' division sometimes finds it necessary to convince customers to honor their obligations. That may be accomplished in many ways, but not by murder. Quite simply, dead men don't pay their bills."

Donatello's face took on an expression of defiance as he continued.

"As for narcotics, absolutely not. Yes, there are those in the organization who are involved in that trade and no I will not tell you who they are. However, personally I do not engage in that part of the business and I have refused to do so. That stand has probably made me some enemies, but that is my affair. As to your question of whether someone else could suspect that Sam had somehow been involved through me, I cannot answer that." At this point his eyes turned ice cold. "What I can tell you is that if I should find out that someone I know killed Sam for that reason, they will not have a future, and I assure you there will be no evidence that they had ever existed."

"Mr. Donatello," I said quietly. "I sincerely hope that you never give me any reason to have to arrest you. I also hope that I find Sam's killer before you do, for his sake."

I stood up and came around the desk to open the door. "Have a nice stay in Key West, Mr. Donatello. Come back and see us again, but please use the parking lot. And remember, Frankie and Tony can pick up their toys on the way out of town."

Donatello's face softened again as he stood and he smiled as we shook hands. "Thank you, Lieutenant. I have enjoyed our chat. Please let me know if I can be of assistance in your investigation."

He collected his boys and left.

I went back into the office and sat down. There was a lot to go over, but right then I was thinking of the phrase about family and friends that Donatello had uttered. It was one I'd heard often enough and had seen almost every day of my life, certainly every day while I was growing up. And hearing Donatello recite it felt like a fist hitting me square in the chest such that it'd been hard to keep a poker face. It was the exact phrase that my mother had stitched on a sampler for my father when they were first married and that he'd framed and hung on the wall in our living room where everyone could see it. It was still there. How the hell did Donatello know that phrase? And who was the other person from Key West that he said he could trust? I had a feeling I knew, but I wasn't ready to believe it.

The door opened slightly and Amy stuck her head in.

"I saw your 'guests' leave so I figured it was safe to come out from under my rock. Who were those guys?"

"The distinguished looking gentleman was Salvatore Donatello," I replied. "And the other two were his boys Frankie and Tony."

She came in. "Which was which?"

"Does it matter?"

"No, I guess not. Either one would be enough to take care of anyone I know. Jeeze, Tom, they were both twice the size of Mikey."

"I noticed." I was still puzzled over Donatello's use of the family and friends phrase. "If it'd just been those two I don't think this would have been a friendly chat."

Amy sat down on the couch that Donatello had recently vacated and took out her notebook. The reporter was back on duty.

"So, what was it all about?"

Remembering my promise to give her full access to everything, I told her about my conversation with

Donatello, including his admissions, with the caution that they were off the record and were for her notes only. Without proof, she couldn't make any reference to them in any story she might publish. At the very least she'd be opening herself to a charge of libel and the worst, well, I didn't want to think about that. Amy grudgingly agreed, but I could tell she was intrigued with Salvatore Donatello and wanted to know more. So did I, but not for the same reason.

When I finished, Amy looked at me while she chewed on the end of her pencil and I could see the wheels going around as she tried to put pieces of this puzzle together. I waited for her to come up with something because right then nothing was making sense to me. We were missing some of the pieces and part of me was convinced that Andy Hardy was one of them, not just because I wanted to nail his ass. Andy Hardy was a thorn in my side that I wanted to pluck out any way possible. The problem was how he could be involved in Sam's death. There was no way he could have been on *Greta*. I knew that for a fact. First, he'd been at the paper all day Friday. That had been confirmed by Amy and Larry. Second, you couldn't get Andy on a boat for love or money. I have never known anyone to be so violently sea sick as Andy Hardy. He even had difficulty stepping out onto a floating dock in a dead calm. No, if Sam left Friday morning on *Greta* there was no way Andy killed him. But did he know who did?

"Tom?"

I came back to the present. "What?"

"How exactly did Sam die?" Amy asked. "I mean, what was the official cause of death according to Doc Elliott?"

"You know, I still don't know. Every time I've been back in here to look at the report something else has come up."

I punched the intercom and asked for the autopsy report on Sam Torres. Sally brought it in together with a small envelope. I gave the latter a glance and looked up with a raised, questioning eyebrow.

"It's from your visitor," she said. "One of his boys just dropped it off."

Opening the envelope, I pulled out a small, plain white card on which the following was written in a precise hand:

> 'Tom,
> I would be pleased if you and Miss Petersen would join me for dinner this evening. 7 p.m., Bungalow 4, Key West Lodge.
> S.D.'

"It's from Donatello. He wants us to join him for dinner." I handed Amy the card.

My expression must have given me away because Amy said, "We didn't say anything to him when he left. How does he know me, let alone that I was here?"

"My guess is that he doesn't and he didn't. But your name was on the piece he read in Miami." With that, Amy relaxed and I told her what he'd said about her piece.

"I don't mind fans of my work," she said. "But I would rather they not be from the criminal element."

I agreed, but I also reasoned this could be an opportunity to learn more about Salvatore Donatello.

"Sally," I said, "call Mr. Donatello and tell him that Miss Petersen and I would be happy to meet him for dinner." Then I turned my attention to Doc's report.

Skimming over the preliminaries, I got to the paragraph that mattered. Doc's description of the wound on the back of Sam's head indicated that it had been made by an elongated blunt object that had an edge to it. This was evidenced by the condition of the skull under the scalp where the bone had been caved in along either side of a straight line. The force had been enough to drive bone fragments into the brain. The angle of the wound was downward from right to left indicating that the person who struck Sam had been right handed. Strike three against Andy Hardy as a suspect. He was a southpaw.

The report also indicated that the blow had been delivered from above or in an overhanded manner such as when swinging a hammer. There was little water in the lungs, which ruled out drowning while merely stunned. The conclusion was that the blow to the head was the cause of death and that Sam was dead when he went into the water.

As to the time of death, based on the condition of the body, the water temperature and the location where Sam was found, Doc estimated it was between 7 a.m. and 9 a.m. Friday. With that information and working from tide tables and current charts, we'd be able to make a pretty good estimation of just where *Greta* was when Sam's body was dumped in the water.

Relaxing a bit, I handed the report to Amy so she could read it. Now I knew. I wasn't working on an assumption, even one bolstered by facts and logic. Doc had confirmed that Sam had been murdered.

Amy looked up when she finished reading the report with no hint of pain or disgust. I was impressed. Despite Doc Elliott's clinical description, not everyone can read one of those reports without turning a little pale. "An elongated blunt object with an edge?" she asked. "What could that be? And on a boat? The only thing I can think of that might have that shape would be something like a tire iron or a pry bar. But why would you have one on a boat?"

"Right off hand, I don't know, but let's find out if Sam had one first." I picked up the phone and called Sam's house and was glad that Julio answered since he was the one I wanted to speak to anyway. I asked him if Sam had a crow bar or a pry bar on *Greta* and when he said "yes," I asked him to describe it for me while I doodled a picture. Amy stood up and was watching while my drawing developed and she nodded as I finished it.

I asked Julio if he'd found the charter book. He answered "no" and told me he'd searched the entire house. It was nowhere to be found.

Suspecting the answer, I asked if they normally locked the doors during the day. Julio's response was, "Why? There is always someone in the neighborhood and the women are back and forth to each other's houses all the time." That confirmed it, someone could have slipped in any time and taken the book. I was about to ring off when Julio stopped me, his voice somewhat hesitant and sad but struggling to remain strong.

"Senor Tom, when can we have Papa Sam? Father Stephen came by today to discuss funeral plans but we could not decide on a date because we do not know when we will get Papa Sam back. Can you tell me?"

"Julio, I know this is a difficult time for you and Elyse, but I think Dr. Elliott could release Sam's body now. He's finished the autopsy, so there really shouldn't be any reason to keep him. In the meantime, until we know who killed Sam and why, I'd suggest that you lock your doors when no one is home. It's probably not necessary, but it'd make me feel better."

"Si, I will tell Mama Elyse. And gracias, thank you." He hung up.

I replaced the handset on the cradle and looked at Amy. "Sam had a crow bar on the boat. Julio said it was sometimes useful for getting a hook out of a big fish. He also said it has a multi-sided shaft. I'm thinking that is our murder weapon and I'm hoping it's still on board when we find *Greta*."

"What was all that about locking doors?"

"Julio searched the entire house and found no sign of Sam's charter book. I didn't think he would. Anybody could have walked in and taken it after Julio left for school Friday morning. All they'd have to make sure of was that they weren't seen."

"So who do you think took it and why?"

"I don't know, but I have my suspicions."

Amy scowled and pointed her pencil at me. "Come on Tom. Don't hold out on me. Remember our deal. I get everything."

"I know, I know. Right now it's only an assumption based on very few facts. Let me have some time to think it through and make sure I'm not going off course. In the meantime, we have a dinner to get ready for."

CHAPTER 12

An elegant but unassuming hotel, the Key West Lodge consisted of a main building that housed the lobby, restaurant and normal hotel rooms, with a swimming pool behind and a quartet of bungalows, nestled under palm trees, that made an arc on the other side of the swimming pool. The bungalows were generally popular with families because each included a small kitchen and three bedrooms around an open sitting and dining room. I was a little surprised that the note from Donatello indicated he had taken one of them. I thought he'd have had a room in the main building with the twins on each side.

Not knowing where we would be eating and considering Donatello's sartorial appearance, we'd opted for something a bit more formal than our normal attire. I traded my uniform for a sport coat and tie while Amy pulled out a simple black cocktail dress and strand of pearls. What possessed her to pack those last night, I had no idea. She even had the shoes and purse that went with the dress. When I asked her about it, all she said was, "I used to be a Girl Scout. Now I'm always prepared."

When we stepped up onto the porch of the bungalow one of the twins opened the door and ushered us in. I still couldn't tell them apart. In the combination sitting and dining area, three place settings lay on a table with candles and a small floral centerpiece in the middle. An array of bottles lined a small bar along one wall, opposite which was a couch where Salvatore Donatello sat reading some papers. Mouthwatering smells emanating from the small kitchen perfumed the air.

Donatello rose and approached us. "Lieutenant." He grasped my hand. "Thank you for accepting my invitation to dine." He turned to Amy. "And this, I presume, is Miss Petersen. Enchenté, mademoiselle," he said as he took her hand. "I do hope that neither of you is 'on duty' this evening as I have some particularly nice wines to accompany our meal, or perhaps you would prefer a cocktail before dinner?"

Amy answered first, "Thank you, Mr. Donatello, I think wine would be nice."

"Please, Miss Petersen, Lieutenant, there is no need to be so formal, Sal is fine and I shall call you Amy and Tom. I think by the time this evening has passed, we will be friends rather than mere passing acquaintances." Donatello beckoned to the twin who had let us in. "Frankie, the Spumante."

Frankie was by the bar pouring what, to my eye, looked like champagne into three glasses on a tray which he then brought over to us.

I took the proffered wine. "I presume then that we will not be adjourning to the hotel restaurant and that the menu this evening is Italian."

"Quite right, Tom. Salud." He raised his glass and we responded. "I thought the restaurant would be too public given our respective positions. In addition, our conversation is likely to touch on subjects that, for the present, the three of us would like to keep to ourselves. Besides, it will give you the opportunity to see that Frankie and Tony have skills beyond their obvious talents."

I was hesitant, but Amy took a sip of her wine and her eyebrows rose. "This is nice," she said. "What is it?"

"Ah, you like it," Donatello said after sipping from his glass. "I am glad as it is one of my favorites. It is a slightly dry Prosecco Superiore from the Veneto region of Italy and has the delightful ability to travel well." Turning slightly serious, Donatello added, "Amy, I must thank you for your piece on Sam and for seeing that it got into the Miami papers. I am sure that Elyse appreciated your sensitivity."

"Have you spoken with her yet?" Amy asked.

"Alas, no, not yet. We just arrived in town this afternoon and I had hoped to get more information on the case during my visit with Tom earlier this afternoon. As it is an ongoing investigation, he was understandably reluctant to discuss it. Perhaps you could prevail upon him so that I may be able to help in some way." He cocked an eye in my direction.

"I'll do my best, Sal," Amy replied. "But you must understand that our Lieutenant can be extremely stubborn when it comes to procedure."

"I can ask for nothing more, my dear." Donatello said. "Ah, dinner begins."

I looked toward the kitchen and couldn't believe it. There in the door in full chef whites, complete with a tall toque-blanche, stood Tony with a tray of appetizers. I knew it was Tony because Frankie came over from the bar and held Amy's chair for her while Donatello and I took the other seats.

Dinner was an adventure. Tony had created a true Italian menu from the antipasti through the pasta and fish dishes on to gelato. I hadn't had a meal like this since a farewell dinner with Lou just before I left Miami. How Tony did it in the small bungalow kitchen I couldn't guess but every bite was delicious. When I congratulated him I was rewarded with a smile that I hadn't expected. According to Sal, that was the only time Tony had ever smiled at a cop.

At the table after the final course, and with both Frankie and Tony in the room I said to Donatello, "When I first saw those two this afternoon, I never would have thought that this evening I'd be served by Jeeves a meal cooked by Escoffier. What the hell are they doing in your organization? They could be running the most successful Italian restaurant in Florida. They'd certainly never have to worry about anyone arguing about the service or the bill."

Sal smiled at me. "You're not too far off the mark Tom. When I retire, that is exactly what they intend to do."

"When they're ready, let me know," said Amy. "I'll write their reviews." She stood up, went to each of them and standing on her tip toes with they, in turn, bending down to meet her, she gave each of them a kiss on the cheek. She returned to her seat as Frankie cleared the last dishes. "Tom, we have to find them a location here in Key West. Just think what a draw it would be to have the best Italian restaurant in Florida down here."

"Do you think people would drive two hours from Miami for dinner?" I asked.

"For the right dinner, Tom, people from Miami go to New York," said Sal. "This is closer."

Frankie placed a decanter of brandy and three glasses on the table and left us alone. A pot of coffee and three cups were on the sideboard. The sounds of dishes being washed and put away came from the kitchen, then the back door opened and closed. We were apparently alone and I figured the important discussion was about to begin. Our conversation during dinner had been light, mostly Donatello learning Amy's history. We, in turn, tried to get information out of him but without success.

I took a sip of Sal's excellent brandy and turned to him. "Okay, Sal. We've been wined and dined. What do you want?"

Donatello looked first at Amy, then at me. "I want to tell you a story," he said.

"Fact or fiction?" I asked.

"I think Amy will be able to answer that question when I'm finished," Donatello replied. He sipped his brandy and began.

"Many years ago a young man began his job with a family run business. His father knew the owner and had been able to get him the position. The young man's duties were varied and were calculated so that he would learn the business from the ground up and inside out. He proved to be of a higher than average level of intelligence and to have a good head for figures. As a result, it wasn't too long before he had moved up to a minor management position. Recognizing the young man's abilities, the owner of the business sought to further his education and, being unable to get him into a good American school, placed him at a school in England where he would learn finance and economics.

"For four years he pursued his studies and made friends which brought him invitations to country houses and contact with individuals he otherwise would never have met. One of these contacts proved to be the captivating daughter of a prominent family who, knowing nothing of our lad's background, nevertheless permitted him to 'call upon' the young lady whenever he was in the area or she was in town, albeit always with a chaperone of some sort. During this period he also learned the finer points of society: what to wear, when to wear it, what wines went with what foods, how to address those at different levels of society. In short, all the things considered necessary by those in the upper echelons. Our young man evolved into a gentleman.

"Completing his studies and receiving his degree, he prevailed upon the father of the young lady to recommend him for a position in a London banking house, having first secured his patron's permission to remain for an additional two years to obtain practical experience. Concurrently, one or two of his friends had secured positions, through family contacts, with American banking houses and this enabled the young gentleman to develop, through them, his own contacts in those institutions. During this time, the relationship with the young lady was growing and flourishing to the point that he had reached an understanding with her father concerning the couple's future. Although disliking the deception, our young gentleman had been very careful to hide his true family background."

Sal paused and raised the decanter to Amy, who shook her head. He poured a taste into his glass then passed it to me. It truly was an excellent brandy and I couldn't pass it up. Sal then continued.

"This period coincided with the run up to the crash of 1929 and the beginning of the great depression. However, our young gentleman had early on recognized that something was not right in the economy and had been able to warn his patron and make financial recommendations which would later prove sound. Simultaneously he had taken steps with his own finances to weather what he suspected would be a difficult time. The result was that when the economies on both sides of the Atlantic collapsed, he was able to show the young lady's father that he could support her in the proper manner and, thereby, secured permission to marry her.

"Following their wedding and honeymoon trip on the Continent, the couple returned to London and a rather elegant town house which had been procured by her father during their absence. Our young gentleman had also convinced his patron that it would be beneficial to the family business if he were to remain in Europe for the time being and had devised a strategy for improving the company's finances even in those troubled times. It would be necessary for him to occasionally return to the United States for business consultations, but he made his home and began his family in London.

"He and his wife were blessed with two sons, both healthy and alert, about three years apart. As conditions deteriorated in Europe, they talked about moving to the

United States, but business and family kept them in London until one day in September of 1940."

"The Blitz had started." Up to this point, Donatello had been relaxed, but with those words he tensed up. His jaw became set, his gaze was distant and his hands remained flat on the table in front of him. "London was being bombed on a regular basis and those who could get out of the city were doing so. Our young gentleman and his wife had decided that she and the children would go to her father's country house for the duration while he would relocate to a moderately safer part of town. On the day they were to leave, he had just picked up his older son from school when there was an air raid and they were directed to a nearby shelter. With the sounding of the all clear, they made their way home but, upon turning into their street, they were greeted with devastation. The crescent where their house stood had received a direct hit. Only the end houses were still standing. Where their house had been was a gaping hole surrounded by rubble.

"Finding the local Warden, he inquired about survivors. The Warden asked which was his house and the young man could only point. Without another word, the Warden called over a nurse and spoke to her. She led the gentleman and his son to a makeshift shelter in which there were several bodies covered with blankets and identified by the location of their discovery. Taking him to one pair, she gently asked him to identify the two bodies and carefully lifted one corner of each blanket."

At this point Donatello paused in his recitation and I spoke up. "I presume that the two bodies were the wife and younger son."

"Yes," he confirmed quietly and continued. "Upon recovering his composure, he was taken to another tent where he provided the necessary information to the authorities. He and his son then made their way to the railway station to get the train to the country, stopping first at his office to collect various documents and account books. The gentleman had decided to first deliver the sad news to his father-in-law and then to leave England and return to the United States with his remaining son."

"Didn't the father-in-law raise any objection to his grandson leaving?" Amy asked.

"No," said Donatello, relaxing again. "He agreed with the plan. You have to remember that at that time England was bracing for a German invasion and the father-in-law wanted to be sure that his only remaining heir was safe. His own son had been killed previously at Dunkirk. About one month later, our gentleman and his son were able to obtain passage to New York and, as a U.S. citizen, he avoided any problems that may have been faced by other refugees from Europe.

"Arriving in New York, his first visit was to his patron where he delivered certain of the documents and books retrieved from London. During his time in England, the old family business had expanded and, in view of his experience in Europe, he was offered a significant position in the financial department in New York. A suitable apartment was obtained; his son was enrolled in school; and the two set about re-establishing their lives while the rest of the world went to war.

"Two years later, however, their lives changed again due to death. The patron died and with his passing came a significant change to the family business. The patron's son took control and began to establish his own mark on the business. Unfortunately, the new management's style did not follow that of the former and our gentleman's knowledge and abilities were not readily appreciated by those now in power. Realizing this new management would present difficulties if he remained in close proximity, our gentleman considered how he could change his circumstances in a way which would benefit him and give the appearance that it was to the new management's best interests.

"At that time the business had, shall we say, an entertainment division based in Miami which had been underperforming. The gentleman was able to obtain recent reports and determined that what was needed to turn this division into a profitable enterprise was someone who understood its financial underpinnings and could support the current hierarchy without appearing to try to run things.

"Making it appear that he did not want the job and that he would consider it a demotion, he was able to arrange for his transfer to Miami. That move did two things for him. It got him away from the New York office and the new management and it put him in a position where he had the opportunity to establish financial contacts in the Southern Hemisphere, something that had been politely, but firmly, discouraged in both London and New York."

At this point there was a delicate cough from the direction of the kitchen. Frankie had come in to see if we needed anything and to ask if he and Tony could go to the bar on the other side of the pool for a beer. Sal told them it was okay and that we would be fine. His exact words to Frankie were "I will be perfectly safe with the Lieutenant here." The look I got from Frankie as much as told me that if anything happened to Sal, he would hold me personally responsible. Not a pleasant thought. Before leaving, Frankie moved the brandy decanter to the coffee table in front of the couch and we relocated to more comfortable seating, Amy and I on the couch and Sal in an overstuffed armchair where he continued his narrative.

"Life in Miami, even during the war years, was good for the gentleman. His duties to the company were not excessive nor unduly challenging as to require all of his time so he was able to establish side contacts and get involved in other businesses on his own. He discovered that he particularly enjoyed the restaurant business, the challenge of predicting the public's interests and desires, trying new cuisines and flavors and doing it all in a wartime economy. He also discovered the recreational opportunities of Florida. Whereas London society had revolved around clubs and town and country house parties, which, given the English climate invariably occurred indoors, the climate of Florida was far more conducive to outdoor recreation. A particular thrill was the discovery of deep sea fishing with the challenge of taking on a large fish with nothing but a thin line as well as the long hours which could be spent discussing various business strategies in complete privacy."

"Was that when you met Sam?" Amy asked as she rose and went to the sideboard for coffee.

"No, that was later," said Sal.

Amy raised the coffeepot to us. I nodded, but Sal shook his head. "No thank you, my dear. I don't sleep too soundly as it is and that would just keep me awake all night."

Amy poured two cups and brought them over, sat down, looked at Sal over her cup, her eyes sharp and alert. "So what happened next?" she asked.

Sal relaxed against the back of the chair and crossed one leg over the other. "Over the next few years, the performance of the Miami Entertainment Division significantly improved, which kept New York happy, and the gentleman, through his own abilities and unbeknownst to management in New York, established his own not insignificant business presence in Miami, albeit in legitimate circles. He also came to know very well those individuals in local and state government who could be trusted as well as those who could not.

"Knowing that his principal job had hazards which could affect his son, upon arrival in Miami the two had been careful to keep the lad away from any contact with, let's just call it the family business. This included securing accommodations away from others in the business and enrolling his son in a suitable boarding school with the children of society families but under his mother's name, much as he had in London. Being in temperament more English than American, this did not bother the boy. These actions also made it possible for our gentleman himself to meet these society families at school functions and later at their social events without them realizing his other connections. The primary object of this was to establish a footing for his son to enter that strata just as he had done in London.

"All went well. The son did well in school and grew to enjoy sports, particularly football. When it came time to select a college, he decided to stay in Florida and attend the University of Miami. This was to prove disastrous."

Amy leaned forward. "How so?" she asked. She was clearly interested but was choosing her questions and the time to ask them carefully; letting her subject tell the story in his own words and not badgering for facts or details that could sidetrack the narrative.

Sal steepled his fingers, returning her gaze much like a professor about to impart knowledge to a student. "Ah, yes. This probably didn't make it into your history or civics classes up North, but Tom would know. During the 1940's, the demographics of Miami had begun changing with a significant influx of Cuban migration. Just as with the other immigrants who came to this country over the decades, the vast majority of these were decent, hard working people looking for a better life. However, also like their predecessors, some who came did solely to prey on the rest. These individuals saw an opportunity to establish themselves, first within their own community. Then, working their way outward, they expanded into other communities, frequently coming into conflict with those who were there before them and who did not take kindly to invasion. Our gentleman's Entertainment Division was one of those who had more than its share of conflicts. One area was in what was a small but lucrative sideline involving gambling on the outcome of various sporting events, including college football games."

Again Sal tensed up and his gaze became distant. "In the fall of 1952, the University of Miami was favored to win against a team that one of these predatory groups had bet heavily on. In order to save their money and position among their fellows, one group of 'invaders' tried to pressure the Miami quarterback to shave points off the score, if not actually throw the game. Miami won by a considerable margin and the quarterback, or what was left of him, was found a few days later on the edge of the Everglades."

"I remember the case," I said. "The suspicion fell on you, but you were acquitted."

"Yes," Sal said. "The DA had no evidence and later told me that it was purely political that I had been targeted. He had been ordered to prepare the case and go ahead with it."

Amy asked, "Did they ever find out who was responsible?"

"No," said Sal. "I believe it is still what you call 'an open case.'"

"When I left Miami it was still on the books," I confirmed. "I suspect it still is, unless they've found someone to pin it on."

Sal's eyes grew hard and he said, "No, no one else has been charged, yet."

Sal, uncharacteristically, avoided my gaze. Sal Donatello was proving to be an interesting man and something of an enigma. That he was involved in organized crime was a given. He'd just about admitted that in the office earlier. However, there was not one shred of evidence to even hint at linking him to the more violent aspects of that business. In contrast, he repeatedly came off as squeaky clean, even charming, especially with respect to women. He projected what Hollywood has taught us to recognize as the quintessential British gentleman of the upper class. Yet, at times, his eyes could display the ruthlessness of the worst hood you could imagine.

His control over himself appeared to be absolute and I couldn't envision him losing that control even under the worst of circumstances. As for his control over others, I thought of Tony and Frankie and briefly wondered if they were actually his minders, sent by New York to keep an eye on him. Remembering how they'd obeyed him without question at the office and the care they had exercised with dinner this evening, I realized that they were definitely his men; no one else's.

When I returned to the conversation Amy was asking, "Why didn't he send his son back to England after the war?"

"Two reasons, I suspect," Sal said, relaxed once again. "First was probably selfishness. His son was the only part of his wife that he had. The second was practical. There was no one left to send him to. His in-laws had been killed after he left when a V1 buzz bomb fell on the country house one evening."

"And the young gentleman? What happened to him?" she asked. I thought she hadn't picked up that Sal had been telling us his life story until I looked at her and caught the briefest of winks. She wasn't revealing that she'd figured it out.

"Somehow New York found out that the quarterback was his son," Sal said. With a significant look at me he continued, "That organization has resources that are not available to others, the result being that he was transferred out of Miami."

"What about you?" she said. "After the trial where did

you go?"

"Me? I went to Havana for a few years. I ran some businesses there until the revolution, then I came back to Miami to concentrate on my restaurants and fishing. As I told Tom this afternoon, I met Sam in '51 and have been fishing with him on a regular basis since then. When I saw your piece in the *Herald* yesterday, I had to come down to find out what happened and offer my assistance in any way possible. Sam was more than a fishing guide. He was a friend who helped me through some difficult times."

Sal paused to sip his brandy and I calmly asked the question that had been bothering me all evening. "Sal," I said quietly. "When did you meet my father?"

Sal raised an eyebrow. "Ah, I was wondering when you would get to that? At the trial of course. He defended one of the State's witnesses on a related matter."

"No, after that, here at the house in town," I said, "when you saw the sampler in the living room that you quoted this afternoon, 'Value your family and value your friends. Do what you can for them because when all is said and done they are all that matters.'"

"I thought that would get your attention," he said. "However," as he looked at his watch, "I am afraid that is a tale for another time. It is quite late and, since Amy has not been taking notes, I am sure that she will want to get what she remembers on paper as soon as she can." Turning to Amy he said, "Would you be so kind as to call Tony and Frankie back from the bar. I am sure they have finished chatting to the two young ladies they noticed earlier."

Amy stepped out onto the bungalow's back porch and I looked at Sal.

"I'm not going to mince words Sal," I said. "You and I both know that your involvement in organized prostitution and illegal gambling in South Florida is more than just 'advisory.' However, neither I nor any other law enforcement organization has any proof which would stand up in court and your statement this afternoon can't be confirmed. Frankly, if people want to waste their time and money that way, that's their business as long as they can afford it and nobody is harmed."

I smiled at him and continued. "In your favor, as far as I'm concerned, though I can't speak for anyone else, I don't believe that you've had any direct involvement in any significant violence involved in that business. Also, for what it's worth, I believe you with regard to your statements about narcotics smuggling, except for one thing. Sam wouldn't have just thrown you overboard if you'd asked him to carry the stuff, he'd have used you for bait."

Giving him my stern, cop face, I said, "Right now, though, my concern is what was your connection with my father? He was a good man and a good lawyer who cared about the people down here and there is no way that he would've been involved with you and your associates outside of a courtroom, and I don't mean as your defense counsel. Hell, he even warned me about you before I joined the department in Miami."

The back door opened as Amy returned and quickly and quietly Sal said, "Not now Tom. What I tell you about that is for your ears only first. Then you can decide what to tell Amy. She's a good girl, Tom, but she's also a good journalist and the two may not always see things the same way."

Amy and the twins came into the room as I was ready to object and Sal gave me a look that as much as said 'just shut your mouth, we'll talk later' so I did. We rose from our seats, Tony went into the little kitchen to finish cleaning up and Frankie said to Sal, "You want anything else, Boss?"

"Yes, Frankie. Please see that the Lieutenant and Miss Petersen get to their vehicle safely and then we are finished for the evening."

"Sure thing, Boss."

Frankie escorted us out to the car. When we got there he opened the door for Amy and I could almost see him blush when she stood on the doorsill and gave him another kiss on the cheek.

"That's for Tony too," she said. "I mean it. If you two want to open a restaurant down here, I'll help you find a location and write your reviews. You'll be a hit."

Obviously there had been some additional conversation when she had gone out to the pool to get them.

After that, Frankie came over to my side and before I got in he looked at me carefully.

"Lieutenant," he said, "me and Tony, we don't like cops. But the Boss seems to like you. So me and Tony we, how do they say it nice? We 'reserve judgment.' We follow the Boss's lead. He does good by you, you do good by him, okay? Also," he continued, jerking a thumb in Amy's direction, "you take care of her or you answer to me and Tony."

"Fair enough Frankie," I said. "But, if you, Tony or Mr. Donatello break any laws down here, I'll have no choice. I'll have to pursue it. That's my job. As for Miss Petersen, don't worry, she's under my personal 24 hour protection."

Frankie smiled and stuck out a hand that looked the size of a bear's paw and I took it hoping he would be gentle.

"Okay, Lieutenant. Just so's we understand each other."

As we pulled out of the lot, Amy asked me, "What did Sal say while I was out?"

I lied. "Nothing, we just commented on the brandy."

"Tom, you do know that story he told was about himself. I'd like to see the record on that case involving his son."

"Yeah, me too. I'll call Lou Zachiarelli in Miami tomorrow morning and see if he can get a copy sent down. Meanwhile, there might be something in the boxes of Dad's old files in the spare room. I always thought I should get rid of them or send them to storage but never got around to it.

If you want to stay home and go through them I can have one of the boys come over and stay with you while I'm at work."

Truth was I'd tried to go through them several times over the years but could never convince myself to get rid of them. They were part of Dad. I guess keeping them made it seem like he was still there.

"Listen, Tom, I know you're worried about Andy, but I'm a big girl. I can take care of myself."

"I don't know if I'm as worried about Andy now as I am about what Frankie or Tony would do to me if anything happened to you. They like you. That puts you up with Sal in their eyes. Me, I'm just another cop to them, but I'm the cop who's looking after you; so if anything happens to you, I'm the one they're going to come after first."

"Fine," she huffed. "I'll call Sal in the morning and ask if I can borrow one of his boys as a body guard while you're at work. Just think of the dinner that could be waiting when you get home if I get Tony."

"You're joking," I said and then glanced over at her. Even in the dim light of the car I could see the set of her jaw and realized she wasn't.

CHAPTER 13

Tuesday

The phone rang and I reached over to the nightstand and answered it.

"Tom, its Sally."

I'd left word after our dinner with Donatello that I would be in late this morning and Sally wouldn't call me at home unless it was important. I sat up.

"What is it?" I asked while Amy repositioned the pillows to give me some support.

"Mikey just called in; he's got a floater this side of Cow Key Channel."

"Oh Crap!" I said and then immediately apologized to both Sally and Amy. "Is anyone with him?"

"Dennis was here and just left to assist," Sally said. "I'm trying to locate Doc Elliott, but no luck so far."

"He may have been on call last night. You know what he's like to wake up after an all-nighter. Call the hospital and see who they can send over just to make the pronouncement for the record. Not even Doc could tell us much about a floater on site, then call Mike back and tell him I'll be there as soon as I can. Meanwhile he's the lead on this and I don't want any statements given out." Like most investigators, I don't believe in coincidence, so the first question in my mind was is this connected with Sam's murder and, if so, why?

"Okay, Tom," Sally said and rang off.

I turned to Amy, "We've got another body, in the water over by Stock Island. O'Neil's there and Dennis is on his way. Get dressed, we have to get up there too. We'll pick up some coffee on the way."

"You go, Tom. You have to. I'm going to stay here and

go through your Dad's files; see if I can find his notes on that case. Something tells me there might be a connection with Sam's murder. I don't know how, who or what yet, but there's something. Also, Sal knows more than he's told us so far."

"That last bit I agree with. But how could my Father's involvement in a side issue in that case be relevant to Sam's death? That's what I can't figure."

"Neither can I, yet. But you know me, if it's there I'll find it. Also, I'll feel like I'm contributing something to this investigation. Meanwhile, you have to go meet Mikey. Don't worry about me. I'll be fine."

Without answering her I picked up the phone, called Sally back and asked if there was anyone available who could come over and stay with Amy, but she told me everyone was out on duty. I hung up and turned to Amy with a certain amount of resignation.

"I guess you better call Sal and see if you can borrow one of the twins." I said. "It's that or I don't go."

As I got out of bed, Amy reached for the phone and dialed the number for the Lodge. Fifteen minutes later, when I walked out of the house, a cab pulled up and Frankie got out. As we passed I gave him my toughest cop look and he said, "Don't worry, Lieutenant. Nothing'll happen to her while I'm here."

Heading up Flagler toward the Route 1 Bridge over Cow Key Channel, I got on the radio with Mike. He told me he had the body corralled in a basin on the Key West side of the channel by the bridge waiting for an ME to be on hand before pulling it out while Dennis and a couple other officers had a perimeter set up to keep people off the dock.

I saw a Sheriff's car as I pulled in and hoped we wouldn't get into an argument over jurisdiction since the body had obviously been in the channel and the other side was his domain. A deputy came up to me as I got out of the car.

"Lieutenant," he said. "I just talked to the Sheriff and he said if you want this one it's yours. We've got enough on our plate, but he would like a copy of your report."

I thought, 'Yeah, in case we blow it, then he's got an out with the county.'

The body was already covered on a stretcher preparatory to being carried away to the morgue and Mike was taking notes while he listened to a man who, I presumed, was the one who had found my latest problem. Leaving Mike to his interview, I walked down the dock to the body where a youngish person was packing up a medical bag. I recognized him from having seen him with Doc Elliott on occasion, but I couldn't remember his name.

"Can you tell me anything Doctor?" I asked.

"Not much right now, Lieutenant, except that he's dead and he didn't get that way by drowning."

He pulled the sheet back and I saw two holes in the body's chest just right of center.

"Looks like both shots hit the heart," the doctor continued. "I'm guessing a .38. There are no exit wounds so the slugs should still be in him. I'll send them over with the report."

"Any guess as to time of death?"

The doctor looked down at the body and thought.

"Judging strictly by the amount of putrefaction necessary to lift a body of this size to the surface, I would say sometime Friday. No later than Saturday morning. Sorry, Lieutenant, that's the best I can do for you right now."

"Thanks Doctor," I said and walked back to where Mike and his witness were waiting for me.

"Lieutenant," Mike said, keeping things formal with a witness present, "this is Captain Nick Shay of the *Nancy Sue*. He spotted the body and radioed the dock master who called us."

I shook Captain Shay's hand and noted the strong grip and well calloused hands of a working commercial fisherman.

"Thank you for cooperating with us Captain. Is there anything you can tell us about the deceased?"

"Nope, Lieutenant. Like I told your officer here, I've never seen him before. I just saw something floating as I was on my way in and thought it was a bale. They've been seen before in the channel. After I tied up, I took my dingy back out to grab it and bring it in. To be honest, I was figuring on selling some of it to make up for a few lousy fishing runs. It was only when I got close that I saw what it was so I got a line around it, pulled it back to the dock, and then called the dock master."

"Okay, Captain. Thanks again," I said. "By the way, next time you see a floating bale, I suggest you just call the Coast Guard and report its location and heading. You know what'd happen to you if any of us catch you with that stuff. You might pass that advice around to the rest of the boat captains."

"Yes sir," he said, but I knew that if the opportunity presented itself he, like many other boat skippers, would take the chance for the extra cash that could be made selling off salvaged marijuana. I had a feeling that it was going to become a bigger problem for us in a few years and made a mental note to bring the subject up with the Chief when he got back.

I turned back to O'Neil. "Mike, was there any ID on the body?"

"No, and his face doesn't ring any bells with me. I hope we can get some prints off him as that might be our best bet for identification unless we can trace his clothes. The jacket had a Miami label. You think this is connected with Sam Torres?"

"I don't know yet. The other possibility is a connection with Andy Hardy; after all, those holes looked like they were made by .38's. If this guy is from Miami, maybe he was Andy's contact and there was an argument that went from bad to worse. You about done here?"

"Yeah. I've got the location where Captain Shay first saw the body plotted and it doesn't appear that anyone else saw anything. Besides if the stiff got dumped in the water Friday night, like the doctor said, there aren't too many people around here to see anything anyway and there're no lights in the channel."

I agreed with Mike. Apart from some lights on the bridge and a few dock lights, at night this area would be pretty dark and deserted.

"Okay, Mike, you may as well wrap it up. I'll be at the station if you need me." I headed to my car and as I passed Dennis I told him to drop back at headquarters when he was finished here before he went off anywhere else.

Back at the office, I called Amy and gave her a summary of the condition of the body and my conversation with Captain Shay. She picked up immediately on the likely caliber of the bullets still to be retrieved by the ME.

".38's? Are you thinking Andy was involved in this?"

"It's a possibility. I just wish we had samples from Andy's gun to check those slugs against. A .38 is one of the most common pistols around and I'd feel better about this if I could rule out Andy's."

"Don't you get a test bullet when you issue a license?" she asked.

"No, it's not required," I said. "All we get is make, model and serial number on the application form. Besides, as many guns as are sold in this state, let alone the country, storage of test bullets would be a problem. Hey, how's Tweedle Dee behaving?"

"Frankie? He's a pussycat and makes great coffee. I'll

have to learn what he does and show you. The stuff you make is like motor oil. Anyway, I've got him going through your Dad's old files looking for anything that references Miami and then I'll go through those to see if they're relevant to our questions."

"Do you really think that's wise? What if he sees something that reflects poorly on Sal? You know where his first loyalty lies."

"Don't worry Tom. I found the important box last night and put it aside. Frankie's going through the others. You were snoring and I couldn't sleep. I wonder if it was the brandy? You didn't snore the other two nights."

"Just make sure he doesn't hide or walk out with anything. I'm still not sure about Sal Donatello. Not until I have more answers. And don't go anywhere without taking Frankie with you. Remember, Andy's still out there."

I hung up, then picked up the phone again and dialed Lou's number in Miami. As it was ringing I remembered that he was on swing shift and probably wasn't in. I was about to hang up when a voice answered, "Miami PD, Sergeant Zachiarelli's desk."

"This is Lieutenant Tom Jackson, Key West PD. Is Lou there?"

"I'm sorry, Sir, Sergeant Zachiarelli doesn't get in this early. This is Officer Niles. Can I help you?"

Niles? That name didn't ring any bells from my days in Miami, so I figured he must be relatively new. "No thank you, officer. I forgot Lou was on swing these days. Just put a note on his desk letting him know I called." I started to hang up then pulled the phone back. "Niles? You still there?"

"Yes, Sir?"

"Is Alice Clare still in records?"

"Yes, Lieutenant, she is. She runs the place now."

"I thought she would. Can you transfer this call to her

phone?"

"Sure thing, and I'll leave a note for the sergeant."

"Thanks, Niles."

I heard the usual sounds of a call being transferred and then a voice so unlike its owner came on the line; a voice so soft and sultry it made a man think of nothing but sex. It was a voice that I knew belonged to a 63 year old grandmother who knew everything there was to know about the Miami Police Department case files and probably everything there was to know about Miami since her husband of forty years was on the city council. "Miami records," the voice breathed, and part of me melted and went back to the first time I heard it before I found out who it belonged to.

"Alice, I keep telling you, if you don't change your phone voice, someone is going to charge you with making obscene telephone calls."

"Tommy Jackson! You big gorgeous hunk of man you. What the hell have you been up to? Lou told me you called Saturday. What's going on down there?"

"Oh, just the usual, laying out in the sun, hobnobbing with the tourists, trying to solve a murder."

"Yeah, Lou told me about that. Any leads yet?"

"I'm not sure, that's why I called. I forgot Lou was on swing so I thought I'd see if you could help. I need a copy of a file, the case from 1952 involving the university quarterback who was found in the 'glades with a pair of .38 slugs in his head."

"I remember that one. It was the only time anyone's ever had the guts to get Donatello in front of a judge and it didn't get very far. That's still an open case, Tom. If you have anything on that one you'll have to go through Central."

"I know that Alice, but I'm not sure I do. I need to check the file first. If it turns out that I've got something I'll let Central know, but why bother them right now when I don't know?"

"Tell you what I'll do, Tom, I'll have one of the girls get a copy ready and I'll talk to Lou when he comes in this afternoon. If he says it's okay, I'll see to it that it's on the evening bus down to Key West with orders to have it hand delivered to you."

"Thanks Alice. I can't ask for more than that. Oh, make sure the ballistics report is in there. I may want to make a comparison with some slugs I should have by tomorrow."

"You bet. Take care of yourself Tommy and come up and see us sometime."

"I will, Alice, and thanks again."

I hung up and wondered how Lou could give the okay to release a copy of an open case file without getting clearance from Central? Either things have changed in Miami or Lou's been holding out on me.

The phone buzzed and Sally's voice came over the intercom. "Tom, Sal Donatello's here to see you. You want me to send him on back? His boy's out back parking the car."

"That'll be Tony 'cause Frankie's at my place keeping an eye on Amy. Send Mr. Donatello back and have Tony come on back when he comes in."

A few moments later there was a knock on the door and when it opened I saw Donatello standing there in what could only be described as tropical elegance. Cream tropical weight wool slacks with a perfect crease, a pale blue guayabera shirt that, this morning, matched his eyes, a snap brimmed Panama hat and, surprisingly, a pair of well-worn boat shoes. In his hands he held a cardboard tray with three large coffees from the shop across the street.

"Good morning, Tom. I thought this would be a good time to continue our discussion since Frankie is guarding Amy. I presume she is getting some work done on our case."

He put the tray on the desk and I smelled the delicious

aroma, not quite as good as the Coffee Shack by the marina, but a close second.

"I also thought you could use a cup of good coffee. I know how department brew can be. The third one is for Tony. He's parking the car out back."

"Yes, I know. Sally told me."

"Smart lady that Sally. Is she seeing anyone?"

"As a matter of fact she is, Sal," I lied. "She's dating our Chief of Police."

"My loss I'm afraid," Sal sighed.

Sal hung his hat on the tree next to the door, took his coffee and sat down on the couch where he'd been yesterday during our first conversation and we engaged in some small talk while we waited for Tony. When he arrived, he took up his position in the corner where he could watch the two of us and the door and sipped his coffee.

Sal began.

"Tom, last night you asked me when I met your Father and I told you that it happened at the trial. That is the truth. That was the first time I met him. However, it was not when I came to know him. That was later and was at Sam's insistence."

There was a knock at the door and I held up my hand to Sal. "Come in." The door opened and Mike came in and dropped a file on the desk.

"Thought you might want this ASAP so I rushed the photos. Maybe these two might recognize him," Mike said, motioning to Sal and Tony.

Sal raised an eyebrow in my direction and Tony looked suspiciously at Mike.

To neither one in particular I said, "We fished a body out of Cow Key Channel this morning. So far no one recognizes him, but his clothes had Miami labels in them. By the way, he didn't drown." I opened the file and turned it around so Sal could see the photo on top and I watched him for any reaction. There was none. Sal looked at the picture and then quickly scanned through the pages of Mike's preliminary report.

"Hmm. Shot twice in the chest. Preliminary assessment of weapon a .38 pending confirmation. Body believed to have entered the water sometime after noon on Friday. May have been tied to weight but slipped free," Sal mused. "Good preliminary report Officer O'Neil, short and to the point with no conjecture. Sorry, Tom, I can't help you on this one. I don't recognize him and the method of death could be used by anyone. Although I suspect that, given the position of the bullet holes, it was done by someone who was no stranger to that method."

While Sal had been talking Tony had moved over to the desk and was trying to get a closer look at the picture so I said to Sal, "Let Tony have a look. Maybe he knows him or has seen him around."

Sal gave Tony the file and we waited.

It was interesting. Most people, when given a file on a murder, look at the pictures first. Tony read the descriptions then went to the pictures.

"Boss," he said, turning to Sal not to me, "I think this is one of Jimmy O's boys. The face is familiar and I recognize the clothes and the tailor's label. It's from that little place on Calle Ocho just past that restaurant we went to last month. You remember?"

"I remember the restaurant," said Sal. "Good location, so-so food. They need a good chef in there." Looking at me he explained, "I was considering it as an investment in a growing area, but they wouldn't think of changing their kitchen staff."

"Yeah," said Tony. "The kitchen was small but workable if it was organized right. It also needed a good cleaning. But I'm talking about the little tailor shop two doors down from there, Boss. Don't you remember? We went in there looking for shirts."

Sal thought for a moment, then said, "Yes, now I remember. There was barely enough room for us in front of the counter, but he did have good quality merchandise, unfortunately not in your size." Tapping the photograph he continued, "But what makes you think he works for Jaime Ortega?"

"Well, when we came out of the tailor shop and you were getting in the car I looked across the street and saw two guys talking to a third guy in front of the corner grocery. It looked like they were telling this third guy that if he didn't do what he was supposed to do they wouldn't be happy with him. You know what I mean Boss. And in that neighborhood nobody does that kind of thing without they work for Jimmy O."

"You do have a point there," said Sal. "That was another reason I turned down the offer on the restaurant. I don't need the headaches that trying to do business in that area would bring."

"Tony," I said, "can you give me a name to go with this picture?"

Tony looked at Sal and got a brief nod in return. "Sorry, Lieutenant, I never met the guy. Just saw him across the street in what you might call 'suspicious circumstances.'"

"Do you think Frankie might know him?" I asked.

"Uh uh," said Tony. "We don't go over there much and that was the only time I ever saw the guy. I just recognized your picture there as looking like him and with the labels in his clothes I just put two and two together."

"You're very observant, Tony. You'd make a good cop."

With that Tony pulled himself up to his full height and, towering over me with a dour look, said, "There's no call to be insulting, Lieutenant."

Looking at Sal I smiled. "I'm sorry, Tony. That was meant as a compliment. I forgot how you feel about the police." Tony harrumphed and returned to his observer position in the corner.

Turning back to Sal I asked, "Who is Jaime Ortega? I don't remember that name from when I was in Miami. Is he competition?"

Sal and Tony looked at each other like they were trying to decide how much they should reveal. Sal wasn't particularly happy that Tony had mentioned Jimmy O, or Jaime Ortega. However, now that the cat was out of the bag they knew they couldn't very well put it back in. It was now a question of just how much to tell me and, in doing so, how much it would affect their position.

Tony, I had observed, had a true poker face in that it was difficult to tell exactly what was going on in his mind. Of course, I hadn't yet seen him in the kitchen. There he could wear a completely different expression. Here, however, there was nothing to read so I turned to Sal.

Again, I was presented with a face on which nothing could be read. While I'd been watching Tony, Sal had obviously run his mind over the situation and had decided how much, or how little, he was going to reveal and the "British gentleman" had replaced the "Miami mobster" that had briefly surfaced during his interchange with Tony.

"To my knowledge," Sal began, "Jaime Ortega, or Jimmy O as he apparently prefers, did not become generally known until after you left Miami, Tom, although I suspect that he had been active for some time before that in Little Havana. What you knew as West Miami. Since my business interests do not extend to that part of town, my knowledge is not by direct contact. Rumors, or hearsay as the lawyers would call it, hold that he started out as a small time hood in his old neighborhood, running numbers and shaking down the local merchants."

Sal crossed his legs, adjusted the crease in his trousers and flicked at a minute bit of dust that had dared to settle on his knee. "Over time, he allegedly moved into other ventures. Running underground poker games, crap games and other illegal gambling operations, continuing to build and extend his reach throughout West Miami. To my knowledge, he has never crossed into downtown or the Beach so there has been no reason to seek him out as it were.

"Since he presents no significant competitive aspect to anyone in my circles, I know of no effort that has been made to exercise any controlling action on his business. We don't look for conflict, Tom. This is not 1920's Chicago. There's enough business in Miami for everyone as long as all the players know their place and keep to their own operations and areas."

I had a feeling that speck of dust had, for one fleeting moment, been Jimmy O and that Sal had been putting him in his place. "That's what you meant about not needing the headaches that getting involved in that restaurant would have brought?" I asked.

"True," said Sal. "Actually, I never had any interest in the place. I was primarily looking it over for a friend who had been asked to invest in it. After that one visit I advised him to put his money elsewhere."

"Probably good advice if this Jimmy O controls that area. Do you know what Jimmy looks like? Any distinguishing features which would make him easy to recognize?"

"No, nothing I know of," said Sal. "I have never seen him. Furthermore, I have no idea why one of his associates would show up dead down here. However, the fact that he has does not bode well for continued peace on this island. One thing I can tell you about Jaime Ortega from those who profess to have had dealings with him, he has a temper. Such a thing makes him dangerous and unpredictable, but I suspect that it will also be his undoing.

Sal sat forward. "As I see it, there are two possibilities with your latest problem." He held up a finger. "One, Mr. Ortega and his associate were here together and, somehow, the associate upset Ortega to the point that Jaime shot him. However, in that scenario I do not see Ortega taking the time to weight the body, even as clumsily as it was done. Based on stories I've heard, he would have either left it where it fell or had it thrown into the mangroves." A second finger was raised. "Two, someone else killed Ortega's associate. Why I cannot guess, and tried, clumsily as previously noted, to hide the body. I have heard that Ortega does not take kindly to anyone dealing so summarily with his operatives such that he is likely to come looking for the responsible party which, as I observed, could affect the peace of this little tropical paradise."

"You know, Sal," I observed, "for someone who professes to know so little about Ortega, you seem to know quite a lot. May I ask just where you obtained this information?"

Sal relaxed against the back of the couch. "As I said, Tom, most of it is hearsay or rumors. I have had no personal contact with Ortega, but I have heard stories about him from others. However, if you need more information, I suggest that you contact your friend Lou Zachiarelli. He should be able to give you much more information than I can about Jimmy O."

"I'll do that when I speak with him this afternoon. I have a few questions for him concerning the quarterback case as well."

At that point the phone on the desk buzzed and Sally's voice said, "Tom, Sheriff's office on line one for you."

I picked up the phone and punched the button.

"Tom Jackson here."

"Hey Tommy, Dan Riley. One of our boys just called in and thinks he might have found *Greta* up on Sugarloaf."

Dan Riley was a detective with the Sheriff's office over in the Court House Annex on Whitehead Street. Outside of the city limits of Key West that office covers the lower Keys and their officers had been looking for Sam's boat since I called them on Saturday.

"What do you mean he only thinks he found her, Dan?"

"It's Jerry Timmins, a local boy. He noticed something odd concerning some vegetation in the cut from the upper Sound and called it in before going into the brush. I'm waiting for his further report, but figured you'd want to know."

"Thanks, Dan. I know Jerry and if he thinks he's on to something, that's a good reason for calling. Can you give me the location? I'd like to get up there in case he's right."

"I'll do better than that, Tom, pick me up and I'll take you there. If it is *Greta*, then you can have the site and anything you need from us. By the way, got anything on that floater yet?"

"Just Mike's preliminary. I'll bring you a copy and see you in fifteen minutes."

As soon as I hung up, Sally buzzed over and said, "Amy called while you were on the line Tom, she sounded concerned."

I picked up the phone again and called home. Amy answered on the first ring.

"Tom, is that you?"

I could hear tension in her voice. "Yes. What's wrong?"

"Nothing, I think, but Frankie's locked me in the den and told me to stay put."

"What! Why'd he do that?"

"He said he thought he heard something that didn't sound right. When I said it was probably the cat next door, he came back with a comment about it being the biggest cat south of the Miami Zoo," she said.

I put my hand over the mouthpiece and said to Sal, "Does Frankie have a spare piece that I don't know about?"

Sal shook his head and when I looked at Tony he did likewise.

I took my hand off the phone. "Amy, I have to go up to

Sugarloaf. The Sheriff's office just called and they think they may have found Sam's boat. I need facts and answers so I have to see that boat before it's moved but I'm sending Tony over as back-up." I looked at Tony as I said this and got a smile in return. "In the meantime, since we have their guns here, in the back of the den closet on the left side you'll find a lock box, the key is taped to the underside of the center desk drawer. Give the contents to Frankie. I know it's not what he's used to, but it'll do in a pinch if it's needed which I hope it isn't. I'll be there as soon as I can."

"Wait a minute Tom," Amy said. "I want to see that boat too. Why don't you pick us up on the way?"

"I don't have enough room for Tony and Frankie in my car, you know that."

Sal rose from the couch. "Tony, bring the car around front, we'll be right with you."

"Right, Boss," said Tony and left the room. Sal looked at me.

Returning Sal's smile, I said, "Amy, we'll be there in ten minutes. Tell Frankie we're bringing Sal's car." Hanging up the phone, I said to Sal, "Are you sure your boys won't mind helping the police?"

Sal shrugged. "They figure they're helping Amy."

On the way out of the office I stopped at the firearms locker and retrieved the boys' .45's.

CHAPTER 14

We pulled up in front of the house where Amy and Frankie were waiting. He got in front with Tony and Amy joined us in back. The first thing Frankie did was turn to me and give me a brief summary of the last half hour.

"We were in the kitchen, Lieutenant, having some coffee when I heard something outside. Amy suggested a cat, but I thought a dog or something bigger, so I figured I'd better look."

"Frankie, I don't have a dog and neither do the neighbors."

"Yeah, that's what Amy said and that's when I put her in the den and went looking around outside. Someone was poking around out there. I found what look like footprints. I figured you'd want pictures and such so I covered them with an old sack."

"Thanks Frankie. I'll have the lab boys check them when we get back. Meanwhile, I believe this is yours." I handed him his gun.

"Thanks," he said. "Here's yours," and he passed me my spare .38 from the closet.

I told Tony to head back downtown to the Court House and in no time he pulled up in front of the Sheriff's office where Dan was standing at the door. I rolled my window down and called to him.

"Dan. Back here."

Executing a perfect double take Dan looked at the car, then me.

"Since when does a KWPD Lieutenant rate a chauffer driven limo? You can barely afford your old Fords."

"It's a loaner. We're trying it out for a few days," I said as I opened the door for him. "Get in."

As he slid into the jump seat next to Amy, I could see Dan take in Sal next to me and the boys in the front seat.

Cautiously he said, "Everything okay here, Tom?"

"Yes, Dan. It's okay, you're not getting taken for a ride."

I made the introductions. "Dan Riley, Detective, Monroe County Sheriff's Office, Florida, meet Salvatore Donatello, business man, Miami, Florida, our automotive host and his associates Tony and Frankie."

I gestured to the front seat. Dan looked at the boys and, like the rest of us had, said "Which one is which?"

Sal answered, "Tony's driving so just let him know where we're going and he'll get us there."

Dan gave the directions to Tony. Truman Avenue to N. Roosevelt, across the bridge to Stock Island then up the Overseas Highway toward Sugarloaf Key.

Dan said, "Take a right just after Bat Tower Road onto County Road 939 and when you get to the end turn left. You'll want to stop this side of the bridge over the cut. There should be a Sheriff's car there."

Tony said, "Got it," made the turn at Whitehead onto Truman and accelerated.

"Now, Dan," I said, "what makes Jerry think he found *Greta*, and of all places in the cut on Sugarloaf?"

"I don't know. He hadn't called back before you pulled up. I thought you'd have your car so I told the dispatcher to put any calls through to you. Now we'll have to wait 'till we get there. He did say that he saw some unusual vegetation in the cut and thought he saw a boat's bridge sticking up out of the mangroves just inside that creek that comes into the cut east of the bridge."

"I know it," I said. "But I wouldn't think *Greta* would fit in there. The water's not very deep except at high tide and even then it'd be barely enough for her. You know what her hull's like."

"Yeah, bit of a deep draft for close in, but perfect for

open water. If it is her, then God only knows what she's doing in that creek."

Dan sat back in the seat and looked around the interior of the limo. Turning to Sal, he said, "This is a nice car, Mr. Donatello, although I wish it had a light and siren on it. We could make better time."

"I'm sorry I cannot accommodate you there, Detective; the Mayor wouldn't let me install them," said Sal.

"Donatello, Miami, hmm," mused Dan. "Wait a minute," he sat up. "The quarterback case, 1952, that Donatello?"

Dan turned to me. "Tom, what's going on here? What are you doing with him?" pointing at Sal.

"Relax, Dan. Mr. Donatello is assisting in the investigation of the murder of Sam Torres and the John Doe we fished out of the channel this morning. In fact, in the case of the latter, he and Tony have provided us with a lead that I'll be following up this afternoon with Lou Zacchiarelli in Miami. Also, he had the only car big enough for all of us."

"Okay, I'll accept that for the moment, but what's the press doing here?" he asked indicating Amy.

Using my official voice I said, "Miss Petersen is in the protective custody of the Key West Police Department as a material witness in a narcotics investigation."

Looking at Amy, Dan said, "My condolences to you if you've got yourself stuck with this lug."

"Oh he's not that bad, Detective, once you get used to him," she said. "Besides, if he gets out of line, I can always call my big brothers up front and they'll set him straight."

"Hoo boy," said Dan. "When this is over, I want the whole story."

Once out of town there was little traffic and the limo flew smoothly up the highway with Tony ignoring the speed limit signs, obviously comfortable that neither Dan nor I would give him a ticket. It seemed in no time that we made the turn off Route 1 onto the County road then the left toward the cut.

Tony pulled up behind a Monroe County Sheriff's car parked just before a one-lane bridge over the cut. Jerry Timmins was leaning against the trunk waiting for us but he straightened up when Tony and Frankie exited from the limo. Before he could do anything, Dan got out and said, "Relax, Jerry. They're with me."

"If you say so, Dan," said Jerry. "Did they come with the car or did the car come with them?" he said eyeing the limo.

Dan made the introductions as I looked around for what had made Jerry stop here. The Deputy handed me a pair of binoculars and pointed off the side of the road.

"Follow the line of the mangroves along the creek about half way through the second curve in from the cut," Jerry said. "You should just be able to see the frame of the upper bridge. I worked my way just far enough in to confirm that it's a boat and it looks like the same hull style as Sam Torres'."

Following his directions I could just see the frame of a flying bridge structure such as those commonly found on charter boats. Sam's was tubular aluminum and normally had a brightly colored canvas Bimini top for protection from the sun. There didn't appear to be a top, but the angle of the mangroves could have obscured it. The vegetation was pretty thick along the creek, which made it difficult to see much. Although I could just barely make out the very tip of the bow through a gap in the trees, nothing else of the boat was visible.

"You didn't go on board?" I asked.

"No, Tom, I figured you'd want to do that first if it is *Greta*," said Jerry. "If it isn't then it'll be our jurisdiction and I figured waiting for you wouldn't make any difference either way. By the way, there's no easy path in there. Whoever left her there must've had a hell of a time getting out. My guess is they followed the creek back to the cut 'cause I didn't see any sign of someone coming out through the mangroves up here to the road."

"Okay, Jerry, you and I'll go in first." Turning to Dan I said, "If it is *Greta*, one of us'll come out and wave so you can call for a lab team. The rest of you just wait here and I'll fill you in later."

"Tom," said Sal, "it looks pretty thick down there. Why don't you take one of the boys to help you get through?"

I looked at Jerry who shrugged his shoulders and said, "They look like they could get through anything and you know what mangrove is like. Besides, I don't have a machete."

If this was Sam's boat then it automatically became a crime scene and the fewer people on board before the lab techs got here the better. However, it had been at least six months since I'd been on her whereas Sal, Tony and Frankie had been out with Sam about a month ago and probably remembered the layout and where things should be better than I did. Tony particularly had recently shown that he was observant such that he should be able to tell me if anything was out of place. Turning to the two of them I asked Tony and Frankie, "Which of you can tell me where Sam kept his log book?"

Frankie and Tony looked at each other before Frankie answered, "Right hand cabinet in the wheelhouse. The log book is red."

"Okay, Frankie, you're with us. If it is *Greta*, you keep your eyes open and tell us what, if anything, is out of place. But don't touch anything unless Jerry or I tell you to do so. Got it?"

"Got it," he said.

With that the three of us started down off the road into the scrub which gave way to mangroves about half way to the creek. The first few feet in were easy but the mangroves and low vegetation thickened the closer we got to the creek. With their exposed and convoluted root system together with the rather soft ground underneath, it became more difficult to get through the further in we went. I began to think it would have been better to wade along the cut and in along the creek. Also, I agreed with Jerry's theory that whoever left this boat here went out that way or had a small boat with them for that purpose.

Jerry had started out leading but, as the vegetation got denser, Frankie took over and used his size to push branches out of the way so we could get through. As he pulled a branch back, I looked through and saw the boat, or at least part of it. It was about the midships area and there was nothing initially distinctive. The color, white with mahogany trim, was the same as *Greta*, but so were most of the other boats working out of Key West.

I worked my way through the hole Frankie had made and stepped into the creek water at the edge. Grabbing the side of the boat I pulled myself up and looked over the gunwale into the open area behind the wheelhouse and cabin. This part of the boat wasn't as clean as Sam would've had it, but it also hadn't been trashed. I noticed that when I grabbed hold of the boat it didn't rock or move, so I bent down to look along the water line and at the creek shore, or rather the mangrove roots along it.

It appeared that the boat was aground on the bottom of the creek, but it also looked like we were at low tide. Judging by the height of the roots above the current water level, at high tide there should be just enough to float her and get her out. Also, as I looked forward and aft, I could see lines extending into the trees. Whoever had left this craft here didn't just run her aground and leave her. They probably planned to come back and retrieve her for whatever purpose they had in mind.

Jerry and Frankie joined me as I stood up. Frankie

started working his way aft between the hull and trees and I watched him peer around the edge of the transom.

"Lieutenant," he called. "It's *Greta* and there's a ladder out back here. It might be easier to get on board that way."

Jerry said, "I'll go out and give Dan a wave" and started to duck back through the trees.

"Okay, Jerry. Make sure he tells the techs to bring a skiff with them. Frankie and I'll get started here."

Jerry disappeared back into the trees and I went around to the transom where Frankie was patiently waiting. "I'll go first," I said. "When you get to the rail, sit down and take off your shoes so you don't track any mud on the deck. Put them next to mine and they'll be in a place I've already checked and cleared. Watch out where you put your feet and try not to disturb anything that may be on the deck as you walk. The best thing to do first is just stand still and look around to note where any obstacles might be and if there's anything interesting or out of place in the immediate area. If you see anything odd, tell me. Remember, you were on this boat more recently than I was."

I went up the ladder and sat on the transom rail. Taking off my shoes, I found a clean spot for them, stepped onto the deck, and looked around. The deck was only mildly littered with leaves from the surrounding trees and a few spots of bird poop, some of which had dried indicating that it had been there at least a day. Some fishing gear that should have been secured was scattered along one side and lines that would have been properly coiled if Sam were on board had been dropped in a pile. As Frankie came along side of me, I looked toward the wheelhouse and, in the corner with the port gunwale, I saw one thing I was looking for, a crowbar with a multi-sided shaft, painted orange.

"Frankie, do you see that crowbar? Can you tell from here if that's Sam's?"

"Looks like it. I remember he used an orange crowbar

to get the hook out of my fish. It should have his initials stamped in it about half way along the shaft. Also, it shouldn't be lying on the deck. Sam kept it in that box on the starboard side," Frankie said pointing to a box about three feet long and a foot wide secured to the deck along the starboard gunwale.

"We'll check that later. Do you see anything else out of place? Anything that would indicate a struggle or fight?"

"Those stains," he said, pointing to some dark spots I had noticed. "They weren't there a month ago and Sam was very careful when we brought a fish aboard. Any blood or other material was immediately washed down and scrubbed with that brush over there." Frankie indicated a long handled scrub brush clipped under the rail on the port side.

"Yeah, I noticed those," I said. "They look like blood, but whose or what, I don't know yet. Keep clear of them. I want to make sure the lab boys get good pictures and samples. They can determine if it's human and, if so, whether it's Sam's or our John Doe's."

"You think he was shot here? I don't see any of the kind of spatter you normally get with a gun shot wound."

"He was shot with a .38, Frankie, not a cannon like you carry. And if it was at close range, any spatter most likely would be on whoever shot him."

"That's possible, Lieutenant, but a .38 doesn't pack that much of a punch, especially if it was a snub-nose. There's a possibility that the guy just dropped to the deck and if they were both heart shots, as Tony says, not through-and-through's, the blood might dribble out a bit but there wouldn't be much. I'm betting most, if not all, of that is from Sam. Head wounds bleed like crazy."

"You're probably right, but we'll check it both ways. Let's take a look at the wheel house."

We moved forward, stepping carefully around the

bloodstains, and into the wheelhouse. With Frankie it was a bit of a squeeze. Using my handkerchief, I opened the cabinet, hoping that both the logbook and charter book were there, even though I knew that Sam never took the latter to sea. The cabinet was empty. Whoever had hijacked *Greta* and left her here had taken the logbook with them. The question was, why?

"Frankie, do you remember the dates for Sam's log book? When the first entry was made?" I asked.

"Unless he got a new one since then, it'd be last year when we went fishing with him in August. I remember we picked him up and stopped at the supply store for some last minute items and they'd just got some new red books in."

So that logbook was less than a year old. What could be in it that someone would want?

On the other side of the wheelhouse was the chart locker where Sam kept his charts of the waters around the Keys. I opened that and looked through them. Sam was always organized and even in the dark could reach into that locker and pull out exactly the correct chart for where he was or where he wanted to go. They were all labeled and on the inside of the locker door was a list of all the charts and their current dates. Comparing the contents of the locker with the list didn't take long. All the charts were present except one, the chart that covered the area around the Torches, Big Pine and No Name Key.

"Frankie," I said. "Look down in the cabin and see if there's a chart down there."

"Which one's missing?" he asked as he opened the door to the cabin and went to the bottom of the short set of steps.

"Big Pine. Thing is, Sugarloaf to Summerland is here and that's the one I'd expect to be out now." I heard him moving carefully around. "Anything?"

"No charts, but it looks like someone was here not too long ago. There're sandwiches on the table that aren't quite stale and it looks like someone was sleeping on the couch. Other than that, it doesn't look much different than when we've been out for a coupla days."

"Okay. Come on back up. We'll let the lab boys take pictures first when they get here. I have a feeling we've seen the important stuff. It just doesn't make sense yet."

Frankie and I returned to the open deck and sat on the stern rail putting our shoes back on. We'd wait there for the technical boys. I don't know what Frankie was thinking, although I did notice he was watching the birds flying over. Myself, I was trying to connect the dots in this case but I wasn't getting a picture. Some things connected, but others didn't. Rather than fall into the trap of assuming something on insufficient facts, I switched to a different subject.

"Frankie, how long have you and Tony been with Donatello?"

"The Boss? About twelve years now, I guess. Why?"

"Curiosity mostly. He's an interesting individual, your Mr. Donatello. Not at all what one normally expects of someone in his business." Twelve years, I thought. That meant they weren't with Donatello in '52 but, presumably, they were with him in Cuba.

"He's a fair man, Lieutenant. You play square with him, he'll play square with you. But, if you cross him, you'll be the one who's going to wind up hurting and it's gonna hurt a lot."

"Has he ever killed anyone or had them killed, Frankie? For any reason?"

"This an official interrogation?" Frankie asked, looking me square in the face.

"No." I shook my head. "No it's not. I'm just trying to understand him. I know you guys fished with Sam Torres for many years. So did a lot of people, even some here in the keys. But your boss came down here the day after seeing Sam's obituary in the Miami paper. He came to my office, the police, to find out what happened and, I think, I hope, to try to help us find out why Sam was killed and who was responsible. You have to admit that's unusual behavior for anyone in your organization."

"What organization is that, Lieutenant?" Frankie asked with a smile. "The Boss is just a business man in Miami. Me and Tony, we work for him. Cook, drive, run errands, take care of the dry cleaning, that sort of thing."

Frankie was a little wary but not downright suspicious. I was glad he was here because I think Tony would've been more difficult to talk to. For some reason, Tony had a deep-seated distrust of the police in general. Frankie, at least, appeared to view police work as just a job and seemed more inclined to consider the person inside the uniform. Of course, he may also be giving me a break because of Amy. Both he and Tony had clearly developed a soft spot for her.

"Okay, we'll leave the business question alone. But back to my original question and strictly off the record. As long as you've known him, has Donatello ever killed anyone or had them killed?"

"Off the record or on, Lieutenant, as long as I've known him, I've never known the Boss to be involved in that sort of thing. He's always told the both of us that, in business, death never solves anything; it just creates more problems. First and foremost, dead men don't pay their bills."

I nodded. "He told me the same thing."

I sat there thinking for a minute. It was clear Frankie wasn't going to tell me much about Donatello, although Sal had told Amy and myself quite a bit the previous evening. The problem with that, though, was that what he told us was what he wanted us to know. I was trying to find out what he didn't say but, at this point, I didn't think I was going to be successful.

Changing the course of the conversation a bit I asked Frankie, "How did you and Tony come to be with

Donatello?"

"Tony's mom. She got us the job."

I looked at him quizzically and he continued.

"Tony and I, we were in the Army together. Korea. And when we got out we had some trouble finding jobs. Back home it was either the cops or the docks. The first didn't want us and we didn't want the second."

Somewhat incredulously I said, "The police didn't want you? From what I've seen, you two would make great cops." Thinking of Tony's reaction when I had complimented him on his observation, I hastily added, "Don't take that as an insult. You and Tony are disciplined, observant and patient. Those are qualities that most good departments look for in their personnel."

"Yeah, well, maybe the departments in North Jersey weren't so hard up for guys," he said with a shrug. "We have incidents in our records that they didn't take too kindly to. Anyway, we got out and couldn't find jobs and Tony's mom said she knew someone in Miami who could probably use two good boys. The next thing we knew we got letters from the Boss inviting us to come down for interviews. He even sent train tickets for us. Turns out Tony's mom wrote to him and told him about us. Apparently she knew him from when he used to come into her place."

"Her place?" I asked. "What did she do?"

"Tony's mom? She had a little neighborhood place in Hoboken. Best food around. The Boss would come across from New York regular to eat there. That's how Tony learned to cook so good. From his mom."

"What about you? Where are you from and how did you and Tony meet? After all, look at the two of you, you could be twins."

"Me? I'm from Secaucus," he said, a bit of pride creeping into his voice. "We didn't meet until the Army. It was basic training. Our sergeant didn't believe we weren't related either. He had to go all the way up to battalion before he was convinced. He was ready to ship one of us to a different camp to separate us thinking we were brothers but eventually he let us stay in the same platoon. Tony did try to get himself transferred to the kitchens so he could cook, but one look at him and the answer was always the same. 'Forget it soldier. You're more valuable on the line.' Turned out good for us, though, 'cause we always ate good in the field. You'd be amazed at what he could do with K-rations and a few herbs and spices."

Remembering the food from my Army days, I thought about what Tony had fixed in that little bungalow kitchen last night with what he could get on short notice in Key West and envied Frankie and his platoon members. Another thing that all this talk about food was doing was reminding me that it was getting on in the day. It had been some time since a hastily grabbed roll and coffee this morning and I was getting hungry when I heard the sound of an outboard. Looking back over the stern of *Greta*, I saw the bow of a skiff come motoring slowly around the bend in the creek. In the front were two men in county uniforms and, as the boat came around the bend, I saw Dennis in the stern.

They pulled up behind *Greta* and one of the county boys tossed us a line which Frankie caught and made fast. Dennis waved up at me and said, "Hi, Lieutenant. These are the Sheriff's lab guys. Their motor was broken and since I had our boat on the trailer Detective Riley suggested I bring it and them when he called in. I can take you and Frankie back to the road and come back for them and any samples. By the way, Sally says you need to get back real quick. You've got another visitor from Miami and she says he's real anxious."

Great, I thought. What now? "Okay. Give me a minute with these guys first," I said as the lab boys came aboard.

I turned to them and asked, "Can you boys lift a few samples that I can take with me? I want to get some tests started as soon as possible."

"Sure, Lieutenant. What do you want? Of course we'll duplicate whatever you take for the record."

I pointed to the bloodstains on the deck indicating which spots I wanted separate samples from and then I indicated the crow bar.

"We haven't touched it, but I suspect there's blood on it somewhere. I need a sample of that and I need to know if there are any fingerprints. I know I can't take the prints with me, but when you get back with them send me copies as soon as possible. I may be able to match them for you." I was thinking about the John Doe from this morning.

Once I had my blood samples all properly bagged and tagged, Frankie and I got into the skiff and Dennis motored back out the creek and up the cut to the bridge where we joined Dan and the others.

Dennis volunteered to stay with *Greta* and get her out at high tide. The lab boys would take his car so Dan rode back with Jerry. Frankie, Amy, Sal and I rode back to the station in the limo with Tony driving. Along the way Frankie and I filled the rest in on what we'd seen on *Greta* and I asked Sal if he had any ideas about who else would come down from Miami.

"Haven't a clue, Tom. Haven't a clue," was all he would say. However, I had a suspicion and looking at my watch I figured the timing would be just about right.

CHAPTER 15

Crossing back onto Key West, I had Tony swing by my house before going to the station so I could see the prints Frankie had found earlier. They were in a patch of soft ground by a side window but were indistinct. Either the feet that made them were smooth or the nature of the ground was such that it couldn't hold a clear sole impression. The best we could get was that they were about a size 10 or 11 which meant it could have been almost anyone, even me, although I didn't remember being on that side of the house in the last few days. A quick look around the rest of the house failed to turn up anything more so maybe the noise Frankie had heard was just a stray dog nosing around and the marks were unrelated. One of the advantages of being a cop was that the local criminals tended to leave your stuff alone so odds were it wasn't one of our regular 'light fingered Louies.'

On the way to the office I told Tony to just park in front. "No ticket this time," I said. "I guarantee it."

However, turning the corner, we saw another car taking up the "No Parking" space, one with Miami tags that I recognized. Without even asking, Tony pulled up next to it, let us out and drove around back to the parking lot.

"I'll come in the back way," he said.

Pausing at Sally's desk, I handed her the blood samples from *Greta*.

"Have someone run a blood type on these and compare them with the reports from Sam and the John Doe. I want to know if there's a match to either one or both. Also, have someone run copies of the prints from both of them over to the Sheriff's office. Their boys will be coming back with some and I want to know particularly if there's a match with

159

our unknown stiff." To Sal, I said, "We may need your prints and the boys' for exclusionary purposes, but I'll wait and see what they lift off the crow bar first."

Turning back to Sally I inclined my head toward the front door.

"How long has he been here?"

"About an hour and a half," she said.

I quickly calculated that he'd left before my phone call this morning.

"Alone?"

"Uh huh," she nodded.

We headed back to the Chief's office, though I was starting to think of it more as mine because I was spending so much time there.

Opening the door I said, "You made good time, Lou. Traffic must have been light."

As Sal, Frankie and Amy filed in behind me, I continued.

"Now maybe you and Sal can tell the rest of us what this is all about and just who the two of you are actually working for."

As I sat down at the desk, Lou and Sal looked at each other, Frankie leaned back in his corner and Amy, sensing another story, pulled out her pad and sat in the chair next to the desk. Meanwhile, Tony came in and took the corner opposite Frankie, like two bookends.

"How much does he know, Sal?" Lou asked.

"I honestly don't know, Lou. I do not believe I have said anything amiss and I doubt that Frankie said anything when they were alone together this afternoon. As far as I know Tom has not spoken with Tony outside of my presence." Sal said looking questioningly at Frankie.

"No, he hasn't Boss, and we just talked about how Tony and I came to work for you after the Army. Then the guys from the lab showed up," Frankie confirmed.

Lou started to pace back and forth. Lou was a pacer. I remembered that from when I was in Miami. Whenever he had to think or was delivering the morning report in the squad room, even when making a report to the Captain, he couldn't do it sitting still. He had to pace. The office isn't large so Sal sat down on the couch and Amy scooted her chair back further. Even with that Lou only had a strip about three feet wide and ten feet long, but it was enough.

Coming to a decision, he stopped in front of me, albeit briefly.

"Okay, Tom, I can see I'm going to have to trust you. However," he said, turning to Amy, "young lady, I'm afraid that you will have to leave."

"That's not going to happen, Lou," I said. "Amy stays here. First, she's a material witness in what I suspect is part of this whole case. Second, she's been physically threatened by a prime suspect who is still at large and, as such, she's under Key West police protection."

"And ours," growled Frankie from his corner to which Tony grunted concurrence.

"And third," I continued. "She's providing an official record of this case. I'm sorry, Lou. You're in my jurisdiction so we play it by my rules. She stays."

Expecting some support, Lou turned and looked at Sal who just sat there impassively, although when Lou turned back to me I caught a hint of a wink from Sal.

Leaning forward over the desk, I looked at Lou and said, "I'll make this easy. You sit down there next to Sal and I'll tell you what I know and what I suspect, based on the facts I have. You can then fill in any missing pieces. Once we're both finished, hopefully, we'll be in a position to solve this case and then everyone can get back to their normal lives." I raised one eyebrow, questioningly. "Does that sound reasonable to you, Lou?"

Lou sat down on the couch and grumbled. He never did

like not being the one in charge.

Looking over at Amy I asked, "Are you ready?" She nodded and I pushed the pencil cup over so she wouldn't have to reach for one if hers broke. I noticed that she had a fresh pad.

Turning back to Lou and Sal, I began.

"This case starts in 1952 with the murder of Sal's son, by person or persons so far unknown, although I have my suspicions as I'm sure you do. However, without absolute proof you, Lou, can't do anything and you, Sal, won't. I trust you brought the file on that case with you Lou?" He nodded. "Good. As I told Alice this morning, I'm particularly interested in the ballistics report.

"Anyway, as I said, Sal's son was murdered, by whom we don't know yet, but the why, for the moment, is more important. The young Donatello was a college quarterback in a game that his school was favored to win. However, someone had some heavy money placed on the other team and didn't want to lose. The fact that he also had bets placed on the favorite meant that, to protect his interest, he had to make sure that the point spread of the final score didn't put him on one side or the other. The only way to do that was to put pressure on the quarterback. What information was used to do that I have no idea. However, I suspect it probably included revealing the nature of his father's true connections as well as his identity, which was not generally known at that time in Miami society.

"Whether or not young Donatello agreed to hold the score back, but got caught up in the excitement of the game, or refused to acquiesce to the demands made on him, we'll never know. Suffice it to say, his team won by a sizeable margin and someone wasn't happy about that with the result that he was found in the Everglades with two bullets in him.

"Since this all happened before my time in Miami I've

had to rely on other sources for some of the facts. One of those is my father's file on the case. He was called on by the State Bar to be defense counsel for a small time numbers runner who worked the route between here and Miami. From that file I learned that the Miami PD either had some minimal evidence, or fabricated some, to link the murder to illegal gambling on sporting events." My suggestion of false evidence brought a scowl to Lou's face. "Based on that evidence, Sal was charged with the murder. As we all know, that charge was bogus and he was acquitted after which he left Miami and went to Havana to run the casinos for his 'employer." I leaned back in the chair, which squeaked.

"By the time I arrived in Miami in 1954, the case had turned cold. Although it was still open on the books, it wasn't being actively pursued. At least not according to anything I remember from those days. It was just one of those cases that we knew about and kept in the backs of our minds in the event anything came up that might sound like it would apply. When it turned warm again, I don't know, but I suspect it was sometime in 1959 after Sal came back to Miami following the Cuban revolution.

"Sometime between 1952 and 1959, Sal, you met Sam and he worked his magic on you." At this, Sal smiled. Not the usual smile that Amy and I had seen, but a more private smile like he was remembering something, and someone, special. "Some day, when you want to, you'll have to tell me what he did that brought you back from the depths and we can compare notes. You also met my father, while I wasn't here I might add, and I suspect that Sam had a hand in that as well."

In response to that piece of information I got a slight nod from Sal.

So far no one had said a word and I was glad as a lot of what I'd said was conjecture based on the story Sal had told us the night before. I took their silence as confirmation.

"Upon your return to Miami, Sal, you managed to keep a low profile. For the few months I was there in '59, nothing directly involving you showed up on the blotter. Indeed, most of the action which could previously have been traced to your operations seemed to be happening in West Miami. It was as if your crowd had turned legitimate. Once I left and came back down here, I lost track of you. Of course, I must admit, I didn't actively follow what was happening in Miami, only watched it peripherally for anything that might have a connection to Key West. It wasn't until Saturday that I had any idea you'd been down here and knew Sam. He never mentioned you."

"You know how reticent he was, Tom," Sal said. "Besides, I had asked him not too. Like anyone else, when I'm on vacation I don't like to be bothered. And, by the way, that Coast Guard stop was a fluke and we had no idea they were taking pictures."

Continuing my narrative I said, "We'll skip over when, how and why you and Lou started working together and fast forward to last Saturday when we found Sam on the beach with his head caved in. That you, Sal, had nothing to do with Sam's death, I am sure. Also, I suspect you were shocked when you read Amy's piece in *The Herald*, probably angry as well, so you headed down here to find out who, what and why." Sal confirmed this with a slight nod.

Turning to Lou, I added, "Whatever the reason for Sam's death, I can guarantee that he was not involved in whatever it is that you've been working on in Miami. Sal can confirm that. However, I do believe that we may be looking at the same suspects. That file," I pointed to the folder on the front edge of the desk, "is on a John Doe we fished out of Cow Key Channel this morning. We haven't identified him yet, but initial indications are that he's one of Ortega's boys."

"Jimmy Ortega?" Lou asked, surprised and looking

accusingly at Sal.

"According to Tony, yes," I said. "It would be helpful if you could get an ID on him."

"If you have a telecopier I can send the file up to Miami and get them started," said Lou.

"You'll have to go over to the Sheriff's office and use theirs," I said gesturing in the general direction. "In the meantime, we're waiting for some lab results to find out if he was on *Greta*. I believe he was and that he and an accomplice had arranged a charter with Sam as a pretext to get Sam and *Greta*. Had they just wanted the boat, they could have stolen it and Sam would still be alive. But, for whatever they were doing, I think they needed Sam. Whether Sam fought back or they got their information and 'took care of a loose end', I don't know yet. I'm inclined to think the former since there were some indications of a fight on Sam's body. Furthermore, the fact that John Doe had two slugs in him and had been weighted down leads me to suspect he was the junior partner in this job and that he did something to piss off his boss who also didn't want Doe found anytime soon. Fortunately, the boss did a lousy job tying knots and John floated up."

"Wait a minute, Tom," Amy chimed in. "You're talking like there were only two bad guys, John Doe and someone else. You know Sam could take two guys easy. We've both seen him do it."

"Yes, I know he could," I replied, "on dry land with a solid floor under his feet. Out on the water, all it'd take would be an unexpected pitch or roll of the boat to put him off his footing and the others could have an advantage. Besides, if one of them got behind him with the crow bar, which is what I suspect happened and we'll know when we get the results of the prints and blood test, not even Sam could win with a broken skull."

Turning back to Lou I continued, "I know I'm breaking

the rules and making assumptions based on too little evidence, but as a theory, here's what I think. John Doe and his partner, let's call him Jimmy, since I have a feeling that your Jimmy O is involved, were looking for something off shore up around Big Pine. We found *Greta* up a rather narrow creek on Sugarloaf that most people would miss and Sam's Big Pine chart is missing, so I'm guessing they needed Sam for something he knew that wasn't on that chart.

"So Jimmy and John Doe arrange a charter with Sam, probably claiming that Sam had been recommended to them by someone Sam would trust," I proposed, looking at Sal. "However, we can't confirm that since Sam's charter book is also missing. They must have started working on him shortly after getting underway and whatever precipitated Sam's murder occurred sooner than anticipated or intended such that they didn't get the information they needed."

"What makes you say that, Tom?" Sal asked.

"The fact that *Greta* was found where she was," I answered. "If they'd gotten what they needed from Sam and found what they were looking for, *Greta* wouldn't have been needed anymore and the logical thing to do would have been to sink her or set her adrift. The fact that we found her up the creek and securely moored, indicates that Jimmy put her there with the idea of maybe using her again. However, since the Big Pine chart is missing, I suspect that he knows that Sam's body washed up and that we're investigating. If that's so, then he probably hid *Greta* to buy time and may be looking for another, less distinctive boat to steal for use in locating what he's after. He may even consider coming back for *Greta* for the heavy work of recovery. Of course that can't happen now that we've got her.

"I'm guessing that John Doe and Jimmy were pressuring Sam for information. Sam fought back and John Doe hit him with the crowbar unfortunately killing Sam.

166

Jimmy is rather upset at this turn of events and, in anger, shoots Doe, dumps Sam overboard, and then continues on to Cow Key Channel and dumps Doe."

"But why not just dump Sam and Doe at the same time and place?" asked Lou. "Why take the time and risk discovery to go into the channel for the second dump? And why not just get rid of *Greta* at that point and steal another boat sufficient to accomplish the task?"

"I don't know," I said with a shrug. "I told you this was just a theory. It may be that Jimmy and any other accomplices will do just that, although I think they'll have to get one with the means to retrieve something from the seabed. Otherwise, why would they need a boat and why take the chart with them? A chart is relatively worthless on land and, if what they're looking for is ashore, why would they need *Greta* in the first place?"

"Well, as to the latter point," said Lou, "booking the charter would be a way of getting Sam away somewhere relatively safe where they could work on him."

"True," I said, sitting up, the chair squeaking, "but that still doesn't answer the question of the missing chart and the fact that *Greta* was clearly stashed rather than disposed of. Besides, you've been on her. Did you notice the outriggers and equipment she has for handling large fish? In addition to marlin and sailfish, Sam sometimes went after shark so he made sure he had the rigging to handle the big ones. Not everyone does that. Short of grabbing a large commercial craft, I can't think of another boat in the lower Keys that would so readily fit their needs, be available and capable of being handled by only two people. One if he knows what he's doing."

"Tom, as Amy noted, you make it sound like there are only two, at most three, people involved in this," said Sal, "John Doe, there," pointing at the file, "Jimmy and maybe a third. Why so few? What is it that you think they are looking for?"

I could tell that Sal was thinking carefully as he phrased his question. I was beginning to think he knew something I didn't and that he thought it had some bearing on the case.

"Despite what Lou may think Sal, you and I both know that it's not drugs. Anytime Sam came across something like that he always called it in. I think it's money in some form and, as you know with found money, the fewer who know about it the better. I also think it was relatively recently lost rather than traditional sunken treasure. And by 'relatively recently' I'm guessing within the last few years, at most ten. Besides, I checked and there've been no major wrecks with potentially valuable cargo, whether Spanish treasure ships or more modern vessels, around the Big Pine area so it's likely something on a smaller scale. Also, for recovery of anything major, like Spanish gold, you'd need a bigger boat and more gear than *Greta* could carry.

"As for the specific number, I think at most three. Jimmy and John Doe on board and one on land. Remember, Sam's truck is missing along with his charter book which, according to Julio, was on the table in the front room right after Sam left for the charter Friday morning. It wasn't there when Amy and I went to talk to Elyse Saturday morning. I think the book was taken to prevent us from identifying Sam's last charter and the truck was stolen as convenient transportation which would blend in to the local scene and provide some means to retrieve Jimmy from Sugarloaf Key."

Sal nodded as I spoke and said, "Yes, that all makes sense. But who is the third individual? You don't think it could be that person who threatened Amy, do you?"

"Andy Hardy? It's possible, except that he's wanted for the drugs found in his desk which doesn't fit with the scenario for Sam's murder. However, until someone better comes along, he's the best candidate I've got, especially since he's local and fits in. He's reasonably well known on the island and anyone seeing him around would figure he was working a story for the paper whereas an out-of-towner would be noticed."

At the mention of Hardy and drugs, Lou sat up.

"Who the hell is Andy Hardy and what does he have to do with all this?" Lou asked.

"Andy is an editor, or rather former editor, at the *Key West Current* and was Amy's immediate boss," I explained. "He tried to implicate her on an embezzlement charge and, when that didn't work, a bogus drug charge. Larry Reynolds, the owner and publisher of the paper, was smart enough to call his bluff on both points and the last time Andy was seen was Sunday. When I got to the paper, we found a significant stash of marijuana in his desk all packaged and ready for shipment and distribution."

"You mentioned 'physical threats' earlier. Is this the guy who made them and in what form?" he asked.

"On his way into the night, he slashed the tires on Amy's car," I said. Lou just raised an eyebrow as if to say 'that's not much of a threat' and I continued, "Not just slashed, Lou, cut to ribbons. All four of them. And, Andy owns a .38 which has not been found."

"Have you got a file on this guy? I'll send his particulars up to Miami with John Doe here," as he reached for the file on the desk, "see if anything shakes out."

"I'll get you what I can on Andy, but don't go anywhere yet." I held up my hand. "I want some information from you on this Jimmy Ortega. Since it looks like there's a connection, I need to know what to expect."

Lou looked at Sal and Sal said, "I think you should tell him everything."

Lou got up and started to pace.

"Jaime Ortega started out as a two-bit gang member,

running a numbers bag in West Miami. He never really got picked up on the radar until we started having some turf wars between rival gangs. One group seemed to be winning more often and absorbing its opponents and the rumors were that it was being orchestrated by one person, Jaime Ortega, but we couldn't get any information on him. No one would talk. At that time, their operations were mostly gambling, prostitution and protection among their own neighborhoods with occasional beatings and knifings for those who didn't pay or broke the rules.

"Then we started to see an increase in drug related incidents and found a few bodies. The body count started to drop off after a couple years, but not the missing persons count. We figured they got smart and came up with better disposal methods. Most likely out in the 'glades."

I interrupted Lou and asked, "What method was used on the dead ones you found?"

"Mostly severe beatings and knife wounds, then we started seeing gunshot wounds. Sometimes a double tap with the shots close together but not close range and usually in the heart," said Lou. "Kind of like your friend here," he said holding up the John Doe file.

"Ever get any with doubles to the head?" I asked.

"Rarely, and those are usually .22's at close range, you know that. Why waste larger slugs on an execution like that?" said Lou stopping in front of me. "I know what you're thinking, that the same gun that was used on Sal's kid was used on John Doe here and on other victims found in the 'glades. We've checked the ballistics every time and never got a match, but I brought you a copy from the Donatello case like you asked anyway. My guess is that, if it is the same shooter, he ditches the gun every time and gets a new one.

He resumed pacing. "Anyway, after the incident with Sal's kid, the Attorney General decided to form a task force with the FBI and things settled down for a while. I think the word got out to those involved and they figured they better take things a little easy. We tried to get some informants inside but that never worked well. We got a few anonymous tips and made some small busts, picking up the little fish, but we were never able to get close to the big ones. Word kept reaching us about one 'Jimmy O' who was running things. We had our suspicions, but it wasn't until Sal came back from Cuba that we finally got a line on him and confirmed that Jimmy O was Jaime Ortega."

"So Sal's been working for you and the Feds since '59," I said.

"Not 'for,' dear boy," said Sal. "Rather 'with'."

"How do your associates feel about such 'cooperation'?" I asked him.

"Since it doesn't involve them, they don't know." replied Sal with a slight shrug. "At least, I haven't told them. If they do know, then, presumably, they don't care since it doesn't impact their business other than to potentially remove a competitor from the marketplace. However, I suspect that if they did know and had some reservations about my 'cooperation,' as you put it, I wouldn't be here."

Turning back to Lou I asked, "So have you got anything current on Ortega?"

Lou's shoulders slumped. "No, we don't even have a current picture of him."

"In short, you've got nothing. All this time, and the resources of the Feds and you couldn't even identify him if he walked in that door," I said gesturing to the office door.

"That's right," said Lou, rather chagrined. "We have a vague description which could fit half the Cuban population of Miami. The male half."

I sat back in my chair, or rather the Chief's chair, and said, "Well that's just great. I've got two murders and a possible drug problem, which could be directly connected to Ortega, and I have no idea what he looks like. No

171

distinguishing features, mannerisms, characteristics, nothing. All of this you could have told me over the phone. Why all the damn secrecy? Even Alice was evasive when I talked to her."

Lou sat down, his hands between his knees. "Blame the FBI, they don't want anything getting out without their say so and there's always one of them in the office so none of our people can say anything without them knowing. Even now, they think I've gone fishing for two days; this is my 'weekend.' They don't know I'm down here or that I brought you a copy of the Donatello file. And when I send your John Doe and Hardy information up, I'm doing it in your name so don't be surprised if one of them shows up here tomorrow."

"Don't worry, Lou," I said. "You're not sending it up, I am. And I'm going to call and let them know it's coming, what it is and why I want it. I'm already on their 'does not play nice with us' list over the missile business a few years ago."

"Yeah, I heard about that," Lou said. "Did you really make them pay those parking tickets?"

"Of course. We need the money and they weren't using official cars. Hell, I even gave Sal a ticket yesterday."

"Which I paid," said Sal.

"Good for you," said Lou. "God knows how many I've given you that you've ignored over the years."

"I'm making up for that now with my cooperation with the City of Miami," replied Sal.

With that comment, Lou relaxed and I decided I wasn't going to get any additional information out of him. I asked if he was going back to Miami tonight and he said no. Since he was supposed to be gone for two days, he was going to have dinner, watch the sunset and sleep. At the mention of food, we all realized how late it was and that none of us had taken a break for lunch.

Then we heard the sirens as the fire truck pulled out next door and smelled smoke.

CHAPTER 16

Sally opened the door, "Amy, it's the *Current*."

Amy was up and out of the office before I could stop her.

Out front, the flames were already above the roofline as the fire truck pulled up at the *Current* a couple of blocks away and started running hoses out. Even with metal roofs, enough of the buildings in Key West are still wood frame and relatively close together, so we take fires here seriously. With a good wind, a small fire can grow with frightening speed and endanger whole blocks of the town.

As Lou and the rest came out, Amy started toward the fire.

I grabbed her arm. "Where do you think you're going?"

She turned to me, her eyes dark like a storm over the Gulf.

"It's news, Tom. I'm a reporter, it's my job, and it's the *Current*, my paper, on fire."

I turned her around so she faced the fire.

"Take a good look at it. Those flames are in the roof already and it's going to collapse soon. Amy, I'm betting that fire was deliberately set. Maybe an act of revenge, maybe as a diversion. I'll let you go, but someone must be with you at all times. I'm going to be busy with the Fire Chief and crowd control."

I called for Frankie. As he came up I said, "Stay with her. She's insistent that she has to cover this for the paper, assuming there's anything left to print one with. Keep her out of trouble. Pick her up and carry her out of the way if you have to, but keep her safe and watch out for anyone or anything suspicious."

Frankie looked at me, understanding in his eyes. "Got you," he said and the two of them ran off up the street.

To Sally, I said, "Get on the radio. I want two men over at Larry Reynolds' house now and as many as we have available down here to keep people away. Any word from Dennis yet?"

Sally was already on her way back inside and called back, "No, nothing."

Damn. I was hoping he would have called in to at least let us know if it looked like *Greta* would float enough to get her out of the creek on the tide. She got in there; she should get out.

"Lou, do you know where the Sheriff's office is?" He nodded. "Good, get over there and find out if their lab boys got back from Sugarloaf and if they have any results yet. Also," I called as he headed off, "did Dennis send any message back with them?"

Sally stuck her head out the door and called to me. "Tom, I got hold of everyone I could but some of the boys who were off duty went fishing together and aren't back yet. Mikey's going over to Larry's, but he's the only one available on that side of the island."

Damn, I thought. Mike's good but he couldn't cover Reynolds' house by himself. He needed help. It was getting dark and I just had a bad feeling about this fire.

"Tom," Sal said, "I've sent Tony for the car. We'll back up Officer O'Neil."

"I can't let you do that, Sal. You're civilians, you're not official."

"Then deputize us."

"Yeah, right. You and Tony carrying badges? Tony would probably punch me at the suggestion and the Mayor would have mine."

"Listen, Tom, as I see it, right now we're all you have and it's just until you can spare some of your people from here. We'll be careful and take our orders from Mike. Now, where is Reynolds' house?"

Tony pulled up. Sal opened the door and looked at me, "Well? What's it going to be, Tom?"

"Okay, Okay. Larry's place is over by Casa Marina." I gave him the address. Looking directly at Tony I said, "You report to Mike O'Neil and take your instructions from him. Tell him I'll send a couple of officers over as soon as I can spare them. In the meantime, keep your eyes open and stay alert, but do not engage any suspects."

Surprisingly, Tony's reply was a crisp "Yes, Sir." And they drove off. Having heard everything, Sally said, "I'll call Mikey and let him know they're coming."

I headed up to the fire.

Nearing the line set up across the street to keep the curious a safe distance away, I could tell that the firemen were putting up a valiant effort but that it was clear they were going to lose the battle. In fact, just as I was asking where the Fire Chief was, the roof of the *Key West Current* fell in and a shower of sparks and embers flew into the air. Immediately, everyone looked upward and tracked where the glowing debris fell to see if their business or home was now in danger.

In the light from the fire, I saw Frankie with Amy and Larry in front. They were at a safe distance. Our Fire Chief, Joe Farto, and the Mayor were headed in their direction, so I made my way over to them as well. When I reached them, Larry was speaking, apparently answering a question from the Chief, and Amy was taking notes.

"No, that's all stored in a fireproof shed out back away from the building. You know that Joe and it's always kept locked." Larry was saying.

One of the firemen came up and handed something to the Chief. He looked at it and then handed it to me, "What do you think, Tom?"

It was a large heavy-duty padlock on which the hasp had been sheared. "Whoever did this didn't need a key. He just used a bolt cutter. I presume you're treating this as arson, Joe?" Although he didn't seem to care, I didn't like his nickname "Bum" and never used it.

"Yeah. In addition to the sheared lock on the flammables shed, witnesses are telling us the entire back wall was a sheet of flames before we could even get the truck out. I'm guessing he used printing solvent. That stuff's basically alcohol with some additives used to clean ink off the equipment. Makes a wonderful accelerant on dry wood."

"You got any suspects," I asked.

"Well, I heard about the business with Andy Hardy on Sunday so he'd be a good place to start. Any sign of the little bastard yet?"

Like the rest of us, Joe'd had his run-ins with Andy. "Unfortunately, no," I replied. "Any other possibilities come to mind?"

Larry answered this time. "Not that I can think of. We haven't run any articles recently that I think would provoke this kind of response."

"If you do come up with anything, let me know as well as the Chief," I said. "Meanwhile, on the chance that this was a case of revenge, whether by Hardy or someone else, I've got some men watching your house for anything suspicious. I presume that Gloria, Davis and Elena are there."

"Davis and Elena are, yes," said Larry. "But, Gloria called earlier to say she was stopping at a friend's house after school to study and would be home late."

"Did she mention the name of this friend or her address?"

"I don't know. I was here and Davis called with her message. He didn't mention a specific name so I can only assume that Gloria didn't give one."

I didn't tell Larry Reynolds, but the fact that his

daughter didn't mention the friend's name, told me where she was. Excusing myself from the group, I went over to a nearby pay phone leaving the Mayor consoling Reynolds. I put a dime in the slot and dialed Sam's number.

Elyse answered, "Si, hello."

"Elyse, it's Tom Jackson. Is Gloria Reynolds there?"

"Si, Mr. Tom, she is still here. Just a minute, please."

I heard her lay the phone down and walk back to the kitchen; then I heard different steps returning and Gloria picked up the receiver.

"Lieutenant, this is Gloria Reynolds, what's wrong?" I could hear fear in her voice.

"It's okay, Gloria," I said. "There's been a fire at the paper but your father is all right. It may be some time before he's finished with Chief Farto so I want you to stay there with Elyse and Julio until I arrive."

There'd been a sharp intake of breath when I mentioned the fire and a release when I said Larry was all right.

"What happened? How did it start?" she asked.

"The Chief and I believe that it was arson and it may have been done as a diversion to keep us occupied."

"You're thinking of Mr. Hardy, aren't you, Lieutenant?"

"Yes, I am. I have Officer O'Neil and some other men watching your house so Davis and Elena should be okay. Your father is with the Fire Chief. As soon as I can get away from here, I'll come and take you home. So please wait for me."

"Yes, sir, I will. But please don't tell my father where I've been."

"Don't worry, I won't. But I still think you should, and soon."

I hung up and walked back over to where Amy and Frankie were standing. The fire was now under control and would soon be out, but it would be morning before Joe and his investigators could start sifting through the debris. I got a description of the printer solvent cans and set a couple of my boys to looking through trash bins and anywhere else they could think of for them with instructions to carefully transport them back to the lab for fingerprints. Then I detailed a couple over to Larry's to help Mike and tell Sal that we would meet him back at the hotel.

I was all set to tell Amy I was going over to the Torres house to get Gloria when someone called for a medic and two ambulance men who had been standing around went running behind the wreckage of the *Current*.

Amy, Frankie and I followed and when we got there the ambulance men were bending over someone lying on the ground.

The medics helped the individual sit up into the light with a bandage on his head, and Amy ran forward.

"Eddie!" she cried, kneeling down next to him with the immediate questions, "What happened? Are you all right? Who did it? What did you see?"

One of the medics pulled her back. "Please miss, stay back and give him some air. He's had a nasty crack on the head and we're going to take him over to the hospital."

I pulled her aside.

"Amy, you and Frankie go with Eddie. If Doc Elliott's there have him check Eddie top to bottom and find out what you can. I have to go over to Sam's, get Gloria and take her home. Then I'll come to the hospital and pick you two up."

To Frankie, I said, "Sal and Tony went over to Larry Reynolds' as back-up for Mike. Now that the fire's out, I've sent some officers over to relieve them and tell Sal that we'll meet back at the bungalow. When you get to the hospital call him and give him an update. Let him know that it's likely to be a late night. He was thinking of something back at the office and I want to know what it was. If it's what I think it is, we may be close to a break in this case."

Frankie just looked at me and nodded, but Amy started in, "What is it, Tom? What have you figured out? Don't hold out on me."

"Calm down. I'm not sure yet. I have to check some things and get some answers from Sal and Julio, but I have an idea as to the underlying reason for all of this. Now, you two better get moving or that ambulance is going to leave without you."

The medics had Eddie on a stretcher and were loading him into the vehicle, so Amy and Frankie hurried over and forced their way in. The medics looked over at me and I waved my assent.

I found Joe to let him know I was leaving the scene. I told him that my men were checking the area for solvent cans and anything else suspicious and that they would report to him if they found anything. I then went back down the street to the office.

Sally was still there, talking to Lou who had just returned from the Sheriff's office. The lab boys had come back and had brought Dennis' car with the boat trailer. He'd kept the skiff to use as a tow if needed to pull *Greta* out of the creek at high tide and would call in on her radio to let us know his progress. Sally handed me a sheet of paper. It was the blood type analysis from the samples I got from the crowbar and the deck. They both matched Sam's.

"Lou, did the lab have a print report from the crowbar and a comparison with the ones we sent over?"

"Yeah. They'd just finished, but didn't have a write up for you. They said it would be over first thing in the morning, but they did tell me that mostly there were a bunch of smudges but some clear ones that matched Sam and your John Doe, so it looks like you've got your murder weapon and your killer."

"We've got the who, kind of, the what, and the where, with respect to Sam, but not the why," I said. "At least not yet, but I think we'll have that by morning as well. Sally, have someone amend Andy Hardy's file to include suspicion of arson and assault and battery in the charges. Chief Farto is pretty sure the fire was deliberate and I'm inclined to agree. The *Current* building is a total loss and we found Eddie Harris unconscious behind the flammables shed; he'd been hit pretty hard but he's alive and they've taken him to the hospital. Amy and Frankie have gone with him."

"I know his mother, Adele," said Sally. "Gene's here so I'll deliver the news and take her over to the hospital."

"Thanks, I'll see you there."

As Sally collected her purse and left, I pulled Lou back to the office. Even with all of the excitement of the fire, finding Eddie, and worrying about Amy and Gloria, I was still thinking about the careful way that Sal had asked his question about how many I thought were involved in this mess and the look on his face when I mentioned money as the likely reason behind Sam's death. It was a very thoughtful look, like he was putting all of the possible variables into a long equation and getting the same answer every time. I wanted to know if he was doing the same math I was and getting the same answer.

Closing the office door, I turned to Lou and asked him point blank, "Do you trust Sal Donatello and his boys?"

"As far as I know he's never lied to me."

My fist hit the desk. "Damn it, Lou, that wasn't my question. You've been working with them for what, six, seven years? Do you trust them?"

Lou backed up a step holding his hands up. "Easy, Tom, easy. Trust like what? To tell us the truth? I suppose so. Like I said, Sal's never lied to me. Everything he's told me or given us has always checked out. To tell me everything he knows? That's a different matter. No. Like anyone else, he'll keep something back if he can until he's ready to tell you."

I calmed down and nodded at this, having seen it myself over the last couple of days.

Lou continued. "As for the boys, I'm not sure they trust me. They're fiercely loyal to Sal and if he says do it, they'll do it. If I tell them to do something and they don't want to or don't think it's their responsibility, they'll dig their heels in and won't budge until Sal says go. Of the two of them, Frankie's the more reasonable when it comes to cops. Tony just plain doesn't like us for some reason I've never been able to find out. However, they're both extremely observant and intelligent. You do know that they both have degrees from the University of Miami don't you?"

"You're joking."

"No, I'm not. They were enrolled when Sal started working with us. Tony's is in literature and Frankie's is in business management."

Thinking about it, although somewhat surprising, it made sense. Sal was well educated and I couldn't see him having the stereotypical dumb hoodlum type around him. As for the particular interests, Frankie had struck me as the more logical of the two whereas the literary interest fit with Tony's obvious creative side evidenced by his culinary abilities. However, I still wanted to know why he didn't like cops.

Summing up, Lou said, "Bottom line, if it came down to me or Sal, I think the boys would let me drown. Probably even throw me an anchor. Sal, on the other hand, I just don't know for sure, Tom. I just don't know. You, however, that's different. Over the years, Sal has sometimes asked me about you and what you were doing, but he never said why. I know he's been down here several times a year, but he never mentioned seeing you or talking to you. I did catch him reading the FBI report on that incident down here even though he wasn't supposed to. One of the Feds got sloppy and left it out. Sal seemed very amused by what was in there about you. I heard him mumble 'Good for you, young lad.' He likes you Tom, which means the boys like you too. I don't think you have to worry about them."

"That's good to know Lou because, for some reason, I've trusted them since they first showed up here on Sunday. That was the first time I'd ever met them, although something tells me that Sal knew my father, apart from and after the trial in Miami, and that Sam was responsible."

I picked up the file on our John Doe. "Now, you're coming with me. We've got a young lady to pick up and deliver home; then we're going to sit down with Donatello and Co. and get some answers. You've missed the sunset and I don't think any of us are going to get much sleep tonight. But, if you're lucky, Tony will be cooking so you'll at least eat well."

On our way out I gave Gene what I thought would be our itinerary, made sure he had the number for Sal's bungalow, and told him that I wanted to know as soon as Dennis reported in. I was getting worried that we hadn't heard from him.

CHAPTER 17

The drive over to the Torres' home, though short, was quiet. I didn't know what was going through Lou's mind, but mine was working overtime. I'd told Sally we knew who had killed Sam, but we didn't really. Yes, I suspected that our John Doe from Cow Key Channel had done it and, as a result, someone else had killed him. But who was he? I didn't know, but I thought I knew someone who might, which was why I'd brought the file with me.

Another part of my mind was trying to figure out what Andy Hardy had to do with all of this. Andy knew Sam and would have known better than to try to get Sam involved in anything to do with drugs. I was convinced that whatever was at the root of Sam's murder did not involve narcotics, which left the question of what, then, was Andy's involvement?

Or, were we chasing two separate cases? Were Sam's murder and Andy's smuggling merely coincidental? So far, there was nothing to put Andy on *Greta*, not that I would expect him to go anywhere near her. But, then, where was Sam's truck? The last report from the officer watching Andy's house was that his car was still there, but Andy wasn't. However, like most people on the island, Andy did have, and used, a bicycle which had not been reported as present.

Then there was Sal and the boys. I'd told Lou I trusted them. Did I? Yeah, I did. But why? Logic told me not to. Despite Sal's gentlemanliness and Tony's and Frankie's apparent education, they were connected with organized crime. My gut said otherwise. Why, I didn't know. I trusted them with Amy. I trusted them to tell me the truth, even if it might not be pretty or what I wanted to hear. I trusted them to not lie to me. They might not tell me everything, unless I asked the right questions, but I didn't think they would outright lie to me. That, I think, had something to do with Sam and my father. Before this was over, I was going to get the answer to that question from Sal, one way or another.

When we pulled up in front of Sam's place, the front door was open and I started to get worried until Julio looked out, saw the police car and stepped out onto the porch. I'd told him to keep the doors and windows closed, but it was a warm evening and the smell from the fire hung in the air. Lou and I met him at the porch steps.

"Is it true about the *Current* building?" asked Julio.

"Yes, I'm afraid so. Is Gloria still here?"

"Yes, sir. She's inside with Mama Elyse."

I could see that Julio was hesitant to say anything else so I introduced him to Lou and explained why he was here.

"Senor Sal called. He said he would be by later, but that if we needed anything we should call him or let you know." Julio looked a little embarrassed as he continued, "He offered to take care of all of the arrangements for Papa Sam."

"Julio," I said, "Sam and Mr. Donatello go back before your time here and your father helped him through something that I know he would have repaid had Sam let him. I suggest that you let Mr. Donatello do this for you and for Sam. It's important to him."

"Si, Senor," Julio said, quietly.

Lou and I followed Julio into the house and found Gloria and Elyse on the couch, a pot of strong Cuban coffee on the table in front of them. Elyse picked up an empty cup and the pot.

"Ah, Senor Tom. Sit down, have some coffee."

I knew Elyse's coffee and it was tempting. "No, thank you Elyse. We don't have time. I have to get Gloria home and then go to the hospital to see what I can find out from Eddie Harris."

At this, Gloria gave a start. "Eddie's in the hospital? What happened?"

I explained about the fire and the discovery of Eddie behind the shell of the *Current* office. I assured her that he was being well looked after and protected, but that now we had to get her home. I did find her reaction to the news about Eddie interesting and stole a glance at Julio, but his expression revealed nothing.

Turning to Elyse, I said, "I would like Julio to come with us and it may be quite late before he gets home. Is there anyone who could stay with you?"

"Si. Rita and Hector should be home. But why do you need Julio, Senor Tom?"

"I'm not sure yet, but I think he may be able to help with the investigation. Sergeant Zacchiarelli and I are meeting with Mr. Donatello shortly and it'd be easier if Julio were with us. I'll make sure he gets home safely."

Julio went next door to get the Gomezes and I brought them sufficiently up to date so they knew what was happening without being too worried about the situation. Although I had no doubt that Hector could take care of anything that might arise, I did warn him, out of earshot of Elyse and Rita, not to take any chances. If he saw or heard anything unusual he was to call the office and they would get word to me and send someone directly over. Hector was a plumber, a good one, and the first one we called if we had a problem at headquarters so he knew everyone there and they knew him.

Comfortable with the arrangements, Julio, Gloria, Lou and I headed over to the Reynolds house. In the car, the kids were in the back seat and Gloria leaned over the back of the front seat, her hands gripping the upholstery between Lou and I.

"Lieutenant, I can't go home. I must go to the hospital to see Eddie. I need to be there if Father isn't."

"No. I promised your Father I would take you home where you'll be safe. I have officers on duty and Davis and Elena will be worried."

"But Eddie needs ..." There was a pause as if she was going to say something then caught herself. "Someone he knows, someone close."

"Relax, Gloria. Miss Petersen is there and I've sent someone for his mother. Doc Elliott's on tonight, so Eddie will be well taken care of. You are going home and that's it."

She gave up arguing and slumped back in the seat. I tried to see her expression in the rear view mirror, but it was just dark enough and her head was down so I couldn't make anything out. In the dark Julio reached over and took her hand. There was definitely something between those three, Julio, Gloria and Eddie, but that was for their respective parents, not me, to figure out.

As we turned off Flagler Avenue into Reynolds' neighborhood, Sal's limo was parked in front of the house. Sal was leaning against the car and Tony was by the front gate. Mike's car was parked by the driveway. Reynolds' house was similar to many of the more affluent houses on the island and had a wall around it that joined the house at the garage. A gate provided access from the street into the front yard. In this case, the gate was actually a double door that matched the front door of the house and had a bell chain hanging along side. I hoped Gloria had her key.

We parked behind Sal's car and then joined him and Tony. I introduced Gloria and looked around for Mike and the two officers I had sent over from the fire. "Where's Mike, Sal?"

"Officer O'Neill is positioning his men and then he will join us back here," said Sal. "He wants to make sure they are where they can clearly see the back of the house. He's going to cover the front. Good evening, Miss Reynolds. Everything here appears to be secure."

"Thank you Mr. Donatello," she replied. Pulling her key from her purse she turned to me, "Is it okay if I go in now, Lieutenant?"

"Just as soon as I confirm Mr. Donatello's report with Mike, Gloria." At that moment Mike came around the corner, saw us and waved.

When he reached the front gate I asked him, "Everything secure?"

"Yeah. I've got the other two positioned so they can both see into the back yard across the back wall and down their respective sides. I'll be across the street at the corner so I can see this side and the garage. If anyone starts sneaking around, we'll catch them before they can do anything."

"That's good, Mike. I'll take Gloria in and make sure Davis has everything locked up. I don't know when Reynolds will be home. I would imagine he's going to have a lot to do. The *Current* building is a total loss."

"Yeah, that's what the boys said. Damn shame, too. The *Current's* a good paper. What's Amy going to do?"

"Don't know yet, Mike. Right now she and Frankie are over at the hospital with Eddie Harris. I'm going to pick them up and then we're all going to be at Sal's bungalow if you need anything. If Tony's cooking, I'll see to it that you all get some."

"Don't worry about that. Tony and I already have that covered. I promised him some of my Mom's old Irish recipes."

Recipes, I thought. Is that all it takes for a cop to get on Tony's good side? No, it can't be that easy.

I motioned toward the gate which Gloria unlocked and we passed through, closing it behind us. Davis met us at the front door. I gave him a quick summary of events and impressed upon him that if anything happened his job was to get Gloria, himself and anyone else in the family out as quickly as possible. I didn't want any more dead bodies.

Returning to the street, I personally thanked Tony for providing backup for Mike and received a surprisingly polite "you're welcome" instead of his usual grunt. I looked quizzically at Sal but all he did was shrug his shoulders. Tony was starting to be positively warm to us cops. I was going to have to ask Mike how he did it, but not now. Leaving him on guard I pushed Lou and Julio into the Limo with Sal, then got in my car and headed to the hospital.

As I pulled up in front of the hospital the car radio crackled and Gene's voice came over the speaker, "Car 12. Come in Car 12. Lieutenant, are you there?"

Hearing Gene on the radio made me think of Dennis and the fact that we'd had no word from him for way too long. I hoped this wasn't more bad news. I picked up the mic and pressed the key, "Car 12 here. Go ahead Gene."

"Hi, Lieutenant. You said to call as soon as I got any word from Dennis," I held my breath as Gene continued. "He just called in to say he's out of the creek and *Greta's* running under her own power."

I exhaled and keyed the mic again, "Did he say what took him so long and why he didn't call sooner?"

"Yes sir. He said it wasn't easy getting *Greta* out. The tide in the creek was barely enough to float her once he got her unstuck. He didn't risk trying her engines until he was in open water and he got stuck a couple times towing her out with the skiff. Also, he didn't want to run the batteries down using the radio until he had her running."

"Okay, Gene. Call him back and tell him to take his time, but to call when he gets in the harbor. I know he's going to be dead tired, but tell him I said to stay aboard. I don't want that boat left alone. Send someone from the night shift over to meet him and keep watch. I'm at the hospital to find out how Eddie's doing then we'll all be at

Mr. Donatello's bungalow; you have the number. Mike is at Reynolds' house and you can get him on his car radio if needed."

"Got it, Sir. I'll call you if anything comes up."

In the hospital, Amy and Frankie were sitting in the waiting room. Knowing that Amy had probably pestered the doctors until they told her what they could before pushing her out of the emergency room, I joined them.

"Any word on Eddie yet?"

"He's in X-ray," Amy said. "Doc Elliott's with him along with Sally and his mother. Doc said he got a nasty crack to the skull and has a concussion. But he wants to check Eddie out thoroughly to make sure nothing more serious is going on." She paused with a look of concern. "Tom, he was pretty much out of it in the ambulance. I couldn't get a coherent answer from him. Doc Elliott didn't say anything specific, but he looked worried when he examined Eddie. I don't think you're going to be able to question him tonight."

I'd had that suspicion when they bundled the kid into the ambulance, but I also wanted to hear what Doc had to say, so I sat down with Amy and Frankie and waited.

It was about thirty minutes before Doc Elliott came out to the waiting room with Sally. As Amy had said, he looked worried.

"Tom, before you even ask, no, you can't talk to him."

"What's the prognosis?"

"Guarded," Doc replied. "Eddie received a pretty hard blow to the skull but the X-ray doesn't show any fracture, which is a good sign. However, there is a discoloration in the area which could just be an artifact from the process. Or it could indicate some bleeding just under the skull, which may or may not create some pressure on the brain. I have a call in to a specialist who happens to be on Marathon and he's on his way down here."

"Any idea what was used?"

189

"Not a crowbar, if that's what you're thinking. Had it been that, Eddie would probably be in the morgue. No, I suspect it was wood, not a dense wood so probably not a baseball bat, but dense enough. Also, it was probably on the order of three or four inches in diameter. So I would say you're looking for something about the size of a bat but of softer wood. Maybe even a discarded tree branch."

"Which, if Hardy was smart, he threw into the fire," I said.

"Are you sure it was Andy?" Amy asked.

"Who else had a reason to set fire to the *Current* building? Most likely this was an act of revenge, like your tires. However, I suspect that Andy was also thinking it would be a way to dispose of the evidence in his desk if he thought we hadn't found it yet. Andy Hardy's not as smart as he'd like people to think and I suspect that he has an idea that the police department in this town has absolutely no imagination." I turned back to Doc Elliott, "Is Mrs. Harris with Eddie?"

At this question Sally spoke up, "Yes, Tom, she is and I'm going to stay with her tonight, so don't expect me in the morning."

"Okay, but you better call Gene and let him know. Also, if anything changes with Eddie's condition call me. I'll be at Sal's."

As I turned to Amy and Frankie there was a commotion at the emergency desk and I heard Larry Reynolds' voice.

"Where is he? Where's my boy? What have you done with him?"

Doc was the first one out of the waiting room and, when I followed, he had Larry by the shoulders trying to settle him down.

"Larry," Doc said. "Calm down. Eddie's all right. He's still in emergency and will be there for the rest of the night so we can keep an eye on him. He received a hard blow to the head and has a concussion. Now, if you settle down I'll give you a full report and let you see him."

Reynolds took a deep breath and collected himself. "I'm sorry, Stearns," he said. "I didn't know anyone had been injured, let alone Eddie. I was with the fire chief when I found out."

At that point Reynolds realized that the rest of us were there and he turned to me.

"Was it Hardy? Did he burn my building and attack Eddie?"

"Right now, Mr. Reynolds, we don't have any evidence to support a contention that Hardy is responsible." Reynolds started to open his mouth to argue the point. "However," I continued, holding up a hand, "we also don't have any evidence to rule him out and, given recent events, I can tell you that he is the prime suspect in this matter. Now, I suggest you go with Doctor Elliott and see Eddie; then go home. Officer O'Neill is there with two other officers to keep an eye out in case Hardy tries anything else and I personally delivered Gloria into Davis' care. We are on top of the case and we will find him."

Doc took Larry's arm and guided him toward the emergency room doors, "Come on, Larry," he said. "Let's go see Eddie and Adele."

At the mention of Eddie's mother, I saw a slight change in Reynolds, a degree of apprehension flickered in his eyes and I must have shown something because, as they passed through the doors, Doc Elliott looked back over his shoulder and gave me a look that said 'we'll talk later.' Then the doors closed.

Frankie, Amy and I went out to the car. Getting in Amy paused, "Interesting choice of words by Larry," she said. "'Where's my boy.' What do you think he meant?"

I was beginning to have my own suspicions, but since it was clearly a personal matter of Reynolds' and I didn't think it important to the case, I replied, "That's just Larry's style, concerned about one of his employees. After all, he refers to his female employees as 'his girls.'"

"Maybe," Amy said and got in the car.

I knew the sound of that 'maybe.' Amy sensed something else in Larry Reynolds and it had raised her investigative antennae. I hoped she'd leave it alone, but I had a sinking feeling that she wouldn't. All I could reasonably expect was that she would be discrete.

On the way to Sal's bungalow, we stopped at the Reynolds house to give all concerned an update. Gloria was somewhat relieved to hear that Eddie didn't appear to be in any immediate danger and that his mother and her father were both there. "Yes, that's where he should be. At her side," she said quietly.

"Excuse me?" I said, giving the impression that I hadn't heard what she said.

"What? Oh, nothing, Lieutenant," Gloria replied. "I was just thinking out loud. Do you think it would be all right if I called Doctor Elliott later to see how Eddie is?"

"I don't think he'll be able to tell you much more than I have. Why don't you wait until your father gets home since I'm sure the Doctor will give him a complete report and the specialist will have had a chance to give his opinion."

"Yes, that is probably best," she said. "Thank you Lieutenant. I think it is time for a family discussion with Father."

As I left, I found myself wondering which family was going to be first on the list and I felt a little sorry for Larry Reynolds. His 'little girl' wasn't so little anymore and she was displaying a level of maturity that I suspected was going to put him at a distinct disadvantage in any such discussions.

CHAPTER 18

The Lodge was only a few blocks over from the Reynolds house so there wasn't much time for talk, not that I had much to say. I put Larry Reynolds' potential family issues away in the back of my brain and tried to focus on my immediate problems. Amy had her notebook out and was scribbling in a shorthand that only she could decipher, while Frankie sat impassively in the back seat.

As I pulled into a space at Sal's bungalow Amy asked me, "Tom, where was Adele Harris 16 years ago?"

"What? What about Adele?"

"Adele Harris. Where was she 16 years ago? Maybe more importantly, where was she 17 years ago?"

The course of her question finally registered.

"Amy," I said, "leave it alone. Except for the likely fact that it was Andy Hardy who hit Eddie over the head, anything else about him, his mother, his family, has nothing to do with our case. I know what you're thinking, but it's none of our business. Stay out of it."

I was probably a little stronger than I needed to be or should have been since I saw the beginnings of a pout at the edge of her mouth and heard an intake of breath that, ordinarily, would have been a prelude to an argument. Then her jaw relaxed and she exhaled.

"Yeah, you're right, it's none of my business," she said, closing her notebook and getting out of the car.

I closed my door and started for the bungalow, then heard Frankie call, "Hey, somebody wanna let me out of here?"

The back doors of police cars don't have inside door handles, for obvious reasons. I opened Frankie's door and apologized.

In the bungalow Sal and Julio sat on the couch talking. Lou was in a chair with a copy of the *Citizen*, Key West's other newspaper, and Tony was just coming out of the kitchen with what looked like a platter of antipasti. Where he had found a market open and carrying the ingredients he needed at this hour I had no idea. Then I remembered Frankie's comment about what Tony could do with rations when they were in Korea and I looked closer at the platter.

Although from across the room it looked like Italian antipasto, on closer examination, everything on the platter was local which was what the Lodge's kitchen was known for. Now I knew. Tony had an in with someone in the Lodge kitchen. I looked at him and smiled. Tony didn't say a word, but his look told me that he knew that I knew his secret. I gave him a discrete thumbs up and winked.

Julio was the first one to speak.

"Senor Tom, how's Eddie?"

"Doc Elliott thinks he'll be okay," I said. "He does have a concussion and they're keeping a close eye on him tonight. His mother is with him and we'll know more in the morning. If anything changes, the hospital will let me know."

"Can I go see him?" Julio asked.

"Not tonight. I need you here for a while; then you go home."

"Yes sir," he mumbled, clearly disappointed.

"Besides," I continued, "Gloria will probably know more before you can find out. In fact, I suspect that young lady has already got Doc Elliott to give her Eddie's complete history. She has a way with people, much like someone else I know," I said glancing at Amy. "I understand she's been accepted at Tulane. Do you know what she's going to study?"

Julio looked at Amy and then me. "Journalism, what else?"

I poured myself a cup of coffee from the pot then turned back to Julio, "I don't know why yet, but I have a suspicion that a key piece of this case is you, or rather the circumstances under which Sam found you at sea. It was something he would never tell me and it happened before I came back to the island so I wasn't involved in any investigation that went on at the time. I want you to tell us what happened and why. It may help to clear some things up."

Julio looked down at the floor; then at Sal as if asking for permission or support. Sal just gave him a slight nod and Julio began.

"Well, Sir, as you know I lived in Cuba and worked on my uncle's boat. We would often take gentlemen from Havana out fishing. One evening shortly after Castro entered Havana, four men came knocking at the door. My uncle was not home. He had sympathies with the Castro forces and had joined the revolution. These men wanted his boat so they could leave Cuba, but since they knew nothing about boats they forced me to take them. Along the way to the dock, we ran into my cousin, Juan Canterra. Not knowing what was going on he called to me and they grabbed him also.

"The men had five large suitcases with them and when we got on the boat, they told me to start the motor and leave. They wanted to go to Miami. I didn't want to go and tried to tell them it was too far. I lied and said the boat didn't have enough fuel. They didn't care and insisted that I obey. Since they had guns, Juan and I had no choice but to do what they wanted. Fortunately my uncle always kept the boat ready so we left.

"It was night time, but I knew how to read the stars and was able to set the proper course. A few hours into the voyage the weather started to turn bad and they were below deck, sick. Even if they had known how to handle a boat,

195

they would not have been able to. They were too busy puking."

I interrupted Julio at that point, "Had they been drinking?"

"Yes, Lieutenant, they had," he replied.

"What happened then?" I asked.

"I was piloting the boat when Juan came up from below. He was very excited and tried to tell me something about money, but I was too busy concentrating on maintaining a course that would prevent us from being capsized. The waves were very high coming in from the east and I had to make sure I maintained the correct angle going into them." Like many of his fellow Cubans, Julio couldn't keep his hands still when telling a story and, in addition to telling us what happened, he mimed the waves, steering the boat and other actions. "Suddenly, just as Juan was pulling on my arm, there was a great blast of wind. The boat heeled over and we both wound up in the water and were separated.

"It was dark and, when I came to the surface, I couldn't see Juan. I saw the boat going down and no sign of the men. Then cases started coming to the surface and were floating. I needed something to hang on to so I just pulled them together and held onto them until morning when Papa Sam came by and found me."

"Did you know who these men were?" I asked. "Who they worked for? Their names?"

Julio shrugged his shoulders. "They were gringos, Americans. They were not Cubans, but I am sure they worked for one of the casinos in Havana. The cases were large, heavy for me but not so for the men. As for names, no Sir, I do not remember any names except the largest one. I had seen him once before, with some other men who came one time to go fishing. The others called him 'Tiny'."

Sal gave a little start but didn't say anything.

I asked Julio why he thought Sam had not wanted

anyone to know about this.

"I don't know," he said. "Perhaps he was afraid that if people knew they would come looking for me, or the authorities here would send me back to Cuba. Mama Elyse made it very clear that she did not want anyone to know so he didn't tell anybody."

Sal at this point piped up, "What happened to the cases?"

"I do not know, Mr. Sal," said Julio. "I think Papa Sam saved them and I assume he put them away somewhere. I never saw them again."

I looked over at Sal and it was clear he was thinking of something. What, I didn't know, and I wasn't going to ask him. I had my suspicions that, while not involved, he knew things that I wanted to know. However, I didn't want the others to know yet, so I kept quiet. With Julio's tale now told, some of my suspicions were getting a little stronger. For one thing, Sal recognized the name 'Tiny' and probably knew who he had worked for.

Lou had been holding the file on our John Doe. I took it from him and opened it to the photo. "Julio," I said, "did you ever see your cousin again after that night?"

"No, Senor Tom. I guess he drowned. I called his name all night, but he never answered."

"This may be difficult. I'm going to show you a photograph of a body we pulled out of Cow Key Channel and I want to know if you recognize him." I turned the file around so he could see the picture and there was a slight intake of breath, not quite a gasp, but definitely a sound of surprise.

Julio looked at me. "It looks very much like my cousin. But it couldn't be; he must have drowned when the boat sank."

"Did your cousin have any distinguishing characteristics or marks?" I asked.

"I remember he had a mark on his thigh, like a "J." We would joke that it was good that his name was Juan."

Looking at the written description of the corpse I said, "Julio, the coroner's report says there is a birthmark shaped somewhat like a "J" on the left thigh of the body. Is that where Juan's mark was?"

"Yes," said Julio, quietly. "Then that is my cousin Juan?" he asked pointing to the file and looking at me.

"I am afraid it looks that way," I said. "Julio, you're what, eighteen? So you were eleven back then. How old was Juan?"

"Juan? I think he was sixteen."

Digesting this information and making a rapid calculation, I figured that would make Juan twenty-three years old which would coincide with Doc's estimate of early twenties in his report.

Looking back at Julio I continued, "Juan was on deck with you when the boat capsized and you lost sight of him in the water?"

"Yes, Sir. I called out but got no answer. The sea was heavy and I thought he had drowned until now. Where has he been?"

"I don't want to say anything right now, but I have my suspicions," I said glancing at Sal. Noticing his slightly raised eyebrow I answered him with one of mine.

Returning to Julio I asked, "Do you remember your location when the boat capsized?"

"I had been making my course by the stars but I think we were a bit north of Big Pine Key."

"You said there were five cases."

Julio nodded. "Yes sir."

"Where were they on the boat?"

"The men took them down into the cabin with them when they boarded and that was the last I saw of them until I was in the water. I was on deck piloting the boat the entire time."

"Then you were extremely lucky that a couple of them popped out as the boat went down," said Lou.

"No sir, not a couple," said Julio. "All five came up and I was able to pull them together and make a kind of raft."

I was surprised at this, "In stormy waters? You were able to hang onto five suitcases and keep them together? How?"

"I used my pants and belt to tie the handles together," said Julio.

"What kind of boat was this?" asked Sal. "Where was the cabin?"

"It was not a big boat. Papa Sam's boat is bigger." Julio drew a picture in the air with his hands. "The cabin was at the front but was not completely below deck. It had a low roof and walls with windows so you could look out."

"With room for the four men and five cases?"

"Not much room. But, yes, that is where they were."

I was thinking that it was rather providential that all five cases had popped out of the cabin. Something in the back of my head said that they couldn't have done that if they'd been in the cabin. They must have been close to the hatchway.

"Julio," I said. "Where was Juan during the voyage?"

"Sometimes on deck, sometimes in the cabin with the men. After they started getting sick, they insisted on having someone with them so he was down there most of the time."

"What happened to the cases? When Sam found you, he pulled you out of the water. Did he retrieve the cases as well?"

"I was barely conscious and just remember being pulled out of the water. When I woke up at Papa Sam's I think I saw the cases there so he must have pulled them in also."

At this bit of news I was now convinced that Sam did retrieve them and I wished I had his logbook from back then. Sam was scrupulous about keeping records and would have included it in his log of the trip.

"Julio, you said the cases were heavy, yet they floated. How heavy were they?" I asked.

"Lieutenant, I was only eleven. Back then, a lot of things seemed heavy to me. Today, I couldn't tell you how much they weighed. The cases themselves were a yellowish tan color, smooth with gold latches across where the top closed on the bottom."

I said, "With the handle in between the latches?"

"Yes."

I turned to Sal, "What kind of suitcases do you have?"

"My cases? Samsonite, and yes, they look like Julio's description," he said, anticipating my next question. "Why?"

"Could I borrow one?"

"I don't know why, but yes. Frankie, bring out one of our cases."

Frankie went into the bedroom and came out with a medium size case.

"Julio," I said, "is that what the cases looked like?"

Julio nodded. "Yes sir, that's exactly what they were."

"Sal, how long have you had these?"

"I think at least ten years. I believe Samsonite has had that design for a long time."

"Do you know if they're waterproof?"

"I couldn't tell you, I've never had the opportunity to find out."

"Do you mind if I do?"

Sal shrugged his shoulders. "If you think it will help. Is there anything in that one Frankie?"

"No, boss, I unpacked it earlier."

"Okay, Tom, do what you think you have to," Sal said.

I motioned to Frankie, "Come with me." We went out the back door to the hotel pool where I threw the case in the water and watched while it bobbed around on the surface.

Frankie looked at it. "Well, Lieutenant, it floats. So what?"

"What do you think it would do if it was full?"

"Full of what?"

"Money."

"Money?" Frankie pondered. "I guess if it was heavy enough it'd sink. What are you getting at?"

"I'll let you know, but first get me that stack of newspapers." I said, gesturing to the pile by the pool house. While Frankie got the newspapers, I grabbed the skimmer pole and retrieved the case from the water, then filled it with the papers and threw it back in the pool.

"It still floats," said Frankie. "Now what?"

"Now we go back inside."

I retrieved the case again and dumped the papers out. Frankie took a towel from the pile by the pool house and dried it off as we headed back to the bungalow.

Inside, Frankie took the case back into the bedroom as everyone else looked at me. Finally, Lou asked the question everyone else was wondering about.

"Well?"

I shrugged my shoulders. "It floats."

"Okay, so it floats. Do you want to tell us what that means?" said Lou.

I saw a hint of a smile on Sal's mouth, "I think I know what Tom's getting at Lou, but I'm going to let him do it in his own good time. Right now I'm thinking it's been a long day and evening. I don't know about the rest of you, but I'm tired and I suggest that we sleep on what we've learned and renew our discussions in the morning when our minds are clearer. What do you think Tom?"

"That might not be a bad idea, but I have one more question. Julio, do you have Sam's old log books from when he picked you up?"

"No sir, they had all of the maintenance records in them so they went with the boat when he sold it."

"He sold the boat?" I said with surprise. "Sam didn't have *Greta* back then?"

"No, he bought her shortly after he found me."

"Who did he sell the old boat to?"

"To Senor Habermann."

"Gus? Sam sold his boat to Gus?"

"Yes sir."

"So then Gus should have the log books from early January 1959. Well, it's too late to talk to him now. I'll have to do that in the morning. Sal, I think you're right, it's a good idea to adjourn for tonight."

With that everyone realized how tired they were and what a long day it had been. I offered Lou a bed at my place but, looking at Amy, he declined so Sal called the front desk and got him a room at the hotel. Lou and Tony went back to headquarters to get Lou's car. I asked Frankie to take Amy and Julio out to my car and stay with them until I got there as I had something to ask Sal. I closed the bungalow door behind them.

"Sal, you and I both know that you know more about this than you're telling and I'm suspecting more than I'm telling."

"Well a good investigator doesn't give out all his information at once."

"Yeah, and neither do you," I said. "We need a one on one, just you and me, no boys, no Lou and, if I can manage it, no Amy."

"Lou won't be a problem, he's going back to Miami in the morning, but Amy might be difficult, she's sticking to you like glue."

"Yeah, well she senses a good story here and I told her to stick to me, at least until Andy's behind bars. I just hope his activities of earlier are it for the night and he doesn't try anything else.

"First thing in the morning I have to talk to Gus, find out if he has those log books and if he knows anything. The books he should have, but I doubt that he can tell us anything. You knew Sam and what it was like trying to get anything out of him and if Amy couldn't do that nobody could. After that, you and I need to talk."

Sal just kind of stood there looking at the floor like one does when one is thinking then he looked at me. "Okay, Tom. If it's just the two of us. I would be willing to take a chance with Amy there, but just you and I would be preferable. I need to tell you some things and I'm sure you have some questions. But there are some things I don't want Lou to know. He's a good cop and needs to stay that way."

"Yeah," I said. "He is. He taught me a lot."

"I know, and I don't want to put him in a position where he might have to tell others."

"Sal, if you're talking about the Feds, don't worry. I'm not going to tell them anything I don't absolutely have to. I'm not working with them."

Sal put his hand on my shoulder, smiled and said, "I know. That's why I'm willing to talk to you tomorrow."

"Yeah, tomorrow. How about 10:30? I'm going to want to know some things about Cuba. What went on there, what was your job in Havana, and who was involved; so be prepared to name names. It won't go beyond us. As for Amy, if I can't get her out of the room then we both make it clear to her that anything she hears is strictly off the record because I don't want anything to get out that may cause a problem for you."

"I appreciate that Tom, I really do, but you don't have to worry about anything. Now, I think you should get going. You still have to take Julio home. I'll see you tomorrow."

Sal opened the door for me and I stepped outside. Frankie looked up and headed back toward the bungalow, his eyes constantly checking the perimeter and the shrubbery and ignoring me as we passed. It occurred to me that the last few minutes, while Sal and I had been talking, was the longest time we'd been alone without one of the boys actually in sight. I realized then just how much Frankie and Tony watched out for Sal and how much they now trusted me with him. Maybe I was becoming one of the 'good guys' to them.

After we dropped Julio off and checked on Elyse, Amy and I headed for my house. She had been a little quieter than usual all evening and I thought she might be sulking, although why I couldn't say. I didn't think I'd done or said anything to upset her. Yet, how she would take the idea of missing out on my meeting with Sal the next morning was quite another thing.

Grabbing the bull by the horns, I asked her what was wrong and was relieved with her answer.

"Wrong? Nothing's wrong. I was thinking about the fire and wondering if my notes had survived."

"Not likely," I said, "especially if they were in your desk."

"Oh, I never keep anything important there. I guess that should be 'kept' now. I have a file drawer to which only Larry and I have keys. That's the way he has things set up with all his reporters, even the freelancers; so we can keep what we're working on separate and no one can poach from anyone else."

"Didn't Andy know what you were working on and oversee everything?"

"Only after we had our assignments from Larry or we cleared suggested stories with him. Larry is really a "hands on" owner and takes a real interest in what goes into the paper. Andy's job was more to ride herd on the staff, make sure deadlines were met and that all the t's were crossed, i's dotted, commas used. Oh, he was also involved in the layout of the paper. Whose story appeared on page 1, that sort of thing, although Larry would sometimes overrule him."

"I would imagine that rankled Andy. He's always seen himself as the one in control of things," I said.

"Maybe in his own little world. Although for the most part we didn't challenge him, all of us have, at one time or another, gone over his head to Larry over issues such as story placement or editing changes. Larry usually sided with us."

"Well then, why did Larry keep him on?" I asked. "I know that you can write ten times better than he can and could handle any editing matters with the other reporters. Surely there's someone else who could handle the deadline and printing issues."

"Sure there is. Eddie could do that part, but it is a full time job and he's still in school. I don't know why Larry's kept Andy on, but it's a moot issue. We don't have an office now, no typewriters, no desks. I just hope we still have our story files. Oh, damn Hardy. I had some good stuff in that drawer that I wasn't finished with." She turned to me and from the corner of my eye I could see the resolve in her face. "Tom, you better find him before I do or you're likely to have another dead body on your hands." And with that she slumped in the seat with her arms crossed and stared out the window until we got home.

In the house I risked raising the subject again. "I hope those file drawers you all use are fireproof, otherwise you're likely to have just a bunch of ash. You won't be able to find out until tomorrow and I'm not sure about that even. Since the fire was likely arson, I doubt that Chief Farto will let you in until he's finished his investigation, but I'll give him a call in the morning. If any of your files could have a connection to the case he'll probably let us in, at least to see if anything survived." We were in the kitchen. Amy perched on a stool while I pulled a bottle of milk out of the fridge and poured a couple of glasses for us. "What were you working on anyway?"

"I had several stories in various stages, but I had a line on something that I probably should have talked to you about. I'm not sure, but it could involve possible smuggling among some of the fishing captains. Mostly small stuff, but also marijuana and maybe other narcotics. I thought if I said anything to you too soon that you'd start a formal investigation. I didn't want to lose my story."

She took a sip of milk and licked the resulting mustache off. "I was going over my notes a couple of weeks ago, getting ready to start typing them up into something more coherent when I realized someone was standing behind me looking over my shoulder. At first, I thought it was Larry because he sometimes does that even though he can't read my handwriting. But it didn't feel right. When I looked up it was Andy. He had an odd expression on his face, like he'd been able to read and understand my notes and was, I don't know, scared. That's the only way I can describe it. It didn't really register then but with what's happened these last few days, I'm beginning to think he's involved in what I may have discovered. I don't have anything that would clearly implicate him but he must have thought I did, which would explain why he attempted to discredit me and burned down the newspaper."

She looked around and held up her glass. "Do you have any cookies to go with this?"

I pointed to the obvious cookie jar on the counter. "You said Larry can't read your handwriting, I know I have difficulty at times, but assuming Andy can, what were you working on? What was on those pages?" I asked.

Amy got up and looked in the jar. "It's empty." She leaned against the counter. "I've been trying to remember just what I had in front of me that day and what he could have recognized. I know I was checking some addresses and those I'm always careful to write clearly so maybe that's what he saw. I just wish I could remember what they were. One thing Tom, I'm beginning to wonder now if he's somehow connected with Ortega's group in Miami. It would make sense, he's bringing the stuff in here and getting it up to Miami and they're distributing it up there. Why else would Ortega come down here?"

She opened the breadbox and pulled out a piece of day-old Cuban bread. I got the butter and some jam out of the fridge and handed them to her and watched as she made a jelly sandwich. Some people just have to have something with their milk.

"Yeah," I said. "That's certainly a possibility. But as long as there was nothing that had upset the pipeline there'd be no reason for him to be here. If he is behind this, I don't think his visit was connected with anything Andy was doing. I think he was looking for something else."

Amy looked at me over her sandwich. "Are you going to tell me what?"

"Not yet. I'm not 100% sure. Like you, I'm putting things together in my mind. Puzzle pieces are starting to fit, but I need some details from Sal that, hopefully, I'm going to get tomorrow morning. The trouble is that I promised him it would be just the two of us because what he tells me could be somewhat sensitive concerning his position."

Amy started to protest and I held up my hand. "No. If he wants you to know, he'll tell you. Once I have what I need and determine that it would help your story and not hurt Sal if it got out, I'll tell you. Right now, though, I need this information to fill in some areas of the puzzle; he's agreed to talk to me, one on one, and he's coming by the office tomorrow morning about 10:30." I started putting things away for the night. "I figure that would be a good time for you to do some digging, see if you can remember what it was that maybe spooked Andy. Take one of the boys with you.

Then anything that I can fill you in on I will. Other than that, if what I tell you raises any questions you'll have to ask Sal. I think he's been about as open as he can be with everyone else around. Yes, he's connected with the mob, but there's something about him. He's not one of the bad guys, I hope."

"I'll think about it," she said, testily. "Let me sleep on it."

That night we both got a few hours of quiet sleep. We were too pooped to do anything else.

CHAPTER 19

Wednesday

In the morning, Amy and I showered and dressed, then stopped for coffee and Danish on the way to headquarters. I wanted to talk to Gus about the logbooks and of course Sal was due at 10:30.

When we walked in Gene handed me a few notes. One was from Sal confirming our meeting. The other two were from Mike and Dennis. Mike had volunteered to run Gloria to school this morning before going home to get some sleep. Dennis had called late from a pay phone on the dock to report that *Greta* was snugged up for the night and he'd be sleeping on board. He'd see me in the morning. In fact, Amy and I would be waking him up. I made a mental note to pick up coffee and cinnamon rolls.

Next I called Chief Farto to find out if the file cabinets had survived the fire and if Amy could have access to them. They had but the contents were still questionable. It would be the afternoon before anyone other than his investigators would be able to enter the site. I had to push Amy away when she tried to grab the phone and argue with Joe, which didn't make her any happier. After checking the desk and the morning reports, she and I went over to the harbor to see Gus.

We stopped at the Coffee Shack then walked over to *Greta's* berth to wake Dennis and give him his breakfast. His report was short. The trip back had been uneventful and, not being that familiar with the craft, he'd taken it slow until he'd figured out a good cruising speed. Leaving Dennis to his breakfast Amy and I went over to Gus's boat.

Gus wasn't aboard so we walked the couple of blocks to his house, a small Conch cottage with a front porch and door opening into a compact and tidy living room off of which were a small galley kitchen and short hallway leading to a single bedroom and bathroom.

We caught Gus just as he was leaving and explained our errand.

"Ja, Tommy," said Gus. "I bought *Inez* from Sammy. It was soon after he found Julio and yes, I have all the books. Come inside. I get them for you."

In the living room, Gus opened an old trunk that he apparently used as a sort of coffee table. Several of the distinctive books that Sam had preferred lay inside. They were dated on their covers and it was easy to find the last in the series. I thumbed through the one titled 'September 1958 – March 1959' until I found the correct page and started reading.

"Stayed previous night Boot Key Harbor to avoid weather. Running 13 kts., course 255° Atlantic side back to Key West. Encountered wreckage off Spanish Harbor Keys. Flotsam, some cases and ..."

I turned the page but the entry had changed. Two pages had been torn out. There was nothing further about the incident. Not even a mention of finding a survivor, description of the cases, or even an exact position. Flipping quickly through the rest of the book, I determined that no other pages were missing. Skimming the later entries found nothing more to be said about that day.

"Gus, have you ever read these?" I asked.

"Nein, Tommy. I was only interested in Sammy's maintenance records."

I returned to the book. Sam had kept his maintenance records and comments on a separate page from the log entries for each date and the record for that date was there. It was the page after the two missing ones. What had he written on those pages and who had torn them out?

"Gus, you read the maintenance records when you

bought *Inez*. Did you notice the missing pages?"

Gus shook his head. "I don't remember, Tommy. Probably, but the maintenance information was there so I was not interested in the rest."

"And these books have been in this trunk since you got them? No one else has had them or read them?"

"Ja, they been there all this time and nein, nobody interested in them. Tommy, those pages, they must have been missing when Sammy gave me the books. He must have torn them out."

"Yeah, Gus. That's what I'm thinking. The question is, why? What was on them that he didn't want anyone else to know? And, if he didn't want it known, why write it down in the first place?"

"Sammy ein gut Kapitan," said Gus, lapsing into his original German. "He was good captain. Always, he kept good records. It was habit for him. So he maybe wrote his entry before thinking about it?"

Amy hadn't said anything, but at Gus's comment she spoke up.

"Tom, you remember what Julio said last night about Elyse making it clear that she didn't want anyone to know about the circumstances under which Sam found him?"

"Yeah. What about it?"

"I'm guessing that Sam, being, as Gus says, a good captain, described it in his log entry to provide a record of everything that happened during the voyage. Perhaps Elyse convinced him to remove the entry or did it herself without Sam's knowledge."

It made sense, except that Elyse wouldn't have taken it upon herself to mess with Sam's logs. No, Sam removed them, but probably at her urging. Since it would have involved the safety of a child under her care, the son she'd never been able to have, she would have been most insistent.

"Yeah, Amy. You're probably right. Still, it would be nice to know what was on those pages." I put the book back in the trunk and closed the lid; I thanked Gus and the three of us walked out the door.

Back at the harbor, Gus and I stood on the dock and I could compare the two boats *Greta* and *Inez*. Amy sat on a bollard, taking notes. The two boats were very similar and I asked Gus about this.

"Ja, Tommy. Sie sind schwesteren, they are like sisters, not twins, but sisters. They came from the same yard."

I looked at the lines of Sam's boat and compared them with Gus's and noted that *Greta* was a little larger and sat lower in the water even though the fuel tanks were likely only half full. "If they're sisters, how come *Greta's* lower in the water? Don't they have the same engines?"

"Nein, Tommy. Ich habe petrol engines. *Greta* hat zwei grosse diesel, two big diesel engines. Sammy got her like that special because he wanted to be able to go further out and stay out longer for big fish. Mit der petrol that is limited. Diesel ist besser. Also, *Greta* has larger fuel tanks."

I knew she was a diesel boat. Sam had told me many years ago that diesel was better due to their simple operation. Also safer since diesel fuel doesn't explode like gasoline fumes can. I'd thought Sam had always had diesel engines. But then I'd also thought, until last night, that *Greta* was the boat Sam had had for years. It occurred to me then that, when I was younger and went fishing with Sam, he'd always opened the engine hatch to air out the bilge a good ten minutes before starting the engines, but I couldn't remember him doing that with *Greta*. He just turned the blowers on then started her up.

I turned to Gus who was packing tobacco in his pipe, "You bought *Inez* directly from Sam, didn't you Gus?"

"Ja, Sammy went to the boat yard in Miami to order *Greta*; then came back and put the "for sale" sign on *Inez*. I asked him how much. We agreed on the price and he signed her over to me right then."

"Did you pay enough to cover the cost of *Greta*?"

Gus struck a match, held it to the bowl and puffed. "Nein." The tobacco caught and I smelled the aroma on the air. "*Greta*, she cost much more. She was custom because of her engines. Sammy told me once he picked the engines first, then the boat. Without the engines, *Greta* not be what she is."

So, I thought, Sam had to have money on hand when he went to Miami. That fit with what I suspected from the discussion last night. I scratched the back of my head, another piece of the puzzle was trying to fit in place. "Gus, just off hand, how far can *Greta* go on a full load of fuel?"

"Ach, Tommy, Ich weis nicht. I do not know. Julio could tell you for sure, but my guess, she could probably make Jamaica," he said, pointing off across the water.

I looked out in the general direction of that island. Jamaica. That would mean going around the end of Cuba far enough to stay out of Cuban waters and avoid their patrol boats.

"Would she have to refuel to get back?"

"That would depend on wind and currents, Tommy. But I think, maybe nein, she might just make it if you were careful; but Sammy he would add fuel to be safe."

So she could make Jamaica, and maybe back without refueling. That meant Cuba would be no problem. "Thank you, Gus." I shook his hand. "Thank you very much."

Gus started back to his boat when Amy looked up from her pad and stopped him. "Gus, I have a question. Why did Sam name this boat *Greta*?"

"Ach, fräulein, das ist die namen von meine Mutter. That was my mother's name. My boat, Sammy's old boat, is named for his mother *Inez*. I agreed not to rename her so Sammy named his boat for my mother. Warum, why?"

"No reason, just a reporter's curiosity."

Frankly, I'd wondered about that too. I just didn't think it was important to the case so I hadn't asked. Amy, always the reporter, went beyond the cold facts and put a human face on the case, reminding me, if that was needed, just who's death we were investigating.

We left Gus to do what he had to and went over to *Greta* for another look around. The lab boys had finished before Dennis brought her back so I didn't have to worry about messing anything up. The officer on watch had found a folding chair and was relaxed in the shadow of the wheelhouse.

Wanting to test a hunch, the first thing I did was lift the hatch over the engine compartment and look. As many times as I had been fishing with Sam since I'd come back to Key West I had never looked at the engines. There were two of them and they were big. A pair of straight-six Allison's. How they shoehorned those behemoths into a hull not much larger than Gus's boat I couldn't figure out unless they built the hull around the engines; but then I'm not an engineer. There was barely room for someone to get in with them for service.

I followed the filler caps and, with a flashlight, stuck my head down the hatch and saw the fuel tanks; one on either side of the hull with just a squeeze space between. As far as I could see, they were connected which would make sense to maintain trim on the boat as the fuel ran down. If you ran one tank down first, you'd wind up with a list on the boat, which could make steering a straight course difficult. With the two tanks connected, they would drain evenly keeping the boat in trim port and starboard.

I couldn't see clearly enough to read the manufacturer's plate, but the tanks were big. At a guess I figured about 150-200 gallons each. The Coast Guard probably had their size in the registration records. Between the tanks and the engines there wasn't much room below deck other than the forward cabin. This boat definitely was not built for smuggling. There was no place to hide anything. Or so I thought.

I closed the hatch and took another look around the wheelhouse and cabin but didn't see anything that struck me as unusual. The only thing missing was the chart for Big Pine. Whoever took it had to be looking for something they thought might have been marked on it. If, as I suspected, it was the location where Sam found Julio, they were out of luck. Sam was nigh on to religious about keeping his charts updated even though he knew the waters around here better than anyone and there had to have been at least two updates since 1959.

Heading for the stern to hop off, I caught sight of a piece of fabric stuck on something just under the gunwale on the right side. It looked familiar. The color and texture were similar to the pants on our John Doe. I had difficulty thinking of him as Julio's cousin. Fortunately I had an envelope in my pocket and fished it out to put the piece of fabric in.

Amy asked, "What was that?"

I showed her the swatch. "If it matches the hole in his pants it definitely places our John Doe on board."

Back at headquarters Sal and the boys were chatting with Sally. Without argument, but with a scowl in my direction, Amy took hold of Frankie's hand and said "C'mon big boy. You're with me. Apparently I'm not wanted at this pow wow so let's get over to Records and put that education of yours to work."

Without a glance at anyone else, Frankie followed Amy like an adoring puppy dog. Tony watched them go and it looked like there was just a little hint of jealousy in his expression. It was amazing, after only a few days she had those two eating out of the palm of her hand.

Tony, with what I'm sure was a prior arrangement between him and Sal, said, "You need me, boss, I'm going across the street for a cup of coffee. Then I'll be here with Sally. I've got a couple of recipes she wants."

As Tony left he gave me the kind of look that clearly said 'If anything happens to the Boss, you're mine.' Not a pleasant thought.

Sal and I went back to the office and closed the door.

"Now, Tom," said Sal, taking his usual spot on the couch. "Where do we start?"

I sat behind the desk and pulled a pad close in case I wanted to take notes. "I think Sam's death is tied to his finding Julio adrift which happened because the kid was shanghaied by individuals trying to get themselves and their "valuables" out of Cuba immediately after the revolution. Let's start there. What exactly was your job in Havana? And yes, that's out of my jurisdiction so this is completely off the record."

Sal, relaxed and crossed his legs, unconsciously setting the crease in his trousers straight as he did so. "My job, to put it mildly and accurately, was, is and has always been, that of a financial advisor. Some would say a combination of an accountant and an investment counselor. You may not appreciate this, but the organization for which I work is first and foremost a business. They have officers, middle management and employees and their aim is to generate a profit. As a business, they need someone with financial acumen or savvy to see that that happens.

"I was sent to Havana by my employers to oversee certain financial issues involving investments they had in the entertainment industry that was being built there. As you know, a group of businessmen, for lack of a better term," Sal said with a wink, "seeing how Las Vegas had developed, had the idea to duplicate that success on this side of the country. However, not finding a location in the

United States receptive to their ideas, they looked to the islands of the Caribbean and settled on Cuba, specifically Havana, given its proximity to the States."

"By 'businessmen,' I presume you're referring to the likes of Meyer Lansky, Santos Trafficante and their associates."

Sal nodded. "Those and others. Anyway, my company had invested considerable sums in this venture and had an interest in seeing that their investment was properly managed and that they received the expected return. This was early 1953." I noted the date. "That being a difficult time for me, the company determined that a change in location was advisable. Having me on site would be to their advantage, so I was sent to Havana as their financial representative."

"Yeah. But gangsters from the U.S. had been involved in Havana gambling for some time by then. What was it that changed things and got you involved?"

"One man," said Sal as he leaned back, his hands behind his head. "Meyer Lansky. Havana's gaming industry was a free-for-all and was receiving bad press up here as being rife with scams, come-ons and illegalities. It was, in general, only interested in swindling and cheating its customers. President Batista realized that to save the industry and, not to put too fine a point on it, his own cut, from competition in other Caribbean countries, he had to clean up the action at home. So he hired Lansky as Cuba's gambling advisor. Whatever else Meyer Lansky may be, he knows how to run a business."

With little prodding from me, Sal continued his narrative and I learned more about the mob's investments and activities in Cuba and South Florida than I ever knew or could use in any case against any of the individuals he mentioned. I also learned more about Sal Donatello himself.

We finally got to the events of the revolution, specifically December 1958 and January 1959.

"I had come back to Miami the week before Christmas for a regular meeting with my company's directors," said Sal, sitting forward, both feet on the floor. "My plan had been to return to Havana on December 29th so as to be there for the New Years festivities. However, matters with my own businesses in Miami delayed that, fortunately. When word came that Havana had fallen my directors called for a complete audit of their position to determine their current and projected losses. Although the revolutionary government did not immediately close the casinos, there were restrictions on the movement of money and other assets out of the country."

"And you never went back?"

Sal shook his head. "No, Tom. I never went back. There was nothing to go back for."

"Did your people lose much?"

"No, not like others. Before any investment was made by my company, we did a full risk analysis and, although it was determined to be a project that had potential, there was enough concern given the governmental history of the island and the blatant fact that it could not proceed, much less succeed, without payoffs to Batista and his cronies. Accordingly, my recommendation had been that we keep only what was absolutely necessary in the country. Anything else was moved elsewhere."

"Switzerland?" I asked with a raised eyebrow.

"There and other safe locations," said Sal. "Because of that, my company came off better out of the venture than many others did. Mostly we just lost the infrastructure. The actual buildings and fixtures and what cash we had to keep on hand. The profits made over the years were safe. I had brought some back with me and the last delivery made it out on the last flight from Havana to Miami on December

30."

"I suppose you got all of your assets out before everything fell apart?" I said, smiling. Sal didn't strike me as the type of person who lost money.

"Well, to be honest, I didn't keep all that much in Cuba beyond what I actually needed. Even then I had my own business interests back here. But apart from that, when you get right down to it Tom, I tend to be somewhat fiscally conservative. I'm not going to keep my profits in the business that generated them if that business is, shall we say, questionable. Even with my restaurants in Miami, a certain percentage of the profits go back in to keep the business operating, but most of it is diversified. So, no, I kept very little in Cuba and I was not affected by the revolution other than to lose access to a city that I found interesting," he said somewhat wistfully.

"Anyway, on December 31, I was in Miami. Others weren't so lucky. When the revolutionists took Havana, they pretty much shut down all travel out of the country. Meyer and everybody thought they could work a deal with Castro and his faction similar to what they'd had with Batista, but that obviously didn't happen and it was a couple of years before some of them could get out."

"What about all of their investments? Surely they had a lot in there."

"Yes, they did," Sal nodded. "And they lost a lot. They tried to get money out. Some were successful; others weren't."

I leaned back in my chair and asked Sal the question I'd been holding back, but that I suspect he'd been waiting for. "Sal, who was 'Tiny'?"

"Ah, I've been waiting for that one," he said, smiling. "Al 'Tiny' Francetti. He worked for one of my directors, like Tony and Frankie work for me only different if you get my meaning," said Sal with a wink. "I said the company didn't lose too much, Tom. However, a couple of the directors had made their own positions in the venture and, well, let's just say they got greedy. I suspect that Tiny had been ordered to retrieve what he could and get it to Miami while things were still somewhat unorganized down there."

"Any idea how much he may have had?"

"Only a guess. Outside of the company finances there are only a couple of the directors for whom I provide personal investment advice and Tiny's boss wasn't one of them."

"You put him in the past tense. He's not around anymore?" I asked.

"No, he isn't. And not what you're thinking. He died two years ago, of natural causes. A heart attack in his sleep." He smiled. "His girlfriend was very upset when she woke up."

"Okay. But about your 'guess.' How much and would it fit in five suitcases?"

"How much? God only knows. Three, maybe five million. Knowing the individual involved, it could have been as high as ten. I just know that when Tiny failed to arrive, it was not safe to be around that director for some time."

I whistled. "Three to ten million. Dollars or pesos?"

"Dollars. And depending on the denominations and size of the cases, it could fit in one, more likely two or three if it were the higher amount, which would mean the other cases probably held clothes for Tiny and whoever he had with him."

I leaned back and looked at the ceiling trying to visualize what three to ten million dollars would look like. That was a pretty good chunk of change today in 1966 let alone back at the beginning of 1959. It would have been worth a nighttime voyage to get it back. Not only that, it would be one hell of a windfall for anyone who found it and certainly worth going after if someone thought it might still be out there.

"Sal," I said, slowly, sitting up and looking him straight in the eyes. "Assuming Sam retrieved the cases when he rescued Julio, what did he do with the money?"

Equally slowly and deliberately, Sal answered, "I don't know. Other than settling our bill, we never spoke about money. I might have mentioned some things in passing, but he never asked me for investment advice even though he knew that was my business."

"Well, I'm going to go out on a limb and make one suggestion. He bought a new boat." And I told Sal what I'd learned from Gus that morning.

"That is indeed a possibility," he said. "But even at what *Greta* must have cost, there would still have been a considerable amount left. What happened to the rest of it? Neither Sam nor Elyse have ever given any indication of wealth and the times I have been at their home I can't recall seeing anything to indicate unusually expensive purchases."

"Neither have I," I agreed. "And if he put it in the bank on this island, that kind of money, word would have gotten out. No, if it's still here, it's well hidden. But, knowing Sam, I'm betting that most of it isn't here."

Sal opened his mouth to ask a question when we heard the sounds of a scuffle and some shouting out in the squad room. While we'd been talking, Tony had finished his culinary discussions and had slipped silently into the room to take up what had become his usual position in the corner where he could see everything. With the noise from outside, he immediately, and I suspect out of habit, put himself between Sal and the door with his hand on his gun. Motioning him back, I opened the door and saw two officers holding a valiantly struggling Julio who, even though clearly out of breath, was putting up quite a fight to get loose.

Giving the officers a sign to let him go, I said, "Julio, calm down. What's wrong?"

"Gloria," he gasped. "She's missing."

"What do you mean 'missing'? Officer O'Neil said he dropped her off at school this morning and saw her go in. She should still be there."

"No, Senor Tom, not since about eleven. We always meet for lunch and she wasn't there and when I checked she hadn't been in her class before lunch. I found one of the girls in that class and she told me. I can't find her anywhere. I called her home but Davis said she wasn't there. Sir, Gloria would not leave school without a good reason."

I pulled Julio back into the office and sat him down next to Sal, then I called the high school and got the principal on the line. Explaining the circumstances I asked if there had been any message delivered for Gloria Reynolds. I waited while he checked with the secretary. Returning to the phone he told me that, about 10:00 that morning, the switchboard had received a call for Gloria that she was needed at the hospital. Some problem regarding her father. The principal had heard about the fire and thought Larry had been injured so he let her go.

I called the hospital and was told that Mr. Reynolds was not there and neither was his daughter. I asked if Eddie had received any visitors today and they said that only his mother was with him.

"Damn," I said hanging up. "I don't like this. I've got a really bad feeling."

"What?" said Julio. "Tell me. Where is Gloria?"

"I don't know." And before Julio could start in I said, "But I'm going to find her. You stay here." I pointed at Julio as I went out the door toward Sally's desk to give her the details for an urgent APB.

Sally was on the radio to our boys and I was on the phone to Dan Riley when Amy and Frankie came in. I told

Dan I would call him back.

"What's all the excitement?" asked Amy.

"Gloria's missing."

"Oh shit!" said Frankie to Amy. "You don't think…?"

I looked at him. "What do you know?"

"What Amy knows. We've been in records all this time, digging and it's jogged her memory."

I looked at Amy.

"Andy's got to have more money than he could possibly make in a lifetime working at the paper," she said. "He's in the records as an investor in properties all over town and even into the middle and upper keys. That's got to be how he's hiding and moving the stuff, a little at a time."

"What are you talking about?" I said. "Wait a minute. Come on back to the office. I want Sal to hear this too."

Back in the office Amy continued. "Andy has apparently been buying up real estate all over the keys. That story I told you I was working on when I caught him looking over my shoulder was about what was happening to some of the buildings around the island that looked like they were being bought up by speculators. I was going over a list of properties to check out. That must have been what Andy saw and it got him worried. I didn't know at the time that he was involved, but now I do. Given the number of properties, there's no way he could do it on what he makes at the paper and, as far as I know, there's no old money in his family."

I agreed with that. Andy did not come from money.

Amy sat in the spare chair and dug into her bag as she continued talking. "The only way he could have found the money to invest as heavily as the records indicate would be through other means and, in view of what we now know, I suspect that he's been involved in smuggling for some time. We just didn't know about it."

"I knew he'd been acting a bit stranger than usual the

last couple of years," I said. "But that heavy into it? What kind of properties are you talking about?"

She pulled a pad out of her bag and started flipping pages. "Mostly he's an investor in the companies that are listed as the actual owners."

"Well if he's just an investor how did you find out he's connected with them?" I asked.

Frankie chimed in from his corner. "Any company to be, or appear to be, legitimate must register with the county in which they operate. The registration for Monroe County is here in Key West and these companies are required to list their officers and major investors." Frankie looked at Sal who nodded in agreement. "He's not in all of them, but he's in enough; and in some of the initial filings, he's listed as an officer. I'm guessing he started them and had to list himself, but then, as things changed, he managed to get himself off the list. Unfortunately for him, though, a trail was still left."

"That's right, Tom," Amy said. "And it was Frankie who found it. As you said last night, Andy's not always as smart about things as he'd like people to believe."

"So do you have a list?" I asked

"As many as we could dig up," she said as she handed me her notes.

"Amy, I can't read this; it's in shorthand." I gave her the pad back.

"Sorry. Most of them are in town, some empty lots and small houses that are rented out. But there's one that sticks out, the old chandlery over on Stock Island, down Front Street."

"What? You mean Hathaway's?"

"Yes, that's the one. Right in the middle of the commercial area where all the big boats come in and out. Real easy for one of them to come in late and offload a few bales. All Andy has to do is stash them in there before he cuts them into smaller bundles for shipment up the chain."

Sal looked at me. "Are you thinking what I'm thinking?"

I picked up the phone, called the Sheriff's office again, and asked for Riley. "Dan, do you have anyone over by Hathaway's on Stock?"

"I think so. Why?"

"We may have a lead on Gloria's disappearance and I think Andy Hardy's involved. I'm hoping you have someone who can quietly cruise by, give it a look see, and get back to us. We still haven't found Sam's truck and maybe it's hidden over there. Make sure it just looks like a routine patrol, though. If Andy's there and has Gloria I don't want him spooked."

"Okay, but what does Hardy have to do with it?"

"He owns that building and may be using it to receive and hide smuggled goods, particularly drugs."

"You just said the magic word. Let me get on the radio and I'll call you back. I've already put the word out on Gloria, but now I've got cause to activate road blocks further up the highway just in case. That side of Stock is out of your jurisdiction, but I presume you're on your way?"

"Yes, as soon as I can round up a couple of our guys. Listen, Dan, I know that's your territory, but seeing it's Andy Hardy I think I'd better take the point on this. I know him better than you do."

"Agreed, I'll see you there." And he hung up.

I yelled out the door "Sally, are Mike and Dennis here?"

Dennis answered first, "Here, Lieutenant." After which Sally responded that Mike had just called and was on his way.

"Call him back and tell him to meet us at Hathaway's on Stock. Tell him not to give the deputies a hard time; it's their turf and they know we're coming. Andy may be holed up in there with a hostage. So no lights, no siren."

"Right," was all she said and turned to the radio.

Dennis asked, "Your car or mine?"

225

"Both," I said, and he headed out to the parking lot.

Sal and Tony were already on the move to their car. Julio had slipped out during the excitement. Amy and Frankie were waiting for me.

"Frank, why didn't you go with Sal?"

"'Cause I'm on assignment," he said looking at Amy. "You put me on her and that's where I stay until you say otherwise."

"Okay, you two come with me, but stay in the car when we get there." Amy started to protest and I told her, "This is an 'under the rock' time. No arguments."

We took the side streets to avoid traffic then crossed over the bridge to Stock Island, turned off onto Macdonald Avenue, took Maloney to 4th, and made a left onto Front Street where a Sheriff's deputy flagged us down. I pulled over and Jerry Timmins ran over to my window. "Dan is down the street. He wanted me to let you know that it looks like Hardy is there and that he found a blue pickup under a tarp. The plate matches Sam's. Mikey and Dennis are with him. That your Miami friends behind you?"

"Yeah, Jerry. Let them on through." I put the car in gear as he stepped back and gave me a thumbs up.

Hathaway's had been a ships' chandlery since way before my time, but had gone out of business some years ago when old man Hathaway, the last of his family, had died. Since then, the building had languished and served as a flop house for drunks and bums, a place for illegal gambling, even briefly as a bordello. Now, as far as we knew, it was empty.

The building paralleled the street and was a long, two-story wood structure with a shallow pitched roof. The upper floor was originally a sail loft and formed one large room running the length of the building. It could be reached by an outside stair on the backside as well as an inside stair.

Most of the main floor was a large storeroom that

Hathaway had used to hold merchandise for sale. At one end were a sales room, a small office and a couple of smaller rooms where ship owners and captains could meet and discuss voyages, negotiate costs and arrange for supplies from Hathaway and his sources.

The building was old. What paint had been on it was long gone. Clapboards were split and a few were loose and hanging, exposing old tarpaper underneath. Most of the windows were broken and boarded up and there were several entrances which could make it hard to corner Andy if he was in there.

We approached the building on foot, hiding among the clutter and accumulated piles of stuff, old crates, lobster pots, and such, common around boatyards. Jerry and Dennis maintained the roadblock at the head of Front Street and Dan sent a couple of deputies further down to make sure no one came up from the lower slips.

I detailed a couple of my guys to the far end of the building where they could cover both the street and watersides while Mike and I took the near end. If we had to get in quickly, it would be easier through the sales room doors. Also, Sam's truck was at that end and the engine was still warm. Andy had to be here with Gloria.

Despite my warning, Amy had not stayed in the car. I saw her head pop up from behind a pile of boards. I motioned to her to go back when Frankie's hand came up over her and pushed her back down behind the stack. At least he was with her and I could trust him to get between her and anything dangerous.

Turning back to the scene, I was looking around, checking positions when I saw a figure crawling over the roof of Hathaway's. It was Julio, but how he'd gotten here from the station I didn't know.

I thought he was waving to get my attention and I started motioning for him to get down and stay down when

I realized he was signaling me in semaphore. It'd been a while since I'd made use of that language, Sam had taught me years ago and must have taught Julio, but I was able to understand what he was telling me and I immediately signaled back my displeasure. I was too late. He'd already disappeared through a skylight into the sail loft. I waved Mike over.

"Julio's here," I said.

"Yeah. I saw him. You think he can do it?" Mike had read the message too.

"I hope so," I said. "Nothing we can do is going to get him out of there now."

In his message Julio had indicated that he was going inside to 'scout' and would report what he found from the sail loft window. I just prayed that he wouldn't try to be a hero and take on Hardy by himself when Mike tapped my shoulder and pointed.

Julio was in the window signaling. Andy was downstairs, most likely in the office. How he'd found this out I wasn't sure. Maybe he'd looked through cracks in the upstairs floor. I didn't think he'd had time to actually go downstairs, look around and get back up to the loft to signal.

I waved back a one-word question "Gloria?"

Julio's response was inconclusive "Not sure. Think so."

I again signaled for him to stay there and saw him disappear from the window. I looked at Mike and saw the same thing in his eyes that I felt: fear that Julio was going to do something rash. That dictated my next move.

Shifting position closer to the office door on the front of the building, I cupped my hands to my mouth and called out, "Andy Hardy, this is Tom Jackson. Come out now before anything happens to make your situation worse."

Mike and I waited for a reply and when none came I tried again.

"Andy, I know you're in there. I'm not here alone and

neither are you. Let Gloria go and we'll try to keep that part of this mess strictly local." As unlikely as that was to be, given that he would be facing State and probably Federal charges, I figured it was worth a try if it got him to consider releasing her.

I got a reply that essentially confirmed everything else.

"Nice try, Tom. Sorry, she's my ticket out of here."

"Maybe, Andy, but first you have to get past us. Dan Riley's already got roadblocks up between here and Card Sound. And I know you won't try it by water. You can't get out of the Keys so you may as well end this here before anyone else gets hurt. By the way, Eddie's going to be all right despite that crack on the skull you gave him."

I was trying to keep Hardy talking. Keep him focused on us outside in case Julio was moving around inside. I was operating on the assumption that Andy was armed and I didn't want him to hear any noises that would push him to sudden action.

"Yeah. Sorry I had to do that," said Andy. "He's a good kid. Reynolds should do right by him and his mother."

That stopped me a bit until I remembered Larry's behavior at the hospital and what Gloria had said about her father. Andy had a way of digging up things that people would rather stay buried.

"You want to apologize to Eddie, Andy, then come on out and we'll go see him. Maybe then you can also convince Larry of his responsibility."

"No dice, Tom," Hardy's voice came back. "What I want right now is your car and a clear path out of here."

I figured he wanted my car because it was unmarked and had the radio so he could listen in on what we might try to do to stop him.

"I can't do that Andy. You know that. Let Gloria go and I'll come in and we'll talk. Just the two of us."

That got a laugh. Not a happy one.

"Right, Tom. That's rich. I trade the daughter of one of this town's upper class for someone who can beat the crap out of me and who just wants to 'talk'? Sure. How stupid do you think I am? I'm coming out and I'm doing it with my 'insurance.' You try anything and you'll be the one who has to explain to Reynolds why he's lost his little girl."

"Andy, wait," I yelled. "You haven't killed anyone yet. Don't start now."

"Yeah, that's right. I haven't killed anyone yet. At least not directly. And if anything happens here, it won't be because I did it directly either. But you and I both know that won't make one damn bit of difference."

As he talked the sound of his voice changed, like he was moving through the store toward the back. There was more room on that side of the building as well as more piles of crap to hide behind in an effort to escape. Telling Mike to stay where he was, I moved along the end of the building to where I could see the double doors on the back. Passing a window I thought I detected movement inside, but I couldn't tell if it was Andy or Julio. I hoped Julio was hunkered down somewhere safe.

From the corner of the building, I could see the other end and the officer I had positioned there. Motioning to him to keep his position and watch the door, I moved around a pile of debris as one side of the door opened just wide enough to let Gloria ease out. She caught sight of me and with a motion of her head as if to move a stray hair out of the way and a slight smile, she indicated Andy's approximate position. She wasn't gagged but her hands were behind her back and I assumed they were tied.

As Gloria moved away from the door, Andy's hand appeared holding a gun pressed against the base of her skull. It was his right hand, which indicated that he had hold of her with his left, his dominant hand. If Gloria could get some space between them, Andy would have to change hands for any hope at an accurate shot. Right now, though, the only thing we could do was wait. Andy was calling the plays in this game.

Hardy moved himself and Gloria away from the door toward a path through some debris. I stood out from my hiding place with my hands in the air where he could see them. I'd also unholstered my gun and left it in clear sight on the crates I'd been behind. I wasn't taking any chances that Andy might misinterpret my moves.

"Andy," I said with my eyes on Gloria's face. "I'm not going to start anything, but this is your last chance. If you insist on running, my car is over there." I tossed the car keys to his right while I glanced in the opposite direction hoping Gloria would take the hint. The position of the keys also increased the likelihood of him having to release his hold and either switch hands or awkwardly reach across to retrieve them.

It had to be a reflex action on his part, because Andy started to bend over to pick up the keys with his left hand at which point several things happened very quickly.

As Andy bent over, he let go of Gloria, the gun came away from her head, which she felt, and she started to move in the opposite direction. Andy began to straighten up, moving the gun from his right to his left hand. At the same time the other side of the double door burst open as Julio flew out and hit Andy, sending him rolling during which his gun went off. Julio screamed and grabbed his leg, which was enough distraction to let Andy get up and start running. Somehow he'd been able to grab my keys.

Before anyone could get a bead on Andy I yelled, "I want him alive!"

Then I heard what sounded like a cannon go off right behind me. A blossom of red exploded at Andy's right knee and he went down screaming. I looked around and saw Tony holding his .45.

"You said you wanted him alive," Tony calmly intoned. "Well, he's alive, but he's not going anywhere."

"Mike, call an ambulance, tell them we've got two down."

Amy, Sal, Frankie and Tony headed for Gloria, who was already at Julio's side, as Dan and I made a beeline for Hardy. Andy was out and when I saw his knee I realized why. He wouldn't be walking anytime soon, but as soon as he woke up he was going to be in a world of pain. A .45 slug makes a big hole going in and an even bigger one coming out. My guess was that Andy didn't have a right knee anymore.

"He may be alive, but if we don't stop that bleeding he won't be for long," I said to Dan as I started to pull off my shirt.

"I'll get the medical kit from my car," said Dan.

I packed my shirt around what was left of Andy's knee and used my belt as a makeshift tourniquet. He started moaning, then, as consciousness returned, he started screaming again. Even though he was now a known criminal and had tried to harm Amy as well as others, I couldn't forget that we'd known each other just about our entire lives, so I did my best to try to calm him down until Dan returned. Then we proceeded to use our first aid training to bind him up as best we could until the ambulance got there.

During this time, I looked over to where everyone else was huddled over Julio and prayed I wouldn't be making another bad call to Elyse. I couldn't see anything until Frankie and Tony stood up; then I breathed a sigh of relief. Julio was sitting up against Sal, his eyes open and Gloria's skirt wrapped around his left thigh. She was wearing Sal's jacket in its place.

With Andy's knee bound and a proper tourniquet around his thigh, I put a pair of cuffs on his wrists just to be sure and turned my attention to Tony.

"Couldn't you have used something smaller?" I asked. "I'll be surprised if he doesn't lose that lower leg."

Looking a little surprised at my tone, he replied, "Hey, it's all I've got. It's what I'm comfortable with. Besides, he's scum and deserves to be cleaned out."

"Maybe. But that's for the courts to do. Not us."

Tony grumbled, giving me a little more insight into his make-up, "Yeah, that's why I'm not a cop."

"That's probably a good thing," I agreed. "However, right now, you're working for and with one." I pointed to Andy and said, "Keep an eye on him and remember I want him alive."

Leaving Tony and Andy, I went over to Julio and checked Gloria's work. I was relieved to find out that Julio's wound wasn't serious. The bullet had gone clean through the muscle of his thigh without hitting anything major.

I was complimenting her skills when I heard Andy scream and looked over to see Tony fiddling with his bandage.

"Tony, what are you doing?"

"Nothing Lieutenant, just checking the tourniquet, it's a little loose."

"Well leave it alone, the ambulance is coming," I replied hearing the siren in the distance.

Andy screamed again and I went back over to him but he'd passed out. Tony stepped over to the other group and said something to Sal who, I noticed, visibly stiffened and made a brief movement of his hand which caused Tony to stand up and back off. I didn't have a chance to find out what that was about because the ambulance arrived and I got caught up in making sure that Andy was taken care of and had adequate guard. After all he was my prisoner, I was responsible for him and I needed answers from him.

A second ambulance rolled up to take charge of Julio.

After conferring with the medics, who confirmed that Doc Elliott had been alerted, they loaded him into the back and left for the hospital. Gloria insisted on riding with him but not before returning Sal's jacket and wrapping a gurney sheet around herself.

While waiting for the ambulances, Julio had given me a quick appraisal of what he'd seen in the warehouse while he was listening. With the injured now in proper hands, Dan and I went in for a look ourselves.

The storeroom looked more like a barn stocked for the winter. Bales of material were stacked floor to ceiling. I cut a hole in one and handed some of the contents to Dan who took a brief sniff, looked around and gave a low whistle.

"Holy shit, Tom. If all these bales turn out to be what this is, there's no way we'll be able to keep this local. The Feds will want in. They're going to want to know his channels, who's been bringing it in and where it's been going. And God forbid there's any stronger stuff in here. No doubt about it, whether he loses his leg or not, Andy Hardy's going away for a long time."

"I've got a few ideas on his channels. Right now we'd better secure this building, get some forensics, and then move all this to a city or county warehouse."

"I suggest the county facility," said Dan, looking around again. "I don't think the city has room. Besides, it's in our jurisdiction."

"Yeah," I agreed as we walked out into the sunlight. "You guys get this one."

Amy had gone with Gloria and I'd assumed that Sal and the boys had either followed them to the hospital or gone back to their hotel or maybe to the Torres house to let Elyse know what had happened. After securing the site, Dan and I went back to town together.

It wasn't until later that I found out what Tony had gotten out of Andy and what it meant to Sal.

Dan and I stopped at the hospital, and we were told that Doc Elliott had seen Julio and pronounced the wound clean. It had been redressed and Julio was now resting comfortably with Gloria at his side. We could talk to them later. Andy was being prepped for surgery and wouldn't be available for at least 24 hours. I called headquarters, gave Sally a quick rundown of the events and told her to send someone over to 'babysit' Andy and set up a rotation on him until he was released to the county lockup, which Doc told me would be a while. So, at least for the time being, everyone on the force, and probably some of Dan's boys, would get at least a few hours of easy duty.

Amy wasn't there. I didn't know if I was surprised at that or not. She'd left a note letting me know that, with Andy now out of action, she'd gotten a ride home from one of the nurses so she could start writing. Her note didn't say which "home" and I found myself hoping it was mine but the word that formed in my head was actually 'ours.'

With everything settled at the hospital, Dan and I went back to KWPD headquarters to work on our reports. He said we had better coffee.

It was early evening by the time we finished. Dan and I sat back and he looked at me and asked, "What about Donatello and his boys? We're going to need a statement from that gorilla who shot Andy."

"Yeah, I'll make arrangements for that with Sal for the morning. I can have them meet us over at your place unless you want to come here,"

"I'm easy either way," he said, waving one hand.

I picked up the phone and buzzed out to the outer office and Gene picked up. "Gene, call the Lodge and let Mr. Donatello know that Dan and I are going to need to see Tony in the morning to get his statement for the record."

I turned back to Dan, "Tony's statement is really a formality. I've pretty much covered it in my report."

235

"Yeah I know, but you know that if we don't have it someone's going to question it."

The phone rang and I answered. "Sorry, Sir," Gene said. "Mr. Donatello's checked out."

That was a surprise. Sal hadn't mentioned anything about leaving. "Checked out? What do you mean checked out? Where'd they go?"

"Didn't say, sir. I guess it would be back to Miami."

"Okay, Gene, never mind. I'll have to get a hold of them some other way."

Dan looked at me, "Want me to put out the word? Have them stopped?"

I looked at the clock. "Too late now. They're probably back in Miami by now. I'll call Lou in the morning and see what I can find out. But it is interesting. I wonder why they high tailed it out of here so quickly?"

Dan leaned back, stretched and stifled a yawn. "Well this has been an interesting day, but you know something? I'm tired. I think I'm going to pick up a pizza and go home."

"Yeah," I said. "I guess I'll go home too. Find out if I still have a roommate."

Dan stopped at the door and looked at me. "You know something, Tom. I don't think it's going to be easy to get rid of that one and, frankly, I don't think you should try. Set your hook, my boy, and reel her in. She's a keeper. But if you do toss her back, let me know. I may go fishing." And he walked out, leaving me wondering.

CHAPTER 20

It had been a long day; an exciting day; and I suddenly realized I was tired. Here it was, barely Wednesday evening. The case had just started Saturday morning and we now knew who had killed Sam and, most likely, why. We'd put the kibosh on what appeared to be a significant drug smuggling operation and in the process successfully resolved a kidnapping. It was likely that the smuggling was linked to those responsible for Sam's death, but not in the way that most people would expect. There were still a few questions to be answered, but they could wait until morning.

Before following Dan out the door, I made a call to the hospital. Andy was out of surgery. As I'd expected, he'd lost his right leg. The surgeon could do nothing to save the knee and, apparently, there wasn't even enough to let him fuse the leg through the knee. Besides, he reasoned, where Andy was going, by the time he got out there should be some advances in prosthetics. In the meantime, the State would fix him up with a peg leg and it would guarantee him easy jobs in prison.

Eddie had been released from the hospital and Larry and Gloria had taken him and his mother home with them. Someday I might know the whole story there, but a spare part of my brain was slowly putting things together and doing some rough calculations. I had a feeling that in the not to distant future there'd be a wedding in the Reynolds household and a family would be complete.

As for Julio, Doc Elliott was keeping him overnight and had set up an extra bed in his room for Elyse, whom Hector had brought over as soon as Doc had called to tell her what had happened. I suspected Doc wanted to keep more of an eye on her although I got the impression that she was bearing up remarkably well what with all that had happened the last five days. That was another interesting pair.

Doc and Sam had been friends for years and while Doc's wife was alive, the two couples had met regularly for card games. The women went to bingo at the church together and cooked for social events while the two men served. It had been Sam and Elyse who were with Doc when Andrea had finally succumbed to the cancer that he had tried everything to stem. Without that friendship I don't know if Doc would have made it through that period. Now with Sam gone, I was sure that Doc would be doing the same thing for Elyse and Julio. Would that be a new family formed from the remnants of two others? Only time would tell.

And what of the next generation? Julio and Gloria. They were going to have to tread their path carefully. I hadn't seen Larry since the fire and didn't know how much, if at all, today's events had changed his outlook. He could be hard headed and, as they say, old habits die hard. However, I had faith in his daughter. Gloria knows her father and has a good head on her shoulders. If anyone can get him to see things her way, she's the one. And she'll have Doc and Elyse on her side as well as me and Amy.

And what about us? I hadn't spoken to Amy since we were in the car on the way out to Stock Island earlier. My last glimpse of her had been when she got into Julio's ambulance with Gloria and by the time I got to the hospital she'd left. Would I find her at Dad's typewriter when I got home or had she gone back to her place now that Andy was no longer at large? We'd crossed a threshold this weekend and I knew that, from my position at least, we couldn't go back to just being the cop and the reporter that we'd been before. At least I couldn't go back. The question was could we go forward? Should we go forward? Hell, I didn't even know if she wanted to go forward or if we were at an impasse.

What I did know was that I was hungry and tired and, with everything pretty much wrapped up, I could go home and count on a good night's sleep as long as the town stayed quiet.

I turned the light off, closed the office door and walked across the quiet, semi-dark squad room to the reception desk. Saying good night to Gene, I left the building, crossed the street for a sandwich, and went home.

As I turned onto my street, I found myself looking for Amy's car until I remembered that she was still in need of new tires.

I pulled into my driveway. The only illumination I saw was the porch light, which was on a timer. So that was no surprise. But I was disappointed when I opened the front door and didn't hear the distinctive sound of keys hitting paper on that old Royal.

Passing through the house to the kitchen with my sandwich, I stopped at the refrigerator, pulled out the lone carton of milk, gave it a sniff, and poured the contents down the sink. It would be black coffee in the morning. I took a beer and my sandwich out to the patio and sat under the stars.

I took a sip from the beer and started to get moody. Not an unusual occurrence at the end of a case. The last time I'd sat at this table was in the sunshine of Sunday morning, which brought me back to all of the questions about Amy and me and only served to make me feel gloomier that she hadn't been here.

"Thomas Jackson, you are an A number one, first class, Goddamn fool," I said to myself. "Here you are. You've spent the last few days being a 24-hour guardian to a woman who, by all rights, should be able to take care of herself. Now that there's no need for that, you're angry because she wasn't here to meet you at the door, get you your slippers and, in general, take care of you. Put your head on straight. She's not that type and neither are you. Besides, this case isn't done yet. Where's the money?"

I'd told Amy that sometimes in a case it helped to just talk things out. Now I was doing it with myself and had succeeded in reminding myself that, "no, this case isn't over yet." It wouldn't be until we found the money. That thought got my head straight. Amy and I would have to wait until we saw each other again which, depending on what she was writing, could be tomorrow or could be next week.

While she was collecting information, interviewing subjects, doing the necessary research, she could turn it off and do other things like laundry, grocery shopping, having an affair. Once she started writing, though, we could have a hurricane and an earthquake together and it wouldn't register with her. Not until she was finished writing would we be able to sit down and discuss our future. Besides, I still had unanswered questions that needed a clear head in the morning.

I went to bed.

The clock said 3:15 AM. I had awakened from a strange dream where I was swimming, not in water, but in dollar bills. I lay there listening for what had awakened me, but I didn't hear anything. Quietly, I got out of bed and moved through the house alert for anything out of the ordinary but nothing presented itself. Concluding that it must have been some passing sound at just the right time in my dream, I went back to bed and thought about the images that had been playing in my mind. Money, swimming, no one else, just me. Then I remembered there had been a boat in the background. Not any particular boat, just a boat.

Money, boat and swimming. The swimming didn't make any sense, but the images of money and a boat only led me to one conclusion. The money had to be on *Greta*.

The question was where? Sam had to have had a hiding place, a smuggler's hold that only he knew about and that was big enough for the contents of two suitcases given Sal's estimate of how much there could have been. But where was it? The lab boys had been all over that craft and hadn't reported finding anything. Then, of course, they were concentrating on evidence related to two killings. They weren't looking at the construction of the boat.

Tomorrow, today rather, I thought looking again at the clock, I was going to go over *Greta* from stem to stern and I rolled over and went back to sleep.

CHAPTER 21

Thursday

Thursday dawned clear with the promise of a high temperature in the 80's and no rain, normal for our island at this time of year. A slight breeze rustled the palm trees around the house and reminded me that I needed to get the dead fronds trimmed before they fell on someone. In the meantime that breeze would keep the humidity bearable.

After a shower I was ready to solve the final puzzle. Where on *Greta* had Sam hidden the money?

I stopped at headquarters and first placed a call to Lou to bring him up to date. Having been, technically, AWOL from his department, he'd left early yesterday and was surprised when I told him that Sal and the boys had left shortly after we collared Andy.

"I thought they'd at least stay for Sam's funeral," Lou said. "But I'll give him a call and deliver your message concerning Tony's statement. Let me know if you get anything from Hardy."

"Sure Lou, and thanks," I said and hung up.

I arrived at the harbor and picked up a coffee at the Shack where I learned that Gus had taken a charter out early that morning. I was disappointed since I'd wanted to talk to him. His statement that his boat, *Inez*, and *Greta* were sisters, built at the same boat yard, made me think he would be the best one to have with me when I went over *Greta*. Sisters can be different, similar or twins and I wondered how similar *Inez* and *Greta* were. Gus had said they weren't twins, but it would have been helpful to know what the differences were. Fortunately, his charter was only a half-day so he should be back around noon or 1:00 p.m., which gave me a couple hours to go over *Greta* by myself. If

I didn't find anything, then I could always do a comparison of the two boats.

At *Greta's* slip, I sat on a bollard and just looked at her, letting her lines imprint on me like I never had before. All the times I'd been on her with Sam, I'd never really paid attention to her shape, her construction, where things were placed. To me she was just a boat, a conveyance. Now she was something different. A riddle to be solved. A puzzle with a hidden piece. And somewhere on board was either an empty hiding place or, just maybe, a lot of money.

I finished my coffee, then boarded on the starboard side. She was stern in to the dock with a finger pier on either side. Back in the creek, Frankie and I had begun our first investigation at her stern. This time I decided to start at the bow, but first I climbed the ladder to the flying bridge and gave it the once over even though there was clearly nowhere up there to hide anything.

I returned to the main deck, went forward and began a board-by-board search. Knocking here, poking there, looking for anything loose or moveable or out of place. I pulled on every cleat, every stanchion as I moved aft. I checked every seam for a gap, which would indicate a hidden hatch or panel. The only ones I found were the obvious hatches over the engines and the fuel tanks. There was nothing unusual outside so I turned my attention inward.

The wheelhouse was enclosed on each side and had a weather curtain that could be rolled down to block spray coming in from the rear deck area. Across the front were a series of lockers, including the chart locker, in the middle of which was the access to the lower cabin. I opened every locker, knocked on every door, wall, bulkhead, every hard surface listening for any hollowness. Using my flashlight I peered into every dark corner looking for secret latches or switches. Nothing.

The cabin below deck was still a mess. To make sure I didn't miss anything, as I went around I tossed trash into a box and, in the course of my search, succeeded in cleaning up the space. Then I went through the collected trash looking for clues. Again, nothing. I checked everything, opened every locker, every cabinet, every drawer. I thumped and knocked until my knuckles were sore. Checked every cushion and if their covers were removable, I removed them and checked the stuffing. I checked the galley and the head. Nothing.

I sat on the bench along the port side that also served as a bunk, elbows on my knees, chin in my hands, trying to think of what to do next. I couldn't really tear *Greta* apart, not without something more to go on than what I had. Technically the boat belonged to Elyse and I had to eventually return it to her at least in the condition it was in when found.

Greta rocked as another boat went by, a little too fast I thought judging by the feel. That or the mooring lines needed adjusting. But as the angle of sunlight coming in through the portholes and the main hatch changed, I caught sight of something just slightly different on the bulkhead by the hatch up to the wheelhouse. The next second, as the other boat's wake passed and *Greta* settled down, it was gone, but I'd marked the place where it appeared to be.

On either side of the hatchway were decorative rondels the same dark mahogany color as the paneling. Simple round wooden disks, about 3 inches in diameter with carvings of an eagle design, that looked like they were glued to the bulkhead. In the changing light, though, the one on the left had looked slightly different. I'd pressed on them as I went around the cabin methodically pushing and pulling on anything that wasn't flush but they hadn't moved and nothing had happened so I'd moved on. Now I took another look.

In the beam of my flashlight the one on the right didn't look any different. I pressed on it again but it didn't move. The only thing I felt was a very slight flex in the paneling of the bulkhead. No, this one was solid.

I turned my attention to the one on the left. Now in the beam of my flashlight I could see what the quick ray of sunlight hitting just right had revealed. A short arc, a very slight scratch in the paneling closely adjacent to the disk. I pressed it again slowly, gently, feeling for the paneling to flex like the other one had done. It didn't.

Cupping my fingers, I tried to grasp the edges of the disk. It was just thick enough to give me some purchase and I noticed that the edges of my fingernails were against the paneling at exactly the same distance from the disk as the scratch. If I'd been a cartoon, I'm sure a light bulb would have gone on over my head. I tried turning the disk to the right. It didn't move so I turned it to the left. Stiffly, it moved a quarter turn and I heard a very faint click. Something had released.

I was standing on the steps to get a closer look at the rondels. Just three short steps that gave access between the level of the cabin and the main deck through the hatch in the wheelhouse. When I stepped back down to the cabin deck, those steps moved as a single unit, very slightly forward and upward, their edges barely clearing the bulkhead and the deck to which, ordinarily, they appeared securely attached.

Carefully, I got down and inspected the gap looking for anything that might indicate a booby trap. Seeing nothing, I gingerly lifted the steps further. Surprisingly they moved very easily and quietly further outward and upward until I could see the mechanism of pivoting arms and springs, which served as a counterweight. The balance was so good I could lift the steps with one finger and they stayed where I left them.

Raising the steps to their full height revealed a framed opening in the deck about twenty-four inches long and eighteen inches wide. A panel mounted to slide under the deck provided a closure and covered whatever was underneath. With mounting excitement I slid the panel open and found myself looking into a space about a foot deep and what looked to be about three feet square. At a rough guess I figured 20-25 cigar boxes would fit, but not two standard suitcases. You wouldn't even be able to get them through the opening. This was Sam's smuggler's hold but it sure as hell didn't have millions of dollars in it.

There was something in there, however. A package wrapped in an oilskin. I pulled it out and unwrapped two metal boxes, each about a foot wide, 10 inches deep and 5 inches high, like bank or cash boxes. They were locked and I didn't have the keys.

I wanted to know what was in those boxes, but I didn't want to damage them. I tried the keys on my key ring. Some went in but none of them turned. The original keys were probably on Sam's ring, which was with his effects at the morgue unless they'd already been picked up. Sam would have had a spare set but, with what was likely in these boxes, I don't think he would have kept them at home. Then I remembered he kept a spare set of boat keys on board. I went into the galley and looked in the dry goods locker. There they were, behind the coffee, and two of them looked like they would fit the boxes.

Sure enough, and I got them right on the first try.

Sitting there at the cabin table with the boxes unlocked but the lids still closed, I wondered what I would do if the contents were other than what I thought they would be. Yes, if the boxes held cash, I would have to report it, but it would eventually be turned over to Elyse since there was no evidence to show it was other than Sam's property, now hers. However, if the boxes contained anything else, and since yesterday that possibility had crept into my mind, that would mean an investigation which would necessarily involve both Elyse and Julio. An investigation I would not want to undertake.

I breathed a sigh of relief when I lifted the lids.

I counted the bills, put them back in their boxes, locked the lids and pocketed the keys.

Also in one box was a small book which made interesting reading and answered a lot of questions. That I also put in my pocket. But only one other person would see it.

I closed the sliding panel, pushed the steps back down and heard another slight click of the latch as it snapped into place. Once I knew what Julio and Elyse decided to do with *Greta*, I would tell them about her little secret.

I picked up the boxes, then went up the steps and out onto the deck into the afternoon sun. I hadn't realized how much time had passed, but it was clearly after one o'clock. Gus was back and was washing down his boat. I waved to him as I passed, but didn't stop to talk. I would tell him the story later.

Back at headquarters, I taped the keys to their respective boxes and deposited them in the safe, making an entry into the property log at the same time: "Property Description: Two (2) metal lock boxes and keys, contents $55,000.00 cash. Owner: Elyse Torres."

I decided to go home and trim my palm trees.

CHAPTER 22

Friday

Friday morning Doc Elliott called to let me know I'd be able to talk to Andy that afternoon. I called Dan and Steve Barnes and asked them to meet me at the hospital at 2 p.m. Both agreed. Dan and I had sent Steve copies of our reports so he knew the situation.

It had been more than 24 hours since I'd seen or heard anything from Amy. Writing or not, I decided to take the chance and called her. She didn't answer her phone which could mean any number of things. She could be ignoring it; she could be asleep having worked for the last day and half straight; she might not be there although, with the *Current* a smoldering ruin, I didn't know where else she would go to work. I figured I would try again later. With Andy out of the way, I wasn't worried about her safety.

Andy was sullen and, obviously, in pain. Tented blankets were over where his right leg should have been. The surgeon had taken it off just above the knee.

I opened my mouth to speak. He glared at me and pointed to his leg. "Look at what you did to me, you son-of-a-bitch. I'm done for, ruined. I oughta sue you and this city for everything you both have."

At this, Steve Barnes said, "Mr. Hardy, you won't be suing anybody because, pardon the observation, you won't have a legal leg to stand on. We, on the other hand, have you on multiple charges including assault with intent to commit bodily harm, kidnapping, arson, narcotics trafficking and, possibly, murder."

"Murder?" Andy yelled. "What the hell are you talking about murder. I didn't kill anyone. Who the hell am I supposed to have killed?"

"He said 'possibly,'" I said. "We're still waiting for the final reports on ballistics and your fingerprints. But if we get a match to your gun from the slugs we pulled out of his body, then your victim would be one Juan Canterra, a cousin of Julio Torres. I'm also having your fingerprints checked against some we found on Sam Torres' boat and, if they match, we may be adding an accessory charge in the killing of Sam.

Andy laughed, "My fingerprints? On a boat? You know better than that. I hate boats and you know why. There's no way my prints are there." A slight catch in his voice and the way his eyes were shifting from me to Steve to Dan and back told me he was bluffing. "As for Canterra, I don't know any Juan Canterra and I never shot anybody anyway."

"So you're telling us that Jaime Ortega, alias Jimmy O, shot his own man, then took the time to tie him to a weight and throw him into the channel not far from a property you own and where we found you holding a young lady against her will? Why would he want to do that?" Dan asked.

"That's a good question," I said.

"One I'd like to know the answer to myself," said Steve.

"Listen, Andy, all we have to do is put you near Sam's boat and we can make a case against you for his murder and likely Canterra's. You've already got a reputation that would make most people on these islands happy to put you away for a lot less." I pointed at the tent. "And with a murder conviction, missing a leg would be the least of your worries." I looked at Dan and Steve who both nodded in agreement.

Steve added, "Know this Mr. Hardy, given the circumstances, we would ask for the maximum penalty and I am reasonably sure we would get it."

Andy was looking scared, like the cornered rat he was, his eyes jumping between the three of us.

"We're still waiting for an answer, Andy," I growled. "Why would Ortega shoot his own man?"

With the three of us standing over him, pressuring him, and before he could stop himself, Andy screamed, "Because Jimmy's a certifiable nut case. Juan fucked up and killed Sam and Jimmy pulled out his gun and shot him and woulda shot me if ...." Then, realizing that he'd just admitted to being involved in the whole thing, Andy flopped back onto his pillow and said "Oh, shit. I'm screwed."

Like most weasels, Andy couldn't take it when it was dished out to him.

I pulled a chair over and sat down so that I was now eye level with him. "Now, Andy. Be smart for once and tell us everything."

For the next hour, Andy Hardy sang like the proverbial canary while we asked questions and took notes. He told us how, when he was at school in Miami, he'd gotten stuck owing gambling debts to Jimmy O's organization. Not being able to pay them, he was offered a choice of significant bodily injury or work off his debts by going back to the Keys and serving as their contact between smugglers bringing the stuff in and the mainland. They figured his knowledge of the island chain would help more of their merchandise get delivered. It would become his job to receive the incoming shipments, repackage the stuff if necessary and arrange for transportation up the Keys to Miami. Later on, Juan Canterra became his Miami contact.

Although I doubted it, Andy claimed to have come up with the idea of buying up old and abandoned properties through the islands to use as staging areas, meeting places and, when necessary, overnight accommodations. Everything had been working smoothly until he saw Amy's partial list, which included some of his properties and he'd gotten spooked. He thought she was already on to him, so he decided to try and discredit her. When that didn't work and he couldn't get into the file cabinet, he decided to burn the building thinking that would take care of the paper and the stuff in his desk.

But he insisted he had nothing to do with Sam's murder or Juan's.

"I swear," he said. "The only time I was near that boat was when Ortega pulled up behind the warehouse Friday night. Sam wasn't on it, but Canterra was and he was already dead. Ortega was in one of his crazy moods. I think he'd been drinking. He was waving his gun around and I thought he was going to shoot me. I tied Canterra's body to some cinder blocks and set it up so all Ortega had to do was push him overboard when he wanted. I thought he'd wait until he was out in the ocean. I didn't know the crazy son of a bitch was going to dump him in the channel."

Dan asked the next question. "Why did he shoot Canterra in the first place?"

"As near as I could figure from Ortega's ramblings, Canterra had been asking Sam some questions and didn't like the answers he got so he hit Sam and killed him. Ortega went off and shot Canterra. He would do things like that. If you did something to get Ortega pissed off, he was likely to put two in you right then and there without blinking an eye."

"That fits with what I've learned about Jaime Ortega from Lou and Sal," I said to Steve and Dan and turning back to Andy I asked, "So why didn't he dump Canterra over with Sam?"

"How the hell should I know?" said Andy. "I wasn't there. I don't try to figure out why Ortega does things. I just try to keep him from doing them to me. Hell, that's the only reason I snuck round to Sam's and took the charter book, because Ortega told me to and I knew what he'd do if I didn't."

"Where's the book now?" I asked.

"In the channel," replied Andy, sullenly. "I tossed it out the window going over the bridge."

"I, for one, would like to know why Ortega and Canterra were down here in the first place," said Steve. "Did either of them come to Key West on a regular basis?"

"No," answered Andy. "I went up to them on occasion, but as far as I know they'd never been down here. At least no one ever told me if they did. Maybe they wanted to go fishing. The first I knew they were here was when I saw Ortega bringing that damn boat in."

I thought, yeah, fishing for money that Canterra had thought was still on a sunken boat off Big Pine. My guess was that he'd worked his way into Ortega's good graces and told him about the money and the two of them had come down to get it on the side without any of the rest of Ortega's group knowing about it. The question was which one had planned to double cross the other? I didn't think we would ever get the answer to that one. Not that it really mattered.

"How did *Greta* get stuck up the creek on Sugarloaf?" I asked.

"How the Hell should I know? That dumb ass Ortega probably had the chart upside down. All I know is he called me from a phone booth on the highway. He said he was going to Miami, but that he'd be back and expected me to get him another boat like *Greta*, but that right now he wanted her sunk. Before I could find someone to do that, I had my run in with Reynolds and your girlfriend and then you guys found it," he said pointing at Dan.

At this point a nurse came in and told us it was time for Andy's medication and that we would have to leave. Frankly, I was surprised we'd been allowed to stay as long as we had. Before leaving, Steve made it very clear to Andy that this was not the end of the questions and that he would be back with a typed copy of his notes for Andy to sign as a partial statement.

Outside I said, "Well that certainly cleared up some issues. I think my part in this is pretty much done. I'll get you each a copy of my final report and then I guess Andy will be in your hands, Steve. We'll keep a rotation on him until he's transferred to lock-up." Neither of them knew about the money and I hoped to keep it that way. If it was anyone's I figured it belonged to Elyse and Julio. Small payment for the loss of Sam. But if the issue did come up, there was nothing to say that it wasn't still on the bottom of the ocean or spread to the seven seas by now.

Back at headquarters I tried Amy's number again, but with no luck. Damn it, why couldn't she answer. To forestall the inevitable, I set to work transferring my notes into something legible for someone to type with copies for Dan and Steve. Then I went home to what I figured would be an empty house. I was surprised at how quickly I'd gotten used to having Amy there. Sam's funeral was tomorrow; the Chief was due back; the case, at least as far as my part was concerned, was finished and I was tired.

Amy's car, new tires gleaming, was parked in front of the house and my mind started wondering. Was she here to pick up her things and then go home or had she come to stay? I hoped it was the latter. We'd spent more time together this past week than we had the past couple of years. We were comfortable together, at least I thought so. And it had been a long time since the house had felt the warmth of a woman in it.

I got out of my car and walked to hers. The hood was warm, but it was the warmth of the sun, not internal combustion, and the engine wasn't making those ticking sounds as the metal cooled. Amy had been here for a while. Certainly longer than it would have taken her to collect her few belongings and leave.

I opened the front door quietly, stepped inside and was greeted by the warmth and smells of food from the kitchen. Not carryout like I usually had, but real food, roasting chicken, potatoes, vegetables. It smelled good.

I stood there, breathed deep and said loud enough to carry to the back, "Honey, I'm home."

CHAPTER 23

Sunday

In addition to having a very satisfying dinner ready for me Friday, Amy had finished her first story on the events of the week and, instead of coming over to retrieve stuff, had actually brought more, which I considered a good sign.

After dinner, we'd sat and talked, not about the case or about each other separately, but about us together, what we were going to do, where our relationship was going. We discovered that we'd both come to the same decision that, despite being independent, we worked well together and complemented each other. When I asked her if that meant she was staying, she said, "I'm not that easy to get rid of." I told her that's what Dan had said and that he thought I should set my hook and reel her in.

"Very perceptive is our Deputy Dan, but he's got it backwards," she said with a smile.

In the end, we both decided we'd take it one day at a time and see what developed, but that the prognosis looked good for the future. I didn't think we could ask for more.

"Besides," she'd said, looking around the house, "you need a woman here and I like your Dad's office. It'll be a good place for me to work until Larry rebuilds."

It was now Sunday evening. She was at home, our home, pounding out her next story on Dad's old Royal, while Sal and I were sitting on a bench at the edge of Mallory Square smoking cigars and watching the sunset. He and the boys had made it back to Key West in time for Sam's funeral Saturday afternoon and he'd apologized for running out so quick on Wednesday saying he had an urgent matter that required his attention in Miami. After questioning Andy Hardy I'd had an idea what that 'urgent business' had entailed and had asked Tony point blank at dinner earlier what he'd forced out of Andy and then told Sal.

Without even looking at Sal for permission he had said, "I recognized him as the other guy I'd seen with Jimmy O's guy outside that restaurant. So I told him he better tell me where Jimmy was or I'd blow away his other knee. He told me and I told the Boss but by the time we got there he was gone."

Now Sal and I were watching the sunset and I said, "You know there's a state wide APB out for Ortega. You wouldn't care to tell me where he is would you?"

"I can't because I don't know yet, and I won't because I want him more than you do. This is the first lead I've had on him in a long time and I won't let it go to waste. One thing I will guarantee you," he said sternly and with that cold, steely look that I'd briefly seen before, "he won't wash up on some beach and the state won't have to spend any money on his housing."

Sitting forward, I looked sternly at Sal and with my best cop voice said, "That's about as clear an admission of intent as I'm likely to get from you." I paused and he actually paled slightly. Leaning back in my seat and puffing my cigar I continued, "However, as long as it's not within the city limits of Key West, it's outside of my jurisdiction. 'Sides, the only thing I could get him on would be boat theft and even that would be 'iffy' since all indications are that he legitimately arranged a charter."

We sat there, blowing smoke rings and watching the sun sink slowly into the Gulf of Mexico.

In the growing darkness Sal sighed. "I'm going to miss these cigars." He said.

"They are good," I agreed.

"They should be. They're the best hand rolled Cubans from an old guy who makes them for Castro."

I stared at him, my mouth open, and finally gulped and

said, "These are Castro's cigars? How the hell did you get them?"

"From Sam. He told me once he had an arrangement where once a month he would sail to a specific location about three miles off Cuba and meet a small boat at night. The only one in that boat was a young boy about Julio's age. Sam would give the boy an envelope, presumably with money in it, and the boy gave him the cigars. Five to ten boxes at a time and every month he would send me one. I don't know what he did with the other boxes. Presumably he kept them for his clients because I never saw Sam smoke a cigar. Although I tried many times, he would never accept payment for my box. He always told me he'd already been paid. I figured he was referring to the fishing business I sent him. Anytime someone asked me who was a good fishing guide down here, I never hesitated. I just sent them to Sam. I sent him some pretty high rollers too. Speaking of money, have you had any luck finding it?"

I sat there smiling in the dark and enjoying the cigar. "Yeah, I found it. I found Sam's private log along with it."

"Where was it?" Sal asked with what I considered only mild curiosity.

"On *Greta*. Jimmy O had it all along, or rather what was left of it, and didn't know it."

Sal perked up. "What do you mean 'what was left of it'?"

"According to Sam's record, and you know how he was about keeping accurate records, when he fished Julio out he also collected five million three hundred and ninety five thousand dollars in various denominations."

I thought I heard Sal stifle a gasp. "Well, considering whose money it was, I couldn't think of anyone better to find it."

"Me too," I said. "That's why it's not in my official report. I figure it's salvage. Finders, keepers and all that."

"Sounds reasonable," Sal agreed, nodding. "But, what

did Sam do with all that largesse? He certainly didn't spend it around here."

"Part of it he did. He bought *Greta*."

"Good investment," said Sal, puffing on his cigar. "But you said you found 'what was left.' How much was that and what happened to the rest of it?"

"I found fifty five thousand in Sam's hidey hole along with a record book in which he made detailed entries of what he did with the rest of it, down to the penny. You may not have discussed finances with Sam, but he listened to you Sal. Apart from what he spent on the boat, it appears that he took three million and spread it around in various banks and accounts. He did pretty good, too. In almost seven years he doubled the initial investment and all of it in trust for Julio with Elyse as the trustee. I haven't told her yet. I'm leaving that to you because she's going to need someone with your knowledge to advise her. The rest he sent back."

"Sent back?" said Sal, surprised. "How?"

"I'm guessing it was all those trips for cigars. Sam must have figured the money was better off where it came from with those who needed it most. Somehow he worked out a deal with someone, most likely a relative, to distribute it in discrete amounts around villages to the ordinary people. Every month he made a drop, as you would call it, and apparently received a load of cigars in return. I'm sure he didn't ask for them, but they were given to him anyway. As far as I know, it's the only thing Sam ever smuggled."

"Well, I'll be," said Sal with genuine surprise. "All these years and he never mentioned any of this. What about the fifty five thousand you found? What happens to that?"

"Since it was found on Sam's boat, with no evidence to the contrary, as far as the law is concerned it's Sam's which means that once we're done processing everything, it goes to Elyse. Right now it's safely locked up."

"No evidence to the contrary? What about the record

book you found with it?"

I pulled the small book out of my pocket and handed it to him. "The banks, investment houses, account numbers, balances, all the details are in there together with the key to the post office box where Sam received his statements. You and I are the only ones who know about it or about the whole almost six million and that's the way it's going to stay. As I said, salvage of lost goods. You advise Elyse and she and Julio are set for life."

The sun had gone down, it was dark, the tourists had wandered back to their hotels or to the bars on Duval Street and the boys were waiting patiently at the edge of the square. Our cigars were finished and Amy had agreed to leave the typewriter and meet me for a drink in half an hour. I stood up and held out my hand to Sal.

"Mr. Donatello, you consort with crooks and scumbags, but you're an honorable man and you play the game according to the rules. I'm glad we've gotten to know each other. Come back any time."

Sal stood, smiled and took my hand.

"Mr. Jackson, you're a good cop. You are persistent and fair. Sam was right when he said you were a good friend and I am honored to consider you one of mine."

EPILOGUE

July 9, 1966

It was close to lunchtime and I was in the office waiting for Amy. Things were quiet following the July 4 holiday. The typical Keys Summer weather was in place; temperature in the mid to upper 90's and humidity to match. We were now in hurricane season. The first one had come early in June and had just missed us, so the locals were keeping an eye on the barometer. I had the weekend duty and was taking the time to review outstanding warrants, APB's and such.

The Fourth had been quite a celebration for all of us. Julio and Gloria had graduated from high school at the end of May and, with Larry's blessing, had gone into a final sprint of studying for Julio's citizenship test. It paid off. He posted the highest score of anyone in the state of Florida. The formal ceremony had been the morning of the Fourth and that afternoon he was the guest of honor at a neighborhood party organized by Sal and Elyse and catered by Tony. Sal, Frankie and Tony had left the next morning saying they had important business in Miami that couldn't wait. I didn't inquire further.

Going through the papers on my desk, I noticed the outstanding APB on Jaime Ortega. It was interesting that there'd been no reports on him since April. I checked with Lou at least once a week to see if anything on him had turned up. It was almost like he'd disappeared from the face of the earth.

I'd emptied the weekly pouch that Lou sent down from Miami. Since the incident with Andy, he'd convinced the Feds to include us in their briefings and had copies sent down every Friday evening. I was sifting through the contents and had just come across a small envelope when

Amy came into the squad room. Larry had set up a temporary office in a building across the street while he rebuilt the *Current* and she worked there or in Dad's office.

She looked pale, like she hadn't spent any time in the sun, and as she got closer I could see the tracks of tears on her cheeks and quivers at the corners of her mouth as if she was about to start crying if she tried to speak. She handed me a sheet of paper from the telex machine and collapsed into a chair, sobbing.

"Miami Herald July 8, 1966.

Explosion and fire at local marina claims life of local businessman.

An early morning explosion and fire on a boat at Sunrise Marina killed local businessman, Salvatore Donatello. Two associates of Mr. Donatello were severely injured and are in guarded condition at a local hospital. According to a plan filed with the harbormaster, Mr. Donatello was to take a weekend fishing trip to Bimini and had just boarded the craft. Donatello's associates were on the dock tending the mooring lines when the explosion occurred and are reported to have suffered significant burns and multiple injuries. A preliminary investigation by the Coast Guard indicates that a fault in the fuel line allowed fumes to accumulate in the bilge and they were ignited when the engine was started. It is not clear if the bilge fans were running at the time. The craft had recently passed its annual inspection at which time the fuel system was deemed sound. No evidence has been found to indicate that this incident was anything other than a tragic accident."

I looked from the telex to the small envelope that had been in the pouch. It was addressed to me, personally, in a precise hand that I recognized. The back had a Miami PD time and date stamp '07/08/66, 18:35' indicating it had been delivered the previous evening at 6:35 p.m. in time for inclusion in the pouch. Slitting it open, I removed a single card and read the note written in the same hand and smiled. A quiet chuckle escaped from my throat.

Amy looked at me, shocked, and asked, "How can you smile after this news?"

"Because I don't think we've seen the last of Salvatore Donatello," I said and I handed her the card. The note read:

'Miami, July 8, 1966, 4:00 p.m.
Tom, don't believe everything you read.
S.D.'

Thank you for reading.
Please review this book. Reviews help others find
Absolutely Amazing eBooks and inspire us to keep
providing these marvelous tales.

If you would like to be put on our email list to
receive updates on new releases, contests, and promotions,
please go to AbsolutelyAmazingEbooks.com and sign up.

ACKNOWLEDGEMENT

Extreme thanks to family and friends who read this at various stages and gave me encouragement instead of telling me it was crap and not to quit my day job (which I eventually did, but not because of this). You know who you are so, to protect the guilty, I won't name names. Besides, I'd probably forget someone.

ABOUT THE AUTHOR

Bob Haines is a retired patent attorney or, as he puts it, "I was a lawyer but I got better." He grew up in the Virginia suburbs of Washington, DC, escaping in the mid seventies to attend college at Florida Institute of Technology in beautiful Melbourne, Florida. Earning a B.S. in Biology in 1978, he returned to the DC area where he started looking for a job in science which would support further education, a necessity in that field. Landing what he thought was only a temporary clerical job at a local patent law firm, the Powers That Be recognized his abilities and convinced him to go to law school at night while working full time as an intellectual property researcher. Graduation from law school and passing the Virginia Bar (something he promises never to do again) permitted him to enter the exalted (?) ranks of practicing attorneys. Thirty-two years later he found himself able to retire from the practice of law (having never gotten it perfect) and return to the sunshine and warmth of coastal central Florida. Somewhere during those years he discovered that writing wasn't all dry legal briefs and technical patent applications but could be fun, especially when a body was involved. Now, living on the Space Coast with Jeannie on his phone ("Master, I have mail for you") Bob grows mangoes on two trees, makes a yummy jam and killer chutney from the fruit, is researching how to make a mango liqueur and tends his orchids (apologies to Rex Stout and Nero Wolfe) while thinking up new and interesting characters, stories and ways to eliminate people.

Key West Lost and Found is his first novel, hopefully to be followed by many more.

ABSOLUTELY AMAZING eBOOKS

AbsolutelyAmazingEbooks.com
or AA-eBooks.com